Elizabeth Griffith

A Collection of Novels

Vol. III

Elizabeth Griffith

A Collection of Novels
Vol. III

ISBN/EAN: 9783337025281

Printed in Europe, USA, Canada, Australia, Japan

Cover: Foto ©Andreas Hilbeck / pixelio.de

More available books at **www.hansebooks.com**

AGNES DE CASTRO.

Published by G. Kearsly Nº 46 Fleet Street Sepr 1 1777

A
COLLECTION
OF
NOVELS,

SELECTED AND REVISED BY

MRS. GRIFFITH.

VOL. III.

SPARSA COEGI.

LONDON:

Printed for G. KEARSLY, at Nº. 46, in Fleet-Street;
and the other Proprietors.

MDCCLXXVII.

THE

HISTORY

OF

AGNES DE CASTRO.

BY Mrs. BEHN.

CHARACTER OF

AGNES DE CASTRO,

BY THE EDITOR.

THE following little Novel was written in the reign of Charles the Second, by Mrs. Aphra Behn [*].

The scene of this Piece is laid in Portugal, and the manners, as well as the stile, bear some resemblance to the ancient romance; where, though the personages are real, their adventures are fictitious. To the Author, therefore, must be imputed the merit of the Fable, from whence this very just and delicate moral may be drawn : That the indulgence of an unlawful passion in the mind, though restrained within the strictest bounds of conduct, renders the heart incapable of exercising its vitrues, or discharging its duties cordially ; consequently, our dearest connections become sufferers from our estrangement, while the natural tendency of the human mind to palliate its failings, is too apt to flatter us that we remain innocent, because we are not intentionally guilty.

[*] An account of this Author is already given in the first Volume of this Work, in the Preface to the Story of Oroonoko.

Thus

Thus though Don Pedro and Agnes de Caſtro might have ſtood acquitted before an earthly tribunal, of having cauſed the Princeſs of Portugal's death, their own conſciouſneſs muſt have reproached them in ſecret with her ſufferings; and the reader will, therefore, feel himſelf leſs intereſted for the unhappy fate of the fair Agnes, than he might have done, had ſhe not been, however undeſignedly, the fatal cauſe of another's misfortunes.

THE

THE

HISTORY

OF

AGNES DE CASTRO.

THOUGH love, all foft and flattering, promifes nothing but pleafures, yet its confequences are often fad and fatal. It is not enough to be in love, to be happy; fince Fortune, who is capricious, and takes delight to trouble the repofe of the moft elevated and virtuous, has very little refpect for paffionate and tender hearts, when fhe defigns to produce ftrange adventures.

Many examples of paft ages render this maxim certain : but the reign of Don Alphonfo the Fourth, king of Portugal, furnifhes us with one, the moft extraordinary that hiftory can produce.

He was the fon of that Don Denis, who was fo fuccefsful in all his undertakings, that it was faid of him, that he was capable of performing whatever he defigned, (and of Ifabella, a princefs of eminent virtue) who, when he came to inherit a flourifhing and tranquil ftate, endeavoured to eftablifh peace and plenty in abundance in his kingdom.

And to advance this his defign, he agreed on a marriage between his fon Don Pedro (then about eight years of age) and Bianca, daughter of Don Pedro, king of Caftile; whom the young prince married when he arrived to his fixteenth year.

Bianca brought nothing to Coimbra but infirmities, and very few charms. Don Pedro, who was full of fweetnefs and generofity, lived neverthelefs very well with her; but the diftempers of the princefs degenerating into the palfy, fhe made it her requeft to retire; and at her interceffion the Pope broke the marriage, and the melancholy princefs concealed her languifhment in a folitary retreat. Don Pedro, for whom they had provided another match, married Conftantia Manuel, daughter of Don John Manuel, a prince of the blood of Caftile, and famous for the enmity he had to his king.

The princefs Conftantia had beauty, wit, and generofity fufficient to have attached Don Pedro eternally to her; and certainly he had for her an efteem, mixed with fo great a refpect, as might very well pafs for love with thofe that were not of a nice and curious obfervation: but alas! his real affection was referved for another beauty.

Conftantia brought into the world, the firft year after her marriage, a fon, who was called Don Louis: but it fcarce faw the light, and died almoft as foon as born. The lofs of this little prince fenfibly touched her; but the coldnefs fhe obferved in the prince her hufband, went yet nearer her heart; for fhe had given herfelf abfolutely up to her duty, and had made her tendernefs for him her only concern: but thofe virtuous fentiments, which tied her fo entirely to the intereft of the prince

of

of Portugal, opened her eyes upon his actions, where she observed nothing in his caresses and civilities that was natural, or could satisfy her delicate heart.

At first she fancied herself deceived; but time having confirmed her in what she feared, she sighed in secret; yet had so much consideration for the prince, as not to let him see her disorder: which, nevertheless, she could not conceal from Agnes de Castro, who lived with her, rather as a companion than a maid of honour, and whom her friendship made her highly distinguish from the rest.

This maid, so dear to the princess, very well merited the preference her mistress gave her; she was beautiful to excess, wise, discreet, witty, and had more tenderness for Constantia than she had for herself, having quitted her family, which was illustrious, to give herself wholly to the service of the princess, and to follow her into Portugal. It was into the bosom of this maid that the princess unloaded her first sorrows, and the charming Agnes forgot nothing that might give ease to her afflicted heart.

Nor was Constantia the only person who complained of Don Pedro: before his divorce from Bianca, he had expressed some care and tenderness for Elvira Gonzales, sister to Don Alvaro Gonzales, favourite to the king of Portugal; and this amusement of the prince's youth had made a deep impression on Elvira, who flattered her ambition with the infirmities of Bianca. She saw, with secret rage, Constantia take her place, who was possessed with such charms that quite divested her of all hopes.

Her jealousy left her not idle; she examined all the actions of the prince, and easily discovered the little regard he had for the princess; but this brought him not back to her. And it was upon very good grounds that she suspected him to be in love with some other person, and possessed with a new passion; which she promised herself, she would destroy as soon as she could

discover

discover the object of it. She had a spirit altogether proper for bold and hazardous enterprizes; and the credit of her brother gave her so much vanity, as all the indifference of the prince was not capable of humbling.

The prince languished, and concealed the cause with so much care, that it was impossible for any to find it out. No public pleasures were agreeable to him, all conversations were tedious; and it was solitude alone that was able to give him any ease.

This change surprised all the world. The king, who loved his son very tenderly, earnestly pressed him to know the reason of his melancholy; but the prince made no answer, but only that it was the effect of his temper.

But time ran on, and the princess was brought to bed of a second son, who lived, and was called Fernando. Don Pedro forced himself a little to take part in the public joy, so that they believed his humour was changing; but this appearance of a calm endured not long, and he fell back again into his melancholy.

The artful Elvira was incessantly agitated in searching out the knowledge of this secret. Chance wrought for her; and, as she was walking, full of indignation and anger, in the garden of the palace of Coimbra, she found the prince of Portugal sleeping in an obscure grotto.

Her fury could not contain itself at the sight of this loved object; she rolled her eyes upon him, and perceived, in spite of sleep, that some tears escaped his eyes; the flame which burnt yet in her heart, soon grew soft and tender: but oh! she heard him sigh, and after that utter these words: Yes, divine Agnes! I will sooner die than let you know it: Constantia shall have nothing to reproach me with. Elvira was enraged at this discourse, which represented to her immediately, Agnes de Castro with all her charms; and not at all doubting, but it was she who possessed the heart of

Don

Don Pedro, she found in her soul more hatred for this fair rival, than tenderness for him.

The grotto was not a fit place to make reflections in, or to form designs. Perhaps her first transports would have made her waken him, if she had not perceived a paper lying under his hand, which she softly seized on; and, that she might not be surprised in reading it, she went out of the garden with as much haste as confusion.

When she was retired to her apartment, she opened the paper, trembling, and found in it these verses, writ by the hand of Don Pedro; and which, in appearance, he had newly then composed.

In vain, oh! sacred honour, you debate
   The mighty business in my heart:
Love! charming love! rules all my fate;
   Interest and glory claim no part:
The god, sure of his vict'ry, triumphs there,
And will have nothing in his empire share.

In vain, oh sacred duty! you oppose;
   In vain, your nuptial tie you plead:
Those forc'd devoirs LOVE overthrows,
   And breaks the vows he never made:
Fixing his fatal arrows every where,
I burn and languish in a soft despair.

Fair princess, you to whom my faith is due,
   Pardon the destiny that drags me on:
'Tis not my fault my heart's untrue,
   I am compell'd to be undone:
My life is yours, I gave it with my hand,
But my fidelity I can't command.

Elvira did not only know the writing of Don Pedro, but she knew also that he could write verses. And seeing the sad part which Constantia had in these which

were

were now fallen into her hands, she made no scruple of resolving to let the princess see them: but that she might not be suspected, she took care not to appear in this business herself; and since it was not enough for Constantia to know that the prince did not love her, but that she must know also that he was a slave to Agnes de Castro, Elvira caused these few verses to be written in an unknown hand, under those writ by the prince.

> Sleep betray'd th' unhappy lover,
> While tears were streaming from his eyes;
> His heedless tongue without disguise,
> The secret did discover;
> The language of his heart declare,
> That Agnes' image triumphs there.

Elvira regarded neither exactness nor grace in these lines: and if they had but the effect she designed, she wished no more.

Her impatience could not wait till the next day to expose them: she therefore went immediately to the lodgings of the princess, who was then walking in the garden of the palace; and passing without resistance, even to her cabinet, she put the paper into a book, in which the princess used to read, and went out again unseen, and satisfied with her success.

As soon as Constantia was returned, she entered her cabinet, and saw the book open, and the verses lying in it, which were to cost her so dear: she soon knew the hand of the prince, which was so familiar to her; and besides the information of what she had always feared, she understood it was Agnes de Castro (whose friendship alone was able to comfort her in her misfortunes) who was the fatal cause of it: she read over the paper an hundred times, desiring to give her eyes and reason the lye; but finding too plainly she was not deceived, she found her soul possessed with more grief than anger, when she considered, as much in love as the prince was, he had

kept

kept his torment secret. After having lamented her fate, without condemning him, the tenderness she had for him made her shed a torrent of tears, and inspired her with a resolution of concealing her resentment.

She would certainly have done it by her extraordinary virtue, if the prince, who missing his verses when he waked, and fearing they might fall into indiscreet hands, had not entered the palace, troubled with his loss; and hastily going into Constantia's apartment, saw her fair eyes all wet with tears, and at the same instant cast his own on the unhappy verses that had escaped from his soul, and now lay before the princess.

He immediately turned pale at this sight, and appeared so moved, that the generous princess felt more pain than he did : Madam, said he, (infinitely alarmed) from whom had you that paper?---It cannot come but from the hand of some person, answered Constantia, who is an enemy both to your repose and mine. It is the work, sir, of your own hand; and doubtless the sentiment of your heart: but be not surprised, and do not fear; for if my tenderness should condemn your passion, the same tenderness, which nothing is able to alter, shall hinder me from complaining.

The moderation and calmness of Constantia, served only to render the prince more ashamed and confused. How generous are you, madam, (pursued he) and how unfortunate I ! Some tears accompanied his words ; and the princess, who loved him with extreme ardour, was so sensibly touched, that it was a good while before she could utter a word. Constantia then broke silence, and shewing him what Elvira had caused to be written : You are betray'd, sir, (added she) you have been heard to speak, and your secret is known. It was at this very moment that all the forces of the prince abandoned him ; and his condition was really worthy compassion : he could not pardon himself the involuntary crime he had committed, in exposing the lovely and the innocent Agnes. And though he was convinced of the virtue

B 4   and

and goodnefs of Conftantia, the apprehenfions that he had, that this modeft and prudent maid might fuffer by his conduct, carried him beyond all confideration.

The princefs, who heedfully furvey'd him, faw fo many marks of defpair in his face and eyes, that fhe was afraid of the confequences; and holding out her hand in a very obliging manner to him, fhe faid, I promife you, fir, I will never more complain of you, and that Agnes fhall always be very dear to me; you fhall never hear me make you any reproaches: and fince I cannot poffefs your heart, I will content myfelf with endeavouring to render myfelf worthy of it. Don Pedro, more confufed and dejected than before he had been, bent one of his knees at the feet of Conftantia, and with refpect kiffed that fair, kind hand fhe had given him, and perhaps forgot Agnes for a moment.

But love foon put a ftop to all the little advances of Hymen; the fatal ftar that prefided over the deftiny of Don Pedro had not yet vented its malignity; and one moment's fight of Agnes gave new force to his paffion.

The wifhes and defires of this charming maid had no part in this victory; her eyes were juft, though penetrating, and they fearched not in thofe of the prince, what they had a defire to difcover to her.

As fhe was never far from Conftantia, Don Pedro was no fooner gone out of the clofet, but Agnes entered; and finding the princefs pale and languifhing in her chair, fhe doubted not but there was fome fufficient caufe for her affliction: fhe put herfelf in the fame pofture the prince had been in before, and expreffing an inquietude, full of concern; Madam, faid fhe, by all your goodnefs, conceal not from me the caufe of your trouble.----Alas! Agnes, replied the princefs, what would you know? and what fhould I tell you? The prince, the prince, my deareft maid, is in love! The hand he gave me could not beftow his heart; and for the advantage of this alliance, I muft become the victim of it.----What! the prince in love! (replied Agnes, with an aſtoniſhment mixed with indignation) What beauty can diſpute the empire over a heart ſo much your due? Alas! madam, all the reſpect I owe him, cannot hinder me from murmuring againſt him.——Accuſe him not, (interrupted Conſtantia) he does what he can; and I am more obliged to him for deſiring to be faithful, than if I poſſeſt his real tenderneſs. It is not enough to fight, but to overcome; and the prince does more in the condition wherein he is, than I ought reaſonably to hope for: in fine, he is my huſband, and an agreeable one; to whom nothing is wanting, but what I cannot inſpire; that is, a paſſion which would have made me but too happy.----Ah! madam, (cried out Agnes, tranſported with her tenderneſs for the princeſs) he is a blind and ſtupid prince, who knows not the precious advantages he poſſeſſes. Is there any thing, not only in Portugal, but in all Spain, that can compare with you? And, without conſidering the charming qualities of your perſon, can we enough admire thoſe of your ſoul? ---My dear Agnes, (interrupted Conſtantia, ſighing) ſhe who robs me of my huſband's heart, has but too many charms to plead his excuſe; ſince it is thou, child, whom Fortune makes uſe of, to give me the killing blow. Yes, Agnes, the prince loves thee; and the merit I know thou art poſſeſt of, puts bounds to my complaints, without ſuffering me to have the leaſt reſentment.

The delicate Agnes little expected to hear what the princeſs told her; thunder would have leſs ſurpriſed her. She remained a long time without ſpeaking; but at laſt, fixing her looks on Conſtantia, What ſay you, madam? (cry'd ſhe) and what thoughts have you of me? What, that I ſhould betray you? And coming hither only full of ardor for your ſervice, do I bring a fatal poiſon to afflict you? What deteſtation muſt I have for the beauty they find in me, without aſpiring to make it appear? And how ought I to curſe the unfortunate day on which I firſt ſaw the prince? But, madam, it

cannot

cannot be me whom Heaven has chosen to torment you, and to destroy all your tranquillity: no; it cannot be so much my enemy, to put me to so great a trial: and if I were that odious person, there is no punishment to which I would not condemn myself. It is Elvira, madam, the prince loves, and loved before his marriage with you, and also before his divorce from Bianca; and somebody has made an indiscreet report to you of this intrigue of his youth: but, madam, what was in the time of Bianca, is nothing to you.---It is certain, that Don Pedro loves you, (answered the princess) and I have vanity enough to believe, that none besides yourself could have disputed his heart with me: but the secret is discovered, and Don Pedro has not disowned it.---What (interrupted Agnes, more surprised than ever) is it then from himself you have learned his weakness? The princess then shewed her the verses; and there was never any despair like to her's.

While they were both thus sadly employ'd, both sighing, and both weeping, the impatient Elvira, who was willing to learn the effect of her malice, returned to the apartment of the princess, where she freely entered, even to the cabinet where these unhappy persons were; who, afflicted and troubled as they were, blushed at her approach, whose company they did not desire. She had the pleasure to see Constantia hide from her the paper which had been the cause of all their trouble, and which the princess had never seen but for her spite and revenge; and to observe also in the eyes of the princess, and those of Agnes, an immoderate grief: she staid in the cabinet as long as it was necessary to be assured that she had succeeded in her design; but the princess, who did not desire such a witness of the disorder in which she then was, pray'd to be left alone. Elvira then went out of the cabinet, and Agnes de Castro withdrew at the same time.

It was in her own chamber that Agnes, examining more freely this adventure, found it the greatest misfortune of her life. She loved Conſtantia ſincerely, and had not till then any thing more than an eſteem, mixt with admiration, for the prince of Portugal; which, indeed, none could refuſe to ſo many fine qualities. And looking on herſelf as the cauſe of all the ſufferings of the princeſs, to whom ſhe was obliged for the greateſt bounties, ſhe ſpent the whole night in tears and complaints, ſufficient to have revenged Conſtantia for all the griefs ſhe made her ſuffer.

The prince, on his ſide, was in no great tranquillity; the generoſity of his princeſs increaſed his remorſe, without diminiſhing his love; he feared, and with reaſon, that thoſe who were the occaſion of Conſtantia's ſeeing thoſe verſes, ſhould diſcover his paſſion to the king, from whom he hoped for no indulgence: and he would moſt willingly have given his life, to have been free from this extremity.

In the mean time, the afflicted princeſs languiſhed in the moſt deplorable ſadneſs; ſhe found nothing in thoſe who were the cauſe of her misfortunes, but what was fitter to move her tenderneſs than her anger. It was in vain that jealouſy ſtrove to combat the inclination ſhe had to love her fair rival; nor did his weakneſs make the prince leſs dear to her: and ſhe felt neither hatred, nor ſo much as indifference for the innocent Agnes.

While theſe three diſconſolate perſons abandoned themſelves to their melancholy, Elvira, not to leave her vengeance imperfect, ſtudy'd in what manner ſhe might bring it to the height of its effects. Her brother, on whom ſhe depended, ſhewed her a great deal of friendſhip, and judging rightly that the love of Don Pedro to Agnes de Caſtro would not be approved by the king, ſhe acquainted Don Alvaro her brother with it, who was not ignorant of the paſſion the prince had once proteſted to have for his ſiſter. He found himſelf very much intereſted in this news, from a ſecret paſſion he had for Agnes; which the buſineſs of his fortune had hitherto hindered him from diſcovering: and he ex-

pected

pected a great many favours from the king, that might render the effort of his heart the more confiderable.

He did not hide from his fifter his paffion; fo that fhe was now poffeft with a double grief, to find Agnes fovereign of all the hearts to which fhe had a pretenfion.

Don Alvaro was one of thofe ambitious men, that are fierce without moderation, and proud without generofity; of a melancholy, cloudy humour, of a cruel inclination, and, to effect his ends, found nothing difficult or unlawful. Naturally he loved not the prince, who, on all accounts, ought to have held the firft rank in the heart of the king, which fhould have fet bounds to the favour of Don Alvaro; who, when he knew the prince was his rival, his jealoufy increafed his hate of him; and he conjured Elvira to employ all her care, to oppofe an engagement that could not but be deftructive to them both; fhe promifed him, and he, not very well fatisfy'd, relied on her addrefs.

Don Alvaro, who had too lively a reprefentation within himfelf of the beauties and graces of the prince of Portugal, thought of nothing but how to combat his merits, he himfelf not being handfome or well made: his perfon was as difagreeable as his humour, and Don Pedro had all the advantages that one man could poffibly have over another. In fine, all that Don Alvaro wanted adorned the prince: but as he was the hufband of Conftantia, and depended upon an abfolute father; and that Don Alvaro was free, and mafter of a good fortune, he thought himfelf more affured of Agnes, and fixed his hopes on that thought.

He knew very well, that the paffion of Don Pedro could not but infpire a violent anger in the foul of the king. Induftrious in doing ill, his firft bufinefs was to carry this unwelcome news to him. After he had given time to his grief, and had compofed himfelf to his defire, he then befought the king to intereft himfelf in his amorous affair, and to be the protector of his perfon.

Though

Though Don Alvaro had no other merit to recommend him to the king, than a continual and blind obedience to all his commands; yet he had favoured him with several testimonies of his vast bounty: and considering the height to which the king's liberality had raised him, there were few ladies that would have refused his alliance. The king assured him of the continuation of his friendship and favour, and promised him, if he had any authority, he would give him the charming Agnes.

Don Alvaro, perfectly skilful in managing his master, answered the king's last bounties with a profound submission. He had yet never told Agnes what he felt for her; but he thought now he might make a public declaration of it, and sought all means to do it.

The galantry which Coimbra seemed to have forgotten, began now to be awakened. The king to please Don Alvaro, under pretence of diverting Constantia, ordered some public sports, and commanded that every thing should be magnificent.

Since the adventure of the verses, Don Pedro endeavoured to lay a constraint on himself, and to appear less troubled; but in his heart he suffered always alike: and it was not without great uneasiness he prepared himself for the tournament. And since he could not appear with the colours of Agnes, he took those of his wife, without device, or any great magnificence.

Don Alvaro adorned himself with the liveries of Agnes de Castro; and this fair maid, who had yet found no consolation from what the princess had told her, had this new cause of being displeased.

Don Pedro appeared in the list with an admirable grace; and Don Alvaro, who looked on this day as his own, appeared there all shining with gold, mixed with stones of blue, which were the colours of Agnes; and there were embroidered all over his equipage, flaming hearts of gold on blue velvet, and nets for the snares of love, with abundance of double A's. His device was a

Love

Love coming out of a cloud, with these verses written underneath :

Love from a cloud breaks like the God of day,
And to the world his glories does display ;
To gaze on charming eyes, and make 'em know,
What to soft hearts and to his pow'r they owe.

The pride of Don Alvaro was soon humbled at the feet of the prince of Portugal, who threw him against the ground, with twenty others, and carried alone the glory of the day. There was, in the evening, a noble assembly at Constantia's, where Agnes would not have been, unless expresly commanded by the princess. She appeared there all negligent and careless in her dress ; but yet she appeared all beautiful and charming. She saw with disdain her name and her colours worn by Don Alvaro at a public triumph ; and if her heart was capable of any tender emotions, it was not for such a man as he for whom her delicacy destined them : she looked on him with a contempt, which did not hinder him from pressing so near, that there was a necessity for her to hear what he had to declare to her.

She treated him not uncivilly ; but her coldness would have abated the courage of any but Alvaro.----Madam, said he, (when he could be heard of none but herself) I have hitherto concealed the passion you have inspired me with, fearing it should displease you ; but it has committed a violence on my respect, and I can no longer conceal it from you.----I never reflected on your actions (answered Agnes with all the indifference of which she was capable), and if you think you offend me, you are in the wrong to make me perceive it.---- This coldness is but an ill omen for me, (replied Don Alvaro) and if you have not found me out to be your lover to-day, I fear you will never approve my passion. Oh ! what a time have you chosen to make it appear to me ! (pursued Agnes.) Is it so great an honour for
me,

me, that you muſt take ſuch care to ſhew it to the world? And do you think that I am ſo deſirous of glory, that I muſt aſpire to it by your actions? If I muſt, you have very ill maintained it in the tournament; and if it be that vanity that you depend upon, you will make no great progreſs on a ſoul that is not fond of ſhame. If you were poſſeſſed of all the advantages which the prince has this day carried away, you yet ought to conſider what you are going about; and it is not a maid like me who is touched with enterprizes, without reſpect or permiſſion.

The favourite of the king was too proud to hear Agnes without indignation; but as he was willing to conceal it, and not offend her, he made not his reſentment appear; and conſidering the obſervation ſhe made on the triumphs of Don Pedro, which increaſed his jealouſies: If I have not overcome at the tournament, replied he, I am not the leſs in love for being vanquiſhed, nor leſs capable of ſucceſs on occaſion.

They were interrupted here: but from that day Don Alvaro, who had opened the firſt difficulties, kept no more his wonted diſtance, but perpetually perſecuted Agnes; yet, though he was protected by the king, that inſpired in her never the more conſideration for him. Don Pedro was always ignorant by what means the verſes he had loſt in the garden fell into the hands of Conſtantia. As the princeſs appeared to him indulgent, he was only concerned for Agnes; and the love of Don Alvaro, which was then ſo well known, increaſed his pain; and had he been poſſeſſed of ſufficient authority, he would not have ſuffered her to have been expoſed to the perſecutions of ſo unworthy a rival. He was alſo afraid of the king's being advertiſed of his paſſion; but he thought not at all of Elvira, nor apprehended any malice from her reſentment.

While ſhe burnt with a deſire of deſtroying Agnes, againſt whom ſhe vented all her venom, ſhe was never weary of making new reports to her brother, aſſuring
him,

him, that though they could not prove that Agnes made any returns to the tenderneſs of the prince, yet that was the cauſe of Conſtantia's grief; and that, if this princeſs ſhould die, Don Pedro might marry Agnes. In fine, ſhe ſo incenſed Don Alvaro's jealouſy, that he could not hinder himſelf from running immediately to the king, with the diſcovery of all he knew and all he gueſſed, and who, he had the pleaſure to find, was infinitely enraged at the news. My dear Alvaro, ſaid the king, you ſhall inſtantly marry this dangerous beauty, and let poſſeſſion aſſure your repoſe and mine. If I have protected you on other occaſions, judge what a ſervice of ſo great an importance for me would make me undertake; and, without any reſerve, the forces of this ſtate are in your power, and almoſt any thing that I can give ſhall be aſſured you, ſo you render yourſelf maſter of the deſtiny of Agnes.

Don Alvaro pleaſed, and vain with his maſter's bounty, made uſe of all the authority he gave him. He paſſionately loved Agnes, and would not on the ſudden employ violence; but reſolved with himſelf to try all poſſible means to win her fairly; yet, if that failed, to have recourſe to force, if ſhe continued always inſenſible.

While Agnes de Caſtro (importuned by his aſſiduities, deſpairing at the grief of Conſtantia, and, perhaps, made tender by that of the prince of Portugal) took a reſolution worthy of her virtue; amiable as Don Pedro was, ſhe found nothing in him, but his being huſband to Conſtantia, that was dear to her; and, far from encouraging the power ſhe had got over his heart, ſhe thought of nothing but removing from Coimbra. The paſſion of Don Alvaro, which ſhe had no inclination to favour, ſerved her as a pretext; and preſſed with the fear of cauſing, in the end, a divorce between the prince and his princeſs, ſhe went to find Conſtantia, with a trouble which all her care was not able to hide from her.

The

The princess easily found it out; and their common misfortunes having not changed their friendship, What ails you, Agnes? said the princess to her, in a soft tone, and with her ordinary sweetness, and what new misfortune causes that sadness in thy looks?--- Madam, replied Agnes, the obligations and ties I have to you put me upon a cruel trial; I had bounded the felicity of my life in hope of passing it near your highness, yet I must carry to some other part of the world this unlucky face of mine, which renders me nothing but ill offices; and it is to obtain that liberty that I am come to throw myself at your feet, looking upon you as my sovereign.

Constantia was so surprised and touched with the proposition of Agnes, that she lost her speech for some moments; tears, which were sincere, expressed her first sentiments, and after having shed abundance, to give a new mark of her tenderness to the fair afflicted Agnes, she, with a sad and melancholy look, fixed her eyes upon her, and holding out her hand to her in a most obliging manner, sighing, cried, You will then, my dear Agnes, leave me, and expose me to the grief of seeing you no more?---Alas, madam! interrupted this lovely maid, hide from the unhappy Agnes a bounty which does but increase her misfortunes: it is not I, madam, that would leave you; it is my duty and my reason that orders my fate; and those days which I shall pass far from you, promise me nothing to oblige me to this design, if I did not see myself absolutely forced to it. I am not ignorant of what passes at Coimbra, and I shall be an accomplice of the injustice there committed, if I should stay here any longer.---- Ah! I know your virtue, cried Constantia, and you may remain here in all safety while I am your protectress; and let what will happen, I will accuse you of nothing. ---There is no answering for what is to come, replied Agnes sadly, and I shall be sufficiently guilty, if my

presence

presence causes sentiments which cannot be innocent. Besides, madam, the importunities of Don Alvaro are insupportable to me; and though I find nothing but aversion to him, since the king protects his insolence, and he is in a condition of undertaking any thing, my flight is absolutely necessary. But, madam, though he is odious to me, I call Heaven to witness, that if I could cure the prince by marrying Don Alvaro, I would not consider of it a moment; and finding in my punishment the consolation of sacrificing myself to my princess, I would support it without murmuring. But if I were the wife of Don Alvaro, Don Pedro would always look upon me with the same eyes; so that I find nothing more reasonable for me, than to hide myself in some corner of the world, where, though I shall most certainly live without pleasure, yet I shall preserve the repose of my dearest mistress.----All the reason you find in this design, answered the princess, cannot oblige me to approve of your absence. Will it restore me the heart of Don Pedro? and will it not fly away with you? His grief is mine, and my life is tied to his; do not make him despair then, if you love me. I know you, I tell you so once more; and let your power be ever so great over the heart of the prince, I will not suffer you to abandon us.

Though Agnes thought she had perfectly known Constantia, yet she did not expect to find so intire a virtue in her, which made her think herself more unhappy, and the prince more criminal. Oh, wisdom! Oh, bounty without example! cried she, Why is it that the cruel destinies do not give you all you deserve? You are the disposer of my actions, continued she, kissing the hand of Constantia, I will do nothing but what you will have me: but consider, weigh well the reasons that ought to determine you in the measures you oblige me to take.

Don Pedro, who had not seen the princess all that day, came in then, and finding them both extremely troubled,

troubled, with a fierce impatience demanded the cause.
Sir, answered Constantia, Agnes, too wise, and too
scrupulous, fears the effects of her beauty, and will live
no longer at Coimbra; and it was on this subject, (which
cannot be agreeable to me) that she asked my advice.
The prince grew pale at this discourse; and snatching
the words from her mouth (with more concern than possessed either of them), cried with a voice very feeble,
Agnes cannot fail, if she follow your counsel, madam;
and I leave you full liberty to give it her. He then
immediately went out; and the princess, whose heart
he perfectly possessed, not being able to hide her displeasure, said, My dear Agnes, if my satisfaction did
not depend on your conversation, I should desire it of
you, for Don Pedro's sake: it is the only advantage that
his unfortunate love can hope; and would not the world
have reason to call me barbarous, if I contribute to deprive him of that?---But the sight of me will prove a
poison to him, replied Agnes, and what should I do,
my princess, if, after the reserve he has hitherto kept,
his mouth should add any thing to the torments I have
already felt, by speaking to me of his flame?---You
would hear him sure, without causing him to despair,
replied Constantia, and I should put this obligation to
the account of the rest I owe you.---Would you then
have me expect those events which I fear, madam? (replied Agnes) Well! I will obey; but, just Heaven,
(pursued she) if they prove fatal, do not punish an innocent heart for it. Thus this conversation ended.
Agnes withdrew into her chamber; but it was not to be
more at ease.

What Don Pedro had learned of the design of Agnes,
caused a cruel agitation in his soul: he wished he had
never loved her, and desired a thousand times to die;
but it was not for him to make vows against a thing
which fate had designed him; and whatever resolutions
he made to bear the absence of Agnes, his tenderness
had not force enough to consent to it.

After

After having, for a long time, combated with himself, he determined to do what was impossible for him to let Agnes do. His courage reproached him with the idleness in which he passed the most youthful and vigorous part of his days; and making it appear to the king, that his allies, and even the prince Don John Emanuel, his father-in-law, had concerns in the world, which demanded his presence on the frontiers, he easily obtained liberty to make this journey; to which the princess gave no obstacle.

Agnes saw him depart without any concern; but it was not upon the account of any aversion she had to him. Don Alvaro began then to make his importunity an open persecution: he forgot nothing that might touch the insensible Agnes, and made use a long time only of the arts of love; but seeing that this submission and respect was to no purpose, he formed strange designs.

As the king had a deference for all his counsels, it was not difficult to inspire him with what he had a mind to: he complained of the ungrateful Agnes, and forgot nothing that might make him perceive that she was not cruel to him on his account, but from the too much sensibility she had for the prince. The king, who was extremely angry at this, reiterated all the promises he had made him.

The king had not yet spoken to Agnes in favour of Don Alvaro; and not doubting but his approbation would surmount all obstacles, he took an occasion to entertain her on that subject: and removing some distance from those who might hear him, I thought Don Alvaro had merit enough, said he, to have obtained a little share in your esteem; and I could not imagine there would have been any necessity of my soliciting it for him. I know you are very charming; but he has nothing that renders him unworthy of you; and when you shall reflect on the choice my friendship has made of him from among all the great men of my court, you will do him at the same time justice. His fortune

is none of the meaneſt, ſince he has me for his protector.
He is nobly born, a man of honour and courage; he
adores you; and it ſeems to me, that all theſe reaſons
are ſufficient to vanquiſh your pride.

The heart of Agnes was ſo little diſpoſed to give itſelf
to Don Alvaro, that all the king of Portugal had ſaid
had no effect on her in his favour. If Don Alvaro, ſir,
anſwered ſhe, were without merit, he poſſeſſes advantages enough in the bounty your majeſty is pleaſed to
honour him with, to make him maſter of all things.
It is not that I find any defect in him that I anſwer not
his deſires; but, ſir, by what obſtinate power would
you that I ſhould love, if Heaven has not given me a
ſoul that is tender? And why ſhould you pretend that
I ſhould ſubmit to him, when nothing is dearer to me
than my liberty?---You are not ſo free nor ſo inſenſible
as you ſay, anſwered the king, bluſhing with anger;
and if your heart were exempt from all ſorts of affection,
he might expect a more reaſonable return than what he
finds. But, imprudent maid, conducted by an ill fate,
added he in fury, what pretenſions have you to Don
Pedro? Hitherto I have hid the chagrin which his
weakneſs and yours give me; but it was not the leſs
violent for being hid: and ſince you oblige me to break
out, I muſt tell you, that if my ſon were not already
married to Conſtantia, he ſhould never be your huſband.
Renounce, then, theſe vain ideas, which will cure him,
and juſtify you.

The courageous Agnes was ſcarce miſtreſs of her firſt
tranſports at a diſcourſe ſo full of contempt; but calling
her virtue to the aid of her anger, ſhe recovered herſelf by the aſſiſtance of reaſon; and conſidering the
outrage ſhe had received, not as coming from a great
king, but a man blinded and poſſeſſed by Don Alvaro,
ſhe thought him not worthy of her reſentment: her
fair eyes animated themſelves with ſo ſhining a viva-
city, they anſwered for the purity of her ſentiments;
and fixing them ſtedfaſtly on the king, If the prince
Don

Don Pedro has weakneſſes, replied ſhe, he never communicated them to me, and I am certain I never contributed wilfully to them; but to let you ſee how little
I regard your defiance, and to put my glory in ſafety,
I will live far from you, and all that belongs to you:
yes, ſir, I will quit Coimbra with pleaſure; and for this
man who is ſo dear to you, anſwered ſhe with a noble
pride and fierceneſs of which the king felt all the force,
for this favourite, ſo worthy to poſſeſs the moſt tender
affections of a great prince, I aſſure you, that into
whatever part of the world fortune conducts me, I will
not carry away the leaſt remembrance of him. At theſe
words ſhe made a profound reverence, and made ſuch
haſte from his preſence, that he could not oppoſe her
going if he would.

The king was now more ſtrongly convinced than ever
that ſhe favoured the paſſion of Don Pedro, and immediately went to Conſtantia, to inſpire her with the ſame
thought; but ſhe was not capable of receiving ſuch
impreſſions, and following her own natural inclinations,
ſhe generouſly defended the virtue of her actions. The
king, angry to ſee her ſo well intentioned to her rival,
whom he would have had her hated, reproached her
with the ſweetneſs of her temper, and went thence to
mix his anger with Don Alvaro's rage, who was totally
confounded, when he ſaw the negotiation of his maſter
had taken no effect. The haughty maid braves me
then, ſir, ſaid he to the king, and deſpiſes the honour
which your bounty offered her! Why cannot I reſiſt ſo
fatal a paſſion? But I muſt love her in ſpite of myſelf;
and if this flame conſume me, I can find no way to
extinguiſh it.---What can I further do for you, replied
the king?---Alas, ſir, anſwered Don Alvaro, I muſt do
by force what I cannot otherwiſe hope from the proud
and cruel Agnes.---Well, then, added the king, ſince
it is not fit for me to authorize publicly a violence in
the midſt of my kingdom, chuſe thoſe of my ſubjects
whom you think moſt capable of ſerving you, and take

by

by force the beauty that charms you; and if she do not yield to your love, put that power you are master of in execution to oblige her to marry you.

Don Alvaro, ravished with this proposition, which at the same time flattered both his love and his anger, cast himself at the feet of the king, and renewed his acknowledgments by fresh protestations, and thought of nothing but employing his unjust authority against Agnes.

Don Pedro had been about three months absent, when Alvaro undertook what the king counselled him to; though the prince's moderation was known to him, yet he feared his presence, and would not attend the return of a rival, with whom he would avoid all disputes.

One night, when the sad Agnes, full of inquietude, in vain expected the god of sleep, she heard a noise, and after saw some men unknown enter her chamber; whose measures being well consulted, they carried her out of the palace, and putting her in a close coach, forced her out of Coimbra, without being hindered by any obstacle. She knew not of whom to complain, nor whom to suspect. Don Alvaro seemed too puissant to seek his satisfaction this way; and she accused not the prince of this attempt, of whom she had so favourable an opinion. Whatever she could think or say, she could not hinder her ill fortune: they hurried her on with diligence, and before it was day, were a considerable way off from the town.

As soon as day began to break, she surveyed those that encompassed her, without so much as knowing one of them; and seeing that her cries and prayers were all in vain with these deaf ravishers, she satisfied herself with imploring the protection of Heaven, and abandoned herself to its conduct.

While she sat thus overwhelmed with grief, uncertain of her destiny, she saw a body of horse advance towards the troop which conducted her. The ravishers did not shun them, thinking it to be Don Alvaro; but
when

when they approached, they found it was the prince of
Portugal who was at the head of them, and who, without foreseeing the occasion that would offer itself of
serving Agnes, was returning to Coimbra, full of her
idea, after having performed what he ought in his ex-
pedition.

Agnes, who did not expect him, changed now her
opinion, and thought that it was the prince that had
caused her to be stolen away. Oh, sir! said she to him,
having still the same thought, is it you that have torn
me from the princess? And could so cruel a blow come
from a hand that is so dear to her? What will you do
with an unfortunate creature, who desires nothing but
death? And why will you obscure the glory of your life
by an artifice unworthy of you? This language astonished the prince no less than the sight of Agnes had
done: he found by what she had said, that she was taken
away by force; and immediately passing to the height of
rage, he made her understand by one look, that he was
not the base author of her trouble. I tear you from
Constantia, whose only pleasure you are! replied he.
What opinion have you of Don Pedro? No, madam,
though you see me here, I am altogether innocent of
the violence that has been done you; and there is
nothing I will not do to rescue you. He then turned
himself to behold the ravishers; but his presence had
already scattered them. He ordered some of his men
to pursue and seize some of them, that he might know
what authority it was that set them at work.

During this, Agnes was no less confused than before:
she admired the conduct of her destiny, that brought the
prince at a time when he was so necessary to her. Her
inclinations to do him justice soon repaired the offence
her suspicions had caused. She was glad to have escaped
a misfortune which appeared certain to her; but this
was not a sincere joy, when she considered that her lover
was her deliverer, and a lover worthy of all her acknowledgments,

knowledgments, but who owed his heart to the moſt amiable princeſs in the world.

. While the prince's men were purſuing the raviſhers of Agnes, he was left almoſt alone with her ; and though he had always reſolved to ſhun being ſo, yet his conſtancy was not proof againſt ſo fair an occaſion : Madam, ſaid he to her, is it poſſible that men born amongſt thoſe that obey us, ſhould be capable of offending you ? I never thought myſelf deſtined to revenge ſuch an offence ; but ſince Heaven has permitted you to receive it, I will either periſh, or make them repent it.----Sir, replied Agnes, more concerned at this diſcourſe than at the enterprize of Don Alvaro, thoſe who are wanting in their reſpect to the princeſs and you, are not obliged to have any for me. I do not in the leaſt doubt but Don Alvaro was the undertaker of this enterprize ; and I judged what I ought to fear from him, by what his importunities have already made me ſuffer. He is ſure of the king's protection, and he will make him an accomplice in his crime : but, ſir, Heaven conducted you hither happily for me, and I am indebted to you for the liberty I have of ſerving the princeſs yet longer. ----You will do for Conſtantia, replied the prince, what it is impoſſible not to do for you ; your goodneſs attaches you to her, and my deſtiny engages me to you for ever.

The modeſt Agnes, who feared this diſcourſe as much as the misfortue ſhe had newly ſhunned, anſwered nothing but by downcaſt eyes ; and the prince, who knew the trouble ſhe was in, left her, to go to ſpeak to his men, who brought back one of thoſe that belonged to Don Alvaro, by whoſe confeſſion he found the truth. He pardoned him, thinking not fit to puniſh him, who obeyed a man whom the weakneſs of his father had rendered powerful.

Afterwards they conducted Agnes back to Coimbra, where her adventure began to make a great noiſe. The princeſs was ready to die with deſpair, and at firſt thought it was only a continuation of the design this fair maid had of retiring ; but some women that served her having told the princess that she was carried away by violence, Constantia made her complaint to the king, who regarded her not at all.

Madam, said he to her, let this fatal plague remove itself, who takes from you the heart of your husband ; and without afflicting yourself for her absence, bless Heaven and me for it.

The generous princess took Agnes's part with a great deal of courage, and was then disputing her defence with the king, when Don Pedro arrived at Coimbra.

The first object that met the prince's eyes was Don Alvaro, who was passing through one of the courts of the palace, amidst a croud of courtiers, whom his favour with the king drew after him. This sight made Don Pedro rage ; but that of the prince and Agnes caused in Alvaro another sort of emotion: he easily divined, that it was Don Pedro who had taken her from his men, and, if his fury had acted what it would, it might have produced very sad effects.

Don Alvaro, said the prince to him, is it thus you make use of the authority which the king my father hath given you ? Have you received employments and power from him, for no other end but to commit rapes on ladies ? Are you ignorant how the princess interests herself in all that concerns this maid? and do you not know the tender and affectionate esteem she has for her ?---No, replied Don Alvaro, (with an insolence that had like to have put the prince past all patience) I am not ignorant of it, nor of the interest your heart takes in her.---Base and treacherous as thou art, replied the prince, neither the favour which thou hast so much abused, nor the insolence which makes thee speak this, should hinder me from punishing thee, wert thou worthy of my sword ; but there are other ways to humble thy pride, and it is not fit for such an arm as mine to

seek

seek so base an employment as to punish such a slave as thou art.

Don Pedro went away at these words, and left Alvaro in a rage which is not to be expressed; despairing to see himself defeated in an enterprize he thought so sure; and at the contempt the prince shewed him, he promised himself to sacrifice all to his revenge.

Though the king loved his son, he was so prepossessed against his passion, that he could not pardon him what he had done, and condemned him as much for this last act of justice, in delivering Agnes, as if it had been the greatest of crimes.

Elvira, whom the sweetness of hope flattered some moments, saw the return of Agnes with a sensible displeasure, which suffered her to think of nothing but irritating her brother.

In fine, the prince saw the king; but instead of being received by him with a joy due to the success of his journey, he appeared sullen and out of humour. After having paid him his first respects, and given him an exact account of what he had done, he spoke to him about the violence committed against the person of Agnes de Castro, and complained to him of it in the name of the princess, and of his own. You ought to be silent in this affair, replied the king; and the motive which makes you speak is so shameful for you, that I sigh and blush at it. What is it to you, if this maid, whose presence is troublesome to me, be removed hence, since it is I that desire it?---But, sir, interrupted the prince, what necessity is there of employing force, artifice, and the night, when the least of your orders had been sufficient? Agnes would willingly have obeyed you; and if she continue at Coimbra, it is perhaps against her will: but be it as it will, sir, Constantia is offended; and if it were not for fear of displeasing you, the ravisher should not have gone unpunished.--- How happy are you, replied the king, smiling with disdain, in making use of the name of Constantia to up-

hold

hold the intereſt of your heart! You think I am ignorant of it, and that this unhappy princeſs looks on the
injury you do her with indifference. Never ſpeak to
me more of Agnes (with a tone very ſevere). Content
yourſelf that I pardon what is paſt, and think maturely
of the conſiderations I have for Don Alvaro, when you
would deſign any thing againſt him.----Yes, ſir, replied
the prince with fierceneſs, I will ſpeak to you no more
of Agnes; but Conſtantia and I will never ſuffer that
ſhe ſhould be any more expoſed to the inſolence of your
favourite. The king had like to have broke out into
a rage at this diſcourſe; but he had yet a reſt of prudence left that hindered him. Retire, ſaid he to Don
Pedro, and go make reflections on what my power can
do, and what you owe me.

During this converſation, Agnes was receiving from
the princeſs, and from all the ladies of the court, great
expreſſions of joy and friendſhip: Conſtantia ſaw her
huſband again with a great deal of ſatisfaction; and
far from being ſorry at what he had lately done for
Agnes, ſhe privately returned him thanks for it; and
ſtill was the ſame towards him, notwithſtanding all the
jealouſy which was endeavoured to be inſpired in her.

Don Alvaro, who found in his ſiſter a maliciouſneſs
worthy of his truſt, did not conceal his fury from her.
After ſhe had made vain attempts to moderate it, in
blotting Agnes out of his heart, ſeeing that his diſeaſe
was incurable, ſhe made him underſtand, that ſo long
as Conſtantia ſhould not be jealous, there were no
hopes: that if Agnes ſhould once be ſuſpected by her,
ſhe would not fail of abandoning her; and that it would
be eaſy to get ſatisfaction, the prince being now ſo
proud of Conſtantia's indulgence. In giving this advice to her brother, ſhe promiſed to ſerve him effectually;
and having no need of any body but herſelf to perform
ill things, ſhe recommended Don Alvaro to manage
well the king.

Four

Four years were paſſed in that melancholy ſtation, and the princeſs, beſides her firſt dead child, and Ferdinando, who was ſtill living, had brought two daughters into the world.

Some days after Don Pedro's return, Elvira, who was moſt dextrous in the art of well governing any wicked deſign, gained one of the ſervants who belonged to Conſtantia's chamber. She firſt ſpoke her fair, then overwhelmed her with preſents and gifts ; and finding in her as ill a diſpoſition as in herſelf, ſhe reſolved to employ her.

After ſhe was ſure of her, ſhe compoſed a letter, which was written over again in an unknown hand, which ſhe depoſited in that maid's hands, that ſhe might deliver to Conſtantia with the firſt opportunity, telling her, that Agnes had dropped it. This was the ſubſtance of it :

" I EMPLOY not my own hand to write to you, for
" reaſons that I ſhall acquaint you with. How happy
" am I to have overcome all your ſcruples ! and what
" happineſs ſhall I find in the progreſs of our intrigue !
" The whole courſe of my life ſhall continually repre-
" ſent to you the ſincerity of my affections ; pray think
" on the ſecret converſation that I require of you : I
" dare not ſpeak to you in public, therefore let me
" conjure you here, by all that I have ſuffered, to come
" to-night to the place appointed, and ſpeak to me no
" more of Conſtantia ; for ſhe muſt be content with
" my eſteem, ſince my heart can be only yours."

The unfaithful Portugueſe ſerved Elvira exactly to her deſires ; and the very next day, ſeeing Agnes go out from the princeſs, ſhe carried Conſtantia the letter ; which ſhe took, and found there what ſhe was far from imagining. Tenderneſs never produced an effect more full of grief, than what it made her ſuffer. Alas ! they are both culpable, ſaid ſhe, ſighing, and in ſpite of

the

the defence my heart would make for them, my reason
condemns them. Unhappy princess, the sad subject of
the capriciousness of Fortune! Why dost not thou die,
since thou hast not a heart of honour to revenge itself?
O Don Pedro! why did you give me your hand without your heart? And thou, fair and ungrateful Agnes!
wer't thou born to be the misfortune of my life, and perhaps the only cause of my death?---After having given
some moments to the violence of her grief, she called the
maid who brought her the letter, commanding her to
speak of it to nobody, and to suffer no one to enter
into her chamber.

She considered then of that prince with more liberty,
whose soul she was not able to touch with the least tenderness; and of the cruel fair one that had betrayed
her: yet, even while her soul was upon the rack, she
was willing to excuse them, and ready to do all she
could for Don Pedro; at least, she made a firm resolution not to complain of him.

Elvira was not long without being informed of what
had passed, nor of the melancholy of the princess, from
whom she hoped all she desired.

Agnes, far from foreseeing this tempest, returned to
Constantia; and hearing of her indisposition, passed the
rest of the day at her chamber-door, that she might
from time to time learn news of her health: for she was
not suffered to come in; at which Agnes was both surprized and troubled. The prince had the same destiny,
and was astonished at an order which ought to have ex-
cepted him.

The next day Constantia appeared, but so altered,
that it was not difficult to imagine what she had suffered.
Agnes was the most impatient to approach her; and the
princess could not forbear weeping. They were both
silent for some time, and Constantia attributed this
silence of Agnes to some remorse which she felt: and
this unhappy maid being able to hold out no longer;
Is it possible, madam, said she, that two days should
have

have taken from me all the goodnefs you had for me ?
What have I done ? And for what do you punifh me ?
The princefs regarded her with a languifhing look,
and returned her no anfwer but fighs. Agnes, offended
at this referve, went out with great diffatisfaction ;
which contributed to her being thought criminal.
The prince came in immediately after, and found Conftantia more difordered than ufual, and conjured her in
a moft obliging manner to take care of her health.
The greateft good for me, faid fhe, is not the continuation of my life ; I fhould have more care of it if I loved
you lefs : but------ fhe could not proceed ; and the
prince, exceffively afflicted at her trouble, fighed fadly,
without making her any anfwer, which redoubled her
grief. Spite then began to mix itfelf ; and all things
perfuading the princefs that they made a facrifice of her,
fhe would enter into no explanation with her hufband,
but fuffered him to go away without faying any thing
to him.

Nothing is more capable of troubling our reafon,
and confuming our health, than fecret notions of jealoufy in folitude.

Conftantia, who ufed to open her heart freely to
Agnes, now believing fhe had deceived her, abandoned
herfelf fo abfolutely to grief, that fhe was ready to fink
under it ; fhe immediately fell fick with the violence
of it, and all the court was concerned at this misfortune : Don Pedro was truly afflicted at it ; but Agnes
more than all the world befide. Conftantia's coldnefs
towards her made her continually figh ; and her diftemper, created merely by fancy, caufed her to reflect
on every thing that offered itfelf to her memory ; fo
that at laft fhe began even to fear herfelf, and to reproach herfelf for what the princefs fuffered.

But the diftemper began to be fuch, that they feared
Conftantia's death ; and fhe herfelf began to feel the
approaches of it. This thought did not at all difquiet
her : fhe looked on death as the only relief from all her
torments ;

torments; and regarded the defpair of all that approached her without the leaft concern.

The king, who loved her tenderly, and who knew her virtue, was infinitely moved at the extremity fhe was in. And Don Alvaro, who loft not the leaft occafion of making him underftand that it was jealoufy which was the caufe of Conftantia's diftemper, did but too much incenfe him againft criminals worthy of compaffion. The king was not of a temper to conceal his anger long : You give fine examples, faid he to the prince, and fuch as will render your memory illuftrious ! The death of Conftantia, of which you are only to be accufed, is the unhappy fruit of your guilty paffion. Fear Heaven after this; and behold yourfelf as a monfter that does not deferve to fee the light. If the intereft you have in my blood did not plead for you, what ought you not to fear from my juft refentment ? But what muft not imprudent Agnes, to whom nothing ties me, expect from my hands ? If Conftantia dies, fhe, who has the boldnefs, in my court, to cherifh a foolifh flame by vain hopes, and make us lofe the moft amiable princefs, whom thou art not worthy to poffefs, fhall feel the effects of her indifcretion.

Don Pedro knew very well that Conftantia was not ignorant of his fentiments for Agnes ; but he knew alfo with what moderation fhe received it : he was very fenfible of the king's reproaches ; but as his fault was not voluntary, and that a commanding power, a fatal ftar, had forced him to love in fpite of himfelf, he appeared afflicted and confufed. You condemn me, fir, anfwered he, without having well examined me ; and if my intentions were known to you, perhaps you would not find me fo criminal : I would take the princefs for my judge, whom you fay I facrifice, if fhe were in a condition to be confulted. If I am guilty of any weaknefs, her juftice never reproached me for it ; and my tongue never informed Agnes of it. But fuppofe I have committed any fault, why would you punifh an

innocent

innocent lady, who perhaps condemns me for it as much as you ?---Ah, villain ! interrupted the king, she has but too much favoured you : you would not have loved thus long, had she not made you some returns.----Sir, replied the prince, pierced with grief for the outrage that was committed against Agnes, you offend a virtue, than which nothing can be purer ; and those expressions which break from your choler are not worthy of you. Agnes never granted me any favours ; I never asked any of her ; and I protest to Heaven, I never thought of any thing contrary to the duty I owe Constantia.

As they thus argued, one of the princess's women came all in tears to acquaint Don Pedro that the princess was in the last extremities of life : Go, see thy fatal work, said the king, and expect from a too-long-patient father the usage thou deservest.

The prince ran to Constantia, whom he found dying, and Agnes in a swoon in the arms of some of the ladies. What caused this double calamity, was, that Agnes, who could suffer no longer the indifference of the princess, had conjured her to tell her what was her crime, and either to take her life from her, or restore her to her friendship.

Constantia, who found she must die, could no longer keep her secret affliction from Agnes ; and after some words, which were a preparation to the sad explanation, she shewed her that fatal billet, which Elvira had caused to be written : Ah, madam ! cried out the fair Agnes, after having read it, Ah, madam ! how many cruel inquietudes had you spared me, had you opened your heart to me with your wonted bounty ! 'Tis easy to see that this letter is counterfeit, and that I have enemies without compassion. Could you believe the prince so imprudent to make use of any other hand but his own on an occasion like this ? And do you believe me so simple to keep about me this testimony of my shame with so little precaution ? You are neither betrayed by your husband nor me ; I attest Heaven, and those

efforts

efforts I have made to leave Coimbra. Alas, my dear
princefs! how little have you known her, whom you
have fo much honoured? Do not believe, that when I
have juftified myfelf, I will have any more communica-
tion with the world: No, no; there will be no retreat
far enough from hence for me. I will take care to hide
this unlucky face, where it fhall be fure to do no more
harm.

The princefs, touched at this difcourfe, and the tears
of Agnes, preffed her hand, which fhe held in her's;
and fixing looks upon her, capable of moving pity in
the moft infenfible fouls, If I have committed any
offence, my dear Agnes, anfwered fhe, death, which
I expect in a moment, fhall revenge it. I ought alfo
to proteft to you, that I have not ceafed loving you,
and that I believe every thing you have faid, giving
you back my moft tender affections.

'Twas at this time that the grief, which equally op-
preffed them, put the princefs into fuch an extremity,
that they fent for the prince. He came, and found
himfelf almoft without life or motion at this fight.
And what fecret motive foever might call him to the
aid of Agnes, it was to Conftantia he ran. The princefs, who finding her laft moments drawing on, by a
cold fweat that covered her all over; and finding fhe had
no more bufinefs with life, and caufing thofe perfons fhe
moft fufpected to retire, Sir, faid fhe to Don Pedro, if
I abandon life without regret, it is not without trouble
that I part with you. But, prince, we muft vanquifh
when we come to die; and I will forget myfelf wholly,
to think of nothing but of you. I have no reproaches
to make againft you, knowing that it is inclination that
difpofes hearts, and not reafon. Agnes is beautiful
enough to infpire the moft ardent paffion, and virtuous
enough to deferve the firft fortune in the world. I afk
her, once more, pardon for the injuftice I have done
her, and recommend her to you, as a perfon moft dear
to me. Promife me, my dear prince, before I expire,

to

to give her my place in your throne; it cannot be better filled; you cannot chuse a princess more perfect for
your people, nor a better mother for our little children.
And you, my dear and faithful Agnes, pursued she,
listen not to a virtue too scrupulous, that may make
any opposition to the prince of Portugal: refuse him
not a heart of which he is worthy; and give him that
friendship which you had for me, with that which is
due to his merit. Take care of my little Ferdinando
and the two young princesses; let them find me in you,
and speak to them sometimes of me. Adieu! live both
of you happy, and receive my last embraces.

The afflicted Agnes, who had recovered a little her
forces, lost them again a second time; her weakness
was followed with convulsions so vehement, that they
were afraid of her life; but Don Pedro never removed
from Constantia: What, madam! said he, you will
leave me then; and you think it is for my good. Alas,
Constantia! if my heart has committed an outrage
against you, your virtue has sufficiently revenged you
on me in spite of you. Can you think me so barbarous?---As he was going on, he saw death shut the
eyes of the most generous princess for ever; and he was
within a very little of following her.

But what grief did this bring upon Agnes, when she
found, in that interval, wherein life and death were
struggling in her soul, that Constantia was newly expired! She would then have taken away her own life,
and have let her despair fully appear.

At the noise of the death of the princess, the town
and the palace were all in tears. Elvira, who saw then
Don Pedro free to engage himself, repented of having
contributed to the death of Constantia; and thinking
herself the cause of it, promised, in her griefs, never
to pardon herself.

She had need of being guarded several days together;
during which time she failed not incessantly to weep.
And the prince gave all those days to deepest mourn-

C 6

ing.

ing. But when the first emotions were past, those of his love made him feel that he was still the same.

He was a long time without seeing Agnes; but this absence of his served only to make her appear the more charming when he did see her.

Don Alvaro, who was afraid of the liberty of the prince, made new efforts to move Agnes de Castro, who was now become insensible to every thing but grief. Elvira, who was willing to make the best of the design she had begun, consulted all her women's arts, and the delicacy of her wit, to revive the flames with which the prince once burnt for her: But it was Agnes alone that was to reign over his heart. She had taken a firm resolution, since the death of Constantia, to pass the rest of her days in a solitary retreat. In spite of the precaution she took to hide this design, the prince was informed of it, and did all he was able to dispose his constancy and fortitude to support it. He thought himself stronger than he really was; but after he had well consulted his heart, he found but too well how necessary the presence of Agnes was to him. Madam, said he to her one day, with a heart big, and his eyes in tears, which action of my life has made you determine my death? Though I never told you how much I loved you, yet I am persuaded you are not ignorant of it. I was constrained to be silent, during some years, for your sake, for Constantia's, and my own; but it is not possible for me to put this force upon my heart for ever: I must once, at least, tell you how it languishes. Receive then the assurances of a passion, full of respect and ardour, with an offer of my fortune, which I wish not better but for your advantage.

Agnes answered not immediately to these words, but with abundance of tears; which having wiped away, and beholding Don Pedro with an air which made him easily comprehend she did not agree with his desires; If I were capable of the weakness with which you would inspire me, you would be obliged to punish me

for

for it: What! said she, Constantia is scarce buried,
and you would have me offend her! No, my prince,
added she, with more softness, no, no; she whom you
have heaped so many favours on, will not call down
the anger of Heaven, and the contempt of men upon
her, by an action so perfidious. Be not obstinate then
in a design in which I will never shew you favour.
You owe to Constantia, after her death, a fidelity that
may justify you; and I, to repair the ills I have made
her suffer, ought to shun all converse with you.----Go,
madam, replied the prince, growing pale, go, and expect the news of my death; in that part of the world,
whither your cruelty shall lead you, the news shall follow close after; you shall quickly hear of it; and I
will go seek it in those wars which reign among my
neighbours.

These words made the fair Agnes de Castro perceive,
that her innocence was not so great as she imagined,
and that her heart interested itself in the preservation of
Don Pedro: You ought, sir, to preserve your life, replied Agnes, for the sake of the little prince and princesses which Constantia has left you. Would you abandon their youth, continued she, with a tender tone, to
the cruelty of Don Alvaro? Live! sir, live! and let
the unhappy Agnes be the only sacrifice.----Alas, cruel
maid! interrupted Don Pedro, why do you command
me to live, if I cannot live with you? Is it an effect of
your hatred?---No, sir, replied Agnes, I do not hate
you; and I wish to God that I could be able to defend
myself against the weakness with which I find myself
possessed. Oblige me to say no more, sir: you see my
blushes, interpret them as you please; but consider yet,
that the less aversion I find I have to you, the more
culpable I am; and that I ought no more to see or
speak to you. In fine, sir, if you oppose my retreat,
I declare to you, that Don Alvaro, as odious as he is
to me, shall serve for a defence against you; and that I
will sooner consent to marry a man I abhor, than to

favour

2

favour a paſſion that coſt Conſtantia her life.---Well
then, Agnes, replied the prince, with looks all lan-
guiſhing and dying, follow the emotions which barbarous virtue inſpires you with; take theſe meaſures
you judge neceſſary againſt an unfortunate lover, and
enjoy the glory of having cruelly refuſed me.

At theſe word he went away; and troubled as Agnes
was, ſhe could not ſtay him. Her courage combated
with her grief, and ſhe thought now, more than ever,
of departing.

It was difficult for her to go out of Coimbra, and not
to defer what appeared to her ſo neceſſary; ſhe went
immediately to the apartment of the king, notwithſtanding the intereſt of Don Alvaro. The king received
her with a countenance ſevere, not being able to conſent to what ſhe demanded. You ſhall not go hence,
ſaid he, and if you are wiſe, you ſhall enjoy here,
with Don Alvaro, both my friendſhip and my favour.
---I have taken another reſolution, anſwered Agnes,
and the world has no part in it.---You will accept Don
Pedro, replied the king, his fortune is ſufficient to ſatisfy
an ambitious maid: but you will not ſucceed Conſtantia, who loved you ſo tenderly; and Spain has prin-
ceſſes enough to fill up part of the throne which I ſhall
leave him.---Sir, replied Agnes, piqued at this diſcourſe, if I had a diſpoſition to love, and a deſign to
marry, perhaps the prince might be the only perſon on
whom I would fix it: and you know, if my anceſtors
did not poſſeſs crowns, yet they were worthy to wear
them. But let it be how it will, I am reſolved to depart, and remain no longer a ſlave in a place, to which
I came free.

This bold anſwer, which ſhewed the character of
Agnes, angered and aſtoniſhed the king. You ſhall
go when we think fit, replied he, and without being a
ſlave at Coimbra, you ſhall attend our order.

Agnes ſaw ſhe muſt ſtay, and was ſo grieved at it,
that ſhe kept her chamber ſeveral days, without daring

to

to inform herself of the prince; and this retirement
spared her the affliction of being visited by Don
Alvaro.

During this, Don Pedro fell sick, and was in so great
danger, that there was a general apprehension of his
death. Agnes did not in the least doubt but it was an
effect of his discontent: she thought at first she had
strength and resolution enough to see him die, rather
than to favour him; but had she reflected a little, she
had soon been convinced to the contrary: she found not
in her heart that cruel constancy she thought there so
well established: she felt pains and inquietude, shed
tears, made wishes, and, in fine, discovered that she
loved.

It was impossible to see the heir of the crown, a
prince that deserved so well, even at the point of death,
without a general affliction. The people who loved
him, passed whole days at the palace-gate to hear news
of him: the court was all overwhelmed with grief.

Don Alvaro knew very well how to conceal a malicious joy, under an appearance of sadness. Elvira,
full of tenderness, and perhaps of remorse, suffered
also on her side. The king, although he condemned
the love of his son, yet still had a tenderness for him,
and could not resolve to lose him. Agnes de Castro,
who knew the cause of his distemper, expected the end
of it with strange anxieties. In fine, after a month had
passed away in fears, they began to have a little hopes
of his recovery. The prince and Don Alvaro were the
only persons that were not glad of it: but Agnes rejoiced enough for all the rest.

Don Pedro, seeing that he must live whether he would
or no, thought of nothing but passing his days in melancholy and discontent. As soon as he was in a condition to walk, he sought out the most solitary places,
and gained so much upon his own weakness, to go every-
where where Agnes was not; but her idea followed him
always, and his memory, faithful to represent her to

him

him with all her charms, rendered her always dangerous.

One day, when they had carried him into the garden,
he fought out a labyrinth which was at the fartheft part
of it, to hide his melancholy during fome hours.
There he found the fad Agnes, whom grief, little different from his, had brought thither: the fight of her,
whom he expected not, made him tremble. She faw, by
his pale and meagre face, the remains of his diftemper;
his eyes full of languifhment troubled her, and though
her defire was fo great to have fled from him, an unknown power ftopped her, and it was impoffible for her
to go.

After fome moments of filence, which many fighs
interrupted, Don Pedro raifed himfelf from the place
where his weaknefs had forced him to fit: he made
Agnes fee, as he approached her, the fad marks of his
fufferings; and not content with the pity he faw in her
eyes, You have refolved my death then, cruel Agnes!
faid he, my defire was the fame with yours; but Heaven
has thought fit to referve me for other misfortunes,
and I fee you again, as unhappy, but more in love than
ever.

There was no need of thefe words to move Agnes to
compaffion; the languifhment of the prince fpoke
enough; and the heart of this fair maid was but too
much difpofed to yield itfelf: fhe thought then that
Conftantia ought to be fatisfied; love, which combated
for Don Pedro, triumphed over friendfhip, and found
that happy moment, for which the prince of Portugal
had fo long fighed.

Do not reproach me for that which has coft me more
than you, fir, replied fhe, and do not accufe a heart,
which is neither ungrateful nor barbarous; and I muft
tell you that I love you: But now I have made you
that confeffion, what is it farther that you require of
me? Don Pedro, who expected not a change fo favourable, felt a double fatisfaction; and falling at the feet

cf

of Agnes, he expressed more by the silence his passion created, than he could have done by the most eloquent words.

After having known all his good fortune, he then consulted with the amiable Agnes what was to be feared from the king. They concluded, that the cruel billet, which so troubled the last days of Constantia, could come from none but Elvira and Don Alvaro. The prince, who knew that his father had searched already an alliance for him, and was resolved on his favourite's marrying Agnes, conjured her so tenderly to prevent these persecutions, by consenting to a secret marriage, that, after having a long time considered, she at last consented. I will do what you will have me, said she, though I presage nothing but fatal events from it; all my blood turns to ice when I think of this marriage, and the image of Constantia seems to hinder me from doing it.

The amorous prince surmounted all her scruples, and separated himself from Agnes, with a satisfaction which soon redoubled his strength: he saw her afterwards with the pleasure of a mystery; and the day of their union being arrived, Don Gill, bishop of Guarda, performed the ceremony of the marriage, in the presence of several witnesses faithful to Don Pedro, who saw him possessor of all the charms of the fair Agnes.

She lived not the more peaceable for belonging to the prince of Portugal; her enemies, who continually persecuted her, left her not without troubles; and the king, whom her refusal enraged, laid his absolute commands on her to marry Don Alvaro, with threats to force her to it if she continued rebellious.

The prince took loudly her part; and this, joined to the refusal he made of marrying the princess of Arragon, caused suspicions of the truth in the king his father. He was seconded by those that were too much interested not to unriddle this secret. Don Alvaro and his sister acted with so much care, gave so many gifts, and made

so

so many promises, that they discovered the secret engagements of Don Pedro and Agnes.

The king wanted but little of breaking out into all the rage and fury so great a disappointment could inspire him with against the princess. Don Alvaro, whose love was changed into the most violent hatred, appeased the first transports of the king, by making him comprehend, that if they could break the marriage, that would not be a sufficient revenge; and so poisoned the soul of the king to consent to the death of Agnes.

The barbarous Don Alvaro offered his arm for this terrible execution; and his rage was security for the sacrifice.

The king, who thought the glory of his family disgraced by this alliance, and his own in particular in the procedure of his son, gave full power to this murderer, to make the innocent Agnes a victim to his rage.

It was not easy to execute this horrid design. Though the prince saw Agnes but in secret, yet all his cares were still awake for her, and he was married to her above a year, before Don Alvaro could find out an opportunity so long sought for.

The prince diverted himself but little, and very rarely went far from Coimbra; but on a day, an unfortunate day, and marked out by Heaven for an unheard-of and horrid assassination, he made a party to hunt at a fine house, which the king of Portugal had near the city.

Agnes loved every thing that gave the prince satisfaction; but a secret trouble made her apprehend some misfortue in this unhappy journey. Sir, said she to him, alarmed, without knowing the reason why, I tremble seeing you to-day, as it were designed the last of my life: preserve yourself, my dear prince; and though the exercise you take be not very dangerous, beware of the least hazards, and bring me back all that I trust with you. Don Pedro, who had never found her so handsome and charming before, embraced her

several.

feveral times, and went out of the palace with his fol-
lowers, with a defign not to return till the next day.

He was no fooner gone, but the cruel Don Alvaro
prepared himfelf for the execution he had refolved on:
he thought it of that importance, that it required more
hands than his own, and fo chofe for his companions
Diego Lopez Pacheo, and Pedro Cuello, two monfters
like himfelf, whofe cruelty he was affured of by the
prefents he had made them.

They waited the coming of the night; and the lovely
Agnes was in her firft fleep, which was the laft of her
life, when thefe affaffins approached her bed. Nothing
made refiftance to Don Alvaro, who could do every
thing, and whom the blackeft furies introduced to Agnes;
fhe wakened, and opening her curtains, faw, by the
candle burning in her chamber, the poniard with which
Don Alvaro was armed: he having his face not covered
fhe eafily knew him, and forgetting herfelf, to think of
nothing but the prince: Juft Heaven! faid fhe, lifting
up her fine eyes, if you will revenge Conftantia, fatisfy
yourfelf with my blood only, and fpare that of Don
Pedro. The barbarous man that heard her, gave her
not time to fay more; and finding he could never, by
all he could do by love, touch the heart of the fair
Agnes, he pierced it with his poniard; his accomplices
gave her feveral wounds, though there were no neceffity
of fo many to put an end to an innocent life.

What a fad fpectacle was this for thofe who approached her bed the next day! And what difmal news
was this to the unfortunate prince of Portugal! He
returned to Coimbra at the firft report of this adventure, and faw what had certainly coft him his life, if
men could die of grief. After having a thoufand times
embraced the bloody body of Agnes, and faid all that
a juft defpair could infpire him with, he ran like a
madman into the palace, demanding the murderers of
his wife, of things that could not hear him. In fine,
he faw the king, and without obferving any refpect,
he

he gave a loose to his resentment: after having railed a long time, overwhelmed with grief, he fell into a swoon, which continued all that day. They carried him into his apartment; and the king, believing that this misfortune would prove his cure, repented not of what he had permitted.

Don Alvaro, and the two other assassins, quitted Coimbra. This absence of theirs made them appear guilty of the crime; for which the afflicted prince vowed a speedy vengeance to the ghost of his lovely Agnes, resolving to pursue them to the utmost part of the universe: he got a considerable number of men together, sufficient to have made resistance, even to the king of Portugal himself, if he should yet take the part of the murderers; with these he ravaged the whole country, as far as the Duero Waters, and carried on a war, even till the death of the king, continually mixing tears with that blood, which he gave to the revenge of his dearest Agnes.

Such was the deplorable end of the unfortunate love of Don Pedro of Portugal, and of the fair Agnes de Castro, whose remembrance he faithfully preserved in his heart, even upon the throne, to which he mounted, by the right of his birth, after the death of the king.

THE

THE

NOBLE SLAVES.

By Mrs. AUBIN.

CHARACTER OF THE
NOBLE SLAVES;
AND
ANECDOTES OF ITS AUTHOR,
BY THE EDITOR.

THE remarkable and interesting adventures contained in the following pages* were, as we have good reason to imagine, received as authentic facts at the time of their publication. Our intercourse with the Mahometan nations, was not then as open and frequent as the extension of our commerce, and a long continued peace with them, have since rendered it: even within less than half a century, many stout hearts have been alarmed at the approach of an Algerine Corsair, as liberty is dearer than life to every True-born Briton.

* Mrs. Aubin, the author of the following Novel, and of many others, is so personally unknown to fame, that though I have used much enquiry, no particulars of her private life have come to my knowledge, farther than that she was the wife of a Mr. Aubin, who held a genteel employment under government, during the reigns of queen Anne and of George the first.

It appears from her dedication, that she had the honour of an intimate acquaintance with the then lord and lady Coleraine, and many other persons of distinction. This circumstance would certainly stamp her character as a decent and a virtuous woman, if her writings had not already fixed her moral merits upon the firmest basis; for from all that I have ever read of them, I think her's, and their character, may be summed up in the words of the wisest and most elegant writer:

" Give her of the works of her hands, and let them
" praise her in the gates."

But

But as our seas are now no longer infested by pirates, (the Buccaniers of America being, 'tis hoped, but a casual and temporary evil) the horrid apprehension of slavery has vanished from our minds; and we read, now, the accounts of our fellow creatures, who were formerly led into captivity, with the same *sang-froid* with which we listen to the story of the Israelites, under Pharaoh.

But whether the misfortunes of the Noble Slaves were real or fictitious, is of little consequence to the Reader, as there is certainly nothing impossible in the whole relation; and even should some particulars of it be deemed improbable, such defect is amply atoned for, by the rich vein of Religion and Virtue which transfuses itself throughout the whole of the narrative.

THE
NOBLE SLAVES.

CHAP. I.

A FRENCH West-India captain, just returned from the coast of Barbary, having brought thence some ladies and gentlemen who had been captives in those parts, the history of whose adventures there are most surprizing, I thought it well worth presenting to the public. It contains such variety of accidents and strange deliverances, that I am positive it cannot fail to divert the most splenetic reader, silence the profane, and delight the ingenious. The Providence of God, which men so seldom confide in, is in this history highly vindicated; his power manifests itself in every passage: and if we are not better by the examples of the virtuous Teresa and the brave Don Lopez, it is our own faults.

These persons, who are the principal subject of this narrative, were both natives of Spain; the Lady Teresa's father was Don Sancho de Avila, a gentleman of Castile; who being a widower, took this young lady, his only child, then but ten years of age, and went for

Mexico, where he resolved to reside the remainder of his days, having received some disgust at his master the king of Spain, who had refused him the government of a place in Castile, which he had asked for.

He left Spain in the year 1708, and arrived safe at Mexico with all his effects and family. There he soon increased his fortune greatly, and the fair Teresa improved in stature and beauty, so that in two years time she was admired by all the men, and envied by all the women. She was moderately fair, but her eyes were black and shining, and inspired love with every glance. Her mouth and features were so sweet, so charming, that her smiles still healed the wounds which her eyes gave. Her shape, her air, her voice, were all divine. Her soul was noble, full of solid sense and honour. She was affable, pious, witty, chaste, and free from pride. Her father was so fond of her, he thought his happiness consisted wholly in her life and welfare; prized her above his wealth, and resolved to sacrifice all he had got, rather than not place her nobly in the world.

But alas! Heaven smiles at our designs, and soon convinced him he could live without her. One evening the fair Teresa being at a country house of her father's, at Segura, going to take the air in a pleasure-boat, with her servants, a strong wind rose, and blew them out to sea: three days and nights they remained tossed to-and-fro, in the extremest danger and despair. At last the boat over-set, and the merciless waves swallowed that, and all her attendants, except a blackamoor slave, who leaping into the sea, cried, My dear lady, throw yourself upon me, and I will bear you up till I die. It was dusk, and no land appeared: but as she held him round the neck, he (swimming) cried, Land, land! hold fast, I tread on land. Then getting nearer to the shore, he found his hopes answered; for they were cast on a desolate island, where no signs of any inhabitants appeared. Here the half dead Teresa fainted, and the poor Black laying her upon the grass, sat down

weeping

weeping by her, having nothing to give her, to comfort her or himself. She at length recovered, and with that weak voice she had left, returned God thanks for her safety.

At break of day they saw an old Indian man come down towards them dreſt in beaſts ſkins, a hat of canes, and ſandals of wood upon his feet: he weit to a tree, dragged a canoe of a ſtrange faſhion, that ſtood againſt it, down to the ſea, and was entering into it when he perceived Tereſa and the Moor: He preſently made up to them, and by ſtrange geſtures expreſſed his ſurprize, ſeeming to admire her habit and beauty; the Black, who was ſkilled in them, by ſigns informed him of their diſtreſs. The Indian, who proved a Japaneſe, caſt on ſhore there with his wife and three children, in the Chineſe language invited them to his home. The Moor underſtood him, and informing his lady, they went with him. They found his wife and children in a poor cottage, or hut; ſhe was dreſſed in beaſts ſkins, and the children were naked: the hut was built of boughs of trees, and hurdles made with canes to fill the ſpaces; the roof was thatched with plaſhes and leaves, yet ſo that the rains could not enter: the Indians were humane, and treated her the beſt they were able, bringing out dried fiſh, and eggs, which the woman roaſted in the embers of a fire they had made to warm them. There was only one room where they muſt all eat and lie; ruſhes and dried leaves, with no coverlid but beaſts ſkins, were their beds; Indian corn, dried in the ſun, their bread; water their drink. This was a hard trial for ſo young a creature as the fair Tereſa, who had been bred with ſuch delicacy and indulgence: but her virtues exceeded her years and ſtrength; ſhe eat thankfully what was ſet before her, was wholly reſigned to the will of Heaven, and murmured not at Providence. Here ſhe and the Moor continued eight days. The poor Indian who was a Chriſtian, converted with his family by the miſſionaries

in

in Japan, and shipwrecked here as he was going with goods for the merchants to China, with a small bark which he was then owner of; he and the Moor went daily out to fish, hoping to get sight of some ship, or bark, that would carry them to Japan, or Mexico. Mean time the lady not being able to converse with the poor Indian woman, whose language she was a stranger to, walked out as far as her weak legs would carry her to view the island, which seemed of no small extent: here she found fruits of divers kinds pleasant and good, especially grapes, which, though wild, were of excellent taste; these she eat and brought home; where pressing out the juice, she mixt it with water, making a pleasant drink of it. This raised a curiosity in the Black to range about the island, hoping to discover something worth his labour. He found nests of young birds, and rice, olives, honey in the hollow trees; and every day brought home something acceptable, and of great use in their melancholy condition. But Providence was determined to deprive Teresa of this comfort also; for one morning she walked out with Domingo (for so was her faithful slave called), to divert herself with the sight of some pleasant walks he had discovered in a woody place about two miles from the house; which being arrived at, they ventured into the thickest part of it: there Domingo espied a tree with fruit he had never seen before, not unlike an European pear; he boldly ventured to gather, and taste it, though Teresa warned him to forbear tasting it till they had shewn it to the Indian: he eat two of them, putting more in his pocket; and in a few minutes after found himself sick, and began to vomit. They hastened to return home; but before they could reach half way, he fell down, and embracing his lady's knees, cried, Farewel, my dear mistress! May God, to the knowledge of whom your dear father brought me, keep you, and deliver you hence, comfort you when I am gone, and have mercy upon the soul of your poor slave! Remember

me,

me, charming Terefa; my foul adored you, but Chriftianity reftrained me from afking what my amorous foul languifhed to poffefs. I brought you to the wood with thoughts my foul now finks at. I was born free as you, and thought I might with honour afk your love, fince Heaven had fingled me out to fave your life, and live your only companion and defender; but God has thought fit to difappoint me. May no other rob you of that treafure which I no longer can protect! Angels guard you! Give me one kifs, and fend my foul to reft. Here he grafped her hand, and ftrove to rife, but fell back and expired. The fair Terefa remained fo afflicted and furprized, that fhe was not able to ftand; her tender foul was fo fhocked, fhe was even ready to follow him; the generofity and love he had fhewn, the defolate condition fhe was left in, diftracted her: yet fhe could not but applaud the goodnefs of God, who had fo wonderfully prevented her ruin; for though he had a foul fair as his face was black, yet Domingo, her father's flave, was not fit to enter her bed.

She was now left alone, no human creature left that could underftand her language; very fmall hopes of ever being delivered from this difmal place, the poor Indians having lived here five years already.

Thefe fad thoughts overwhelmed her for fome time; one while fhe turned her eyes to the infenfible Domingo, then to the diftant fea, and Mexico: at length fhe caft them up to Heaven, and cried,---My God! pity my youth and innocence! Death would be now a favour to me. What fhall I do in this fad place? How fpend thofe wretched hours thou haft allotted me to live? Who fhall clofe my eyes, or lay me decently in my grave? But why do I reflect on that? Who fhall improve by any good that I can do whilft living, or teach me to fuftain the miferies of life as I ought? Oh! thou who madeft and canft not hate me, increafe my faith and patience; or free my foul from this extremity of grief by death. But alas! do I inftruct my God?

Do

Do I point out to him the way to help me? Am I fit to die, and not refigned to him? Forgive me, gracious Heaven! I reft fatisfied: this lonely place fhall henceforth be my Patmos: here, free from temptations that delude mankind, I will live; the woods fhall be my oratory: I will only eat to live, count things the moft diftafteful wholefome and good, and live to die. Here fhe attempted to rife, but was not able. She remained here fome hours. At laft, the poor Indian woman came to feek her, and after having expreffed in her language much concern for Domingo, led her home.

She continued thus ten days, beginning to underftand fomething of their language: the Indian buried Domingo, and Terefa grew very fick, yet refrained not to walk daily to the wood, where fhe offered up her prayers to God.

One morning as fhe was at her devotion, fhe was interrupted by the voice of a woman, who was making fad lamentation in the French tongue for the death of fome perfon. Terefa rofe from off her knees, and following the found of the voice, came to the farther fide of the wood, where fhe perceived a dark valley betwixt two fmall hills, which were fo covered with trees as rendered the valley very obfcure; here fat a woman with her hair difhevelled, her habit rich, but altogether negligent, upon the ground: upon a fcarlet cloak lay a man, whofe habit fpoke him no common perfon, a death-like palenefs reigned in his face, and he appeared as one juft dead. The woman wrung her hands, tore her hair, and fhewed all the fymptoms of a perfon in defpair. Terefa, who fpoke French, after fome time addreffed herfelf to her in this manner: Madam, behold here a perfon, who is, perhaps, wretched as yourfelf, yet not quite unable to help you: tell me your grief, and if I cannot repair your lofs, I may yet comfort you. The woman looking up, difcovered the moft lovely face imaginable. Speak not, faid fhe, to me of comfort; fince the too charming Hautville is no more.

I am

I am inconfolable. See here a man, who has left his country, fortune, and friends to follow me ; and being caft on this fatal fhore by an unfkilful pilot, has perifhted at my feet for want of food. We have been five fad days in this inhofpitable place, where the bruifes he had received againft the cruel fands upon his breaft, bringing me upon his back to fhore, made him unable to go farther. I gathered fruit and honey ; but alas ! he wanted other food, refufed to eat enough to fupport life, and is now departed, leaving me the moft unhappy wretch on earth. Here fhe renewed her tranfport of forrow, kiffed his pale lips, and beat her breaft againft the ground ; which Terefa, who wanted ftrength to hold her, beheld with the utmoft compaffion. At laft the gentleman fetched a deep figh, and opened his eyes. ---Fond woman, faid Terefa, fit not thus to weep, but rife and follow me ; the God, which grief makes you forget, fends you help by me. Make hafte, I will give you food and wine, which, though but poor, will fuftain life. At thefe words Terefa ran back to the hut as faft as her weaknefs would permit, and made the Indian woman follow her with food to the wood, where they found the lady and gentleman, both almoft fenfelefs ; but pouring fome of the grape juice down their throats, which was ftrong, though not purified like wine, they revived, and having got a little food into their ftomachs, made fhift to rife, and walk a little way, but could not reach the hut till evening. Terefa ftaid by them all the day, overjoyed that fhe had company ; and after having eat and drank a fecond time, the gentleman repaid her courtefy with this handfome acknowledgment. Bleft angel ! for fuch you have been to me, and my dear Emilia, how came you here ? Such beauty, and fuch youth and innocence as appears in your face, might furely have fecured you from the miferies of life. What cruel accident brought you to this defert ifle ? Here Terefa recounted her misfortunes, and in return, defired to know their's, if his ftrength would permit.

The

The count de Hautville readily confented to gratify her, and began the fair Emilia's and his own hiſtory in this manner.

CHAP. II.

MADAM, we are natives of France, born both in one province. Poiĉtou is our country; I was the fon of the marquis de Ventadore, a man whofe fortune and quality rendered him vain, and me unhappy. This lady was the daughter of a gentleman, who, though not equal to my father in fortune, was as nobly defcended. He was the younger fon of a general, and related to the duke de Vendome. Emilia was his only child, whofe beauty and virtues made her worthy a prince's bed. I faw, and loved her from her infancy; our affeĉtion was increafed by years, and grew up with us. When I was fourteen, my father carried me to Paris, fhewed me the court, and all the celebrated beauties that fhine there, where art is ufed to improve each charm, and jewels and habit join with nature to fubdue the heart; but Emilia was poffeffed of mine before. I viewed them all unmoved, was impatient to return to Poiĉtou; and then my father firſt began to miftruſt my being pre-engaged to fome perfon there. He carried me back with him, and fet a watch upon my aĉtions. Soon after my return home, Emilia's father died, and fhe was taken by an old aunt to be educated. The fortune left Emilia was about two thoufand pounds, the eſtate was entailed, and could not defcend to a daughter; fo a kinfman enjoys it. This lady was a fordid, malicious old maid, who pretended to devotion and fanĉtity, but was really a vile hypocrite: fhe ufed her with great feverity, and gave my father intelligence of my frequent vifits and prefents to Emilia, hoping to gain his favour and a reward, which she did not fail of. He urged me often to addrefs myfelf to one lady or other; and finding me firm to my firft choice, refolved to put her out of my way. In order to which, he fends for a captain who was going to the French Canada in order to trade, and offers him three hundred crowns to carry her away with him. The villain accepts the offer, vifits the aunt, acquaints himfelf with Emilia, at laft invites them to Rochel, where his fhip lay, to a treat on board: fhe takes my father's coach, which fhe pretended to borrow, and with the innocent Emilia goes to the curfed entertainment, where they gave her wine with an infufion of opium, which foon bereft her of all fenfe; then the vile woman left her on board, and fet out for Paris, where foon after my father went. There they contrived a ftory together to blind the world, pretending Emilia was retired into a monaftery near Paris; which when I heard, who was fufficiently alarmed before with her abfence, I pofted to Paris, fearched every place to find her, and quickly learned the fatal truth: and now, having vented my paffion, I confulted my reafon, and refolved to foothe my father into giving me fome fortune, and then to follow her. Providence, who never fails to punifh fuch enormous crimes, in a fhort time gave me the means of executing this defign. An uncle of my deceafed mother died, and left me a handfome eftate, being a bachelor, and my godfather; I immediately fold it, fecretly put the money into the India company's hands, taking bills; and one morning left a letter for my father on my table, and, attended with one fervant only, went poft for Rochel, where a fhip lay ready to fail with me to Canada, the company having had an account of the other fhip's fafe arrival at Quebec. The letter contained words much to this purpofe:

" My honoured lord and father,

" THAT you may not condemn me unjustly, or
" be surprized at my leaving you and my country so
" suddenly and secretly, I leave this to inform you,
" that I am gone in search of Emilia, whom I have
" promised to make my wife, to repair the inhuman
" injury you have done that charming maid. If I
" never return, it is the will of Heaven. Whether
" ever I am blest with your favour, and a sight of you
" again, or not, I shall never cease to honour, respect,
" and love you as a father, and to be your

Most obedient son and humble servant,
Francis Edward, Count de Hautville.

I left France before those my father sent after me
could overtake me, and in six weeks arrived at Quebec,
where I soon learned where the villain captain lodged
who had robbed me of Emilia. I addressed myself to
the governor, and merchants on whom my bills were
drawn, who all promised to assist me. I obtained an
order from the governor to secure him, and search his
lodgings; but could hear nothing of her. He denied
the fact, pleaded ignorance, so I was forced to let him
go, and use my sword to do myself justice. I got what
money I could of the merchants, discounting the bills,
secured a ship to carry me off, and then one evening
dogged him out of the town with my servant. So soon
as he was at the fields, I came up to him; and demanded satisfaction. We drew, fought, and it was my
fortune to wound and disarm him; he begged his life,
and confessed that he had left Emilia at Panama, designing, so soon as he had dispatched his affairs at Quebec, to return thither and make her his mistress, which
he had in vain attempted when he had her at sea; she
having threatened him with death if he offered to force
her: but now being left in a widow woman's care,
where

where he had placed her, destitute of money and friends, he doubted not of her complying with his desires at his return to her, since she could not subsist in a strange country without him. I was so provoked at this, that I could scarce refrain killing him in the place; however, I governed myself; my servant and I led him to town, and put him into a surgeon's hands: then I went directly to the governor's, and acquainted him with what had past, desiring he would go and hear the villain confess the truth himself. He went with me, and now all the place rung of him, so that had he lived, he must never have returned to Quebec again: but in a few days after I left it he died of his wounds; of which a merchant sent me word to Panama, to which place I went with horses which I hired, and there found the widow's house, but not Emilia. The woman informed me, that some days after the captain left her, she heard of a French captain's arrival, who was come to trade, and bound to New Mexico, and with him she was departed thence. I presently embarked in a small vessel I hired, and went thither, and found her on board the honest gentleman's ship, who had treated her with extraordinary civility, and designed to carry her home to France with him. What joy and transport we both felt at this meeting, you may imagine. I there married my charming Emilia, and resolved to return with her home. The captain was not long before he had dispatched his affairs here, and then set sail for Japan, where he was obliged to deliver goods; but we had not long passed the Straights of California, before a hurricane rose, and our pilot being unskilful, we ran foul of one of those islands that lie near Cape Orientes; there our vessel struck, and split to pieces, every one shifted for themselves; my dear Emilia was my only care. I threw my cloak into the boat, threw her and myself into it, and fortunately got clear of the ship before she split, taking only the captain with us, whom I called to me. We had but eight hands aboard of sailors, and

they

they doubtless all perished in the sea. The poor captain, monsieur de Bonfoy, holding the rudder to steer the boat, was by a wave washed over-board and drowned. We were left to the mercy of the winds and seas, but by Providence preserved; for the boat oversetting, I took Emilia on my back, and seeing myself near this island, made towards it: but my strength was not sufficient, had not God caused the waves to cast me on this shore. We were both so spent, we lay almost senseless for some time: at last we made shift to creep to the wood, being wet, cold, faint, and hungry; I being bruised, and my limbs nummed with lying on the ground, could not rise, or walk farther; so my dear Emilia strove to supply my wants and her own, and finding my cloak on the sands, brought and dried it, in which we wrapped ourselves, and found much comfort: but when God sent you to our relief, nature was no longer able to support us, and we were near dying for want of food.

Teresa embraced Emilia, saying, Now I repent not my own misfortunes in being cast on this place, since it has preserved you both from perishing; we will chearfully support the inconveniencies of it, till Heaven sends some vessel to deliver us. Come, let us try to reach the homely cottage that must shroud us from the cold air, and revive you with food and firing. They got to it, and found the poor Indian and his wife ready to receive them: they made a fire, boiled them eggs and fish, gave them boiled rice; and though they could not converse with, or understand their language, expressed much compassion for them. Here they lay this night much comforted, and Teresa much overjoyed that she had such companions to converse with; conceiving strong hopes of God's delivering her thence, who had so wonderfully provided comforts for her in that dismal place.

CHAP.

CHAP III.

THE next morning the poor Indian went a-fishing; the number of his guests being now increased, it was necessary to use more diligence than usual to get food for them. The Indian woman prepared all at home, whilst her guests walked out in search of fruits and roots, of which they failed not to bring back some, especially grapes, which were of great use to them. Thus they continued to live, though very poorly, for some days.

One night the wind blew hard, and it thundered as if nature had fallen into convulsions, and the world was unjointed. Towards morning it cleared up, and Teresa, Emilia, and the count, walked out to view the shore, to see what havock that dreadful night had made: they found on the shore several coffers, boxes, pieces of timber, &c. which shewed some vessel had been shipwrecked there. By this time the Indians came to them, and the count helped them to bring up some of the chests and vessels, which they could reach, to shore.

Mean time the ladies walked on farther, and at some distance Teresa perceived a man floating upon a chest, which the waves at length threw on the shore. His habit was Spanish, very rich; his shape incomparable; his hands were clenched on the chest, and when she took hold on him, she thought him dead. Emilia and Teresa pitying him, strove to lift him up: but how great was Teresa's surprize, when discovering his face, she knew him to be the brave Don Lopez, a young gentleman, only son to the governor of Mexico; a youth of great hopes, quality, and fortune; who had adored her from the moment he first saw her, and one who had made an impression in her heart, which she had carefully concealed, but could not efface.----My God! she passionately cried, can I see him perish thus without regret? Must Don Lopez charm the undone Teresa no more, nor my ears

ears hear that pleasing voice? Help me, Emilia, to save, if possible, the man I esteem above the world.

By this time the water pouring out of his mouth, his spirits recovered, and with a deep groan gave signs of life. Teresa calling for help, the count and Indians came up; they took the stranger up, and carried him to the hut; there they warmed, chafed, and brought him to himself. And now the Indian having discovered that a vessel of rack was amongst the things they had saved of the wreck, ran and fetched a cup, made of a calabash, full of it; which holding about two quarts, served to revive them all, and mixed with water, made excellent drink for that day.

And now Don Lopez lifting up his eyes, saw the lovely Teresa, who was behind him, supporting his head with a concern that had made her forget the discovery she made of her tender affection for him to the standers by. Blest God! he cried, do I again see Teresa? Is life restored with such a blessing? Here he fainted, at which she was so much surprised, that she turned pale and swooned.

They were in some time both recovered; then he clasped her in his arms, saying, Charming maid, I have sought you every where, resolving to find you, or die in the attempt. I no sooner heard of your disaster, but I procured a ship, have visited all the coast of Peru and Canada. Missing you there, I determined to go to Japan, it being the nearest coast to which you could be drove. I feared, indeed, that the cruel waves had swallowed you; but not being able to live at Mexico without you, I rather chose to range the world, and court death amongst Pagans and Mahometans. I designed to visit the Holy Land, and retire to some desert, and to spend my days in fasting, prayers and contemplation: but indulgent Heaven kindly drove me here, and would not let me perish. Now I am happier than Eastern kings. This place is as paradise, where Teresa's presence makes all things lovely. Say, my good angel!

4

did

did you wish me living when you thought me dead? Am I welcome? Teresa much confused, conscious of the discovery she had made of her passion for him, answered, Don Lopez, I have shewn too much concern for you, not to explain the sentiments I have for you : my thoughts of you are too well discovered by my actions. Here he bowed, saying, I thank thee, gracious Heaven! my vows are heard : if I return in safety with her to my home, I will build a church, and consecrate it to the honour of our God. The count and Emilia joined in congratulating these transported lovers ; and now store of salt meat, biscuit, brandy, wine, and sugar, which was cast on shore, being secured, they prepared such a dinner, as the poor Indians had not tasted of some years.

Don Lopez remembered to ask, what was become of the coffer he was brought to shore upon? which was not once thought of before, saying, It had much treasure in it. When I found, said he, how great the storm was, I caused it to be brought up upon deck. The ship, though small, being not loaded, and a good sailor, held out a long time : at last the lightning fired the shrouds : we got the boat out strait, and had but just time to throw that chest and ourselves into it, before the ship was all on fire. We saw this island, and made for it ; but the waves rose so high, the boat overset near the shore, we leaped into the sea, and I threw myself across the chest, the wind driving to the island. At last losing my breath, I fainted, so the water entered my mouth, and God's providence brought me ashore. They went forthwith, and found the chest where they left it ; but the tide flowing, had they staid much longer they had lost a great treasure, for Don Lopez had put into it much gold, plate, jewels, and clothes, designing to return no more home.

And now nothing was wanting to make this company happy, but a ship to carry them and the poor Indians to Mexico ; for they were resolved to take them and

their

their children with them, in gratitude for the affiftance they had given them. Mean time, to pafs
away the tedious hours, they walked daily out, and
found beyond the wood a ruinous Pagan Temple, in
which were feveral ftrange images, the chief of which
reprefented a man whofe head was adorned with the
rays of the fun : it was rudely cut in black marble,
but the rays were gilded finely. They concluded it to
be the work of fome Chinefe or Perfians, who had inhabited that Place in ancient times. It was a curious
building, and feemed to be founded upon vaults. Near
this place were feveral pits and altars, where facrifices
had been killed and offered. Beyond this place was a
high hill over which the ladies did not dare to venture ;
feveral times they returned to this temple, and ftill
found fomething more of antiquity to admire in it.
One morning the count de Hautville and Don Lopez
walked out very early to this place, refolving to go over
the hill ; and entering the ruined temple, to reft before
they purfued their walk, they confidered it more at-
tentively than ever ; and Don Lopez obferved a door
that went down behind the altar on which the image
of the fun was placed : he boldly pulled it open,
faying, In the name of God let us enter, and fee
what this place contains. They defcended by fome
ftairs, and entered a large room, where a lamp was
burning before a hideous image, whofe face was big-
ger than a buffalo ; his eyes were two lights like
torches ; his mouth ftood open ; his limbs were pro-
portionably large, made of burnifhed brafs ; on his
breaft was a lion's head ; his feet were like a camel's :
he had a bow and arrow in his hands, a mantle of curious feathers hung over his right fhoulder ; he ftood upon
a crocodile of ftone, whofe jaws feemed open to devour
all that entered : fkulls and jaw-bones, with locks of
clotted hair, hung up againft the walls of this dreadful
vault, and fkeletons of cats, wolves, and fcreech-owls :
feveral grave-ftones were in the floor. As they entered,

the bones began to rattle, the image shook, the crocodile's teeth gnashed, and distant thunder seemed to roar.
The Christian heroes, though surprized, went not back,
but falling on their knees, besought God to assist and
keep them. As they prayed, the lightning flashed from
the image, the graves opened, and voices were heard in
the Chinese language, which they understood not. At
last the lion's mouth opened in the image's breast, and
a voice pronounced these words in French : Christians,
you have conquered : Adored by Pagan Indians, long
I have been worshipped here, and human sacrifices
offered to this hideous idol, by which I was honoured.
But now my power is taken from me ; the God you
serve has silenced me. Depart, through this room you
will find a way leads under the great hill, by antient
Persians made : there are christians will assist you to
depart from this sad place and isle. Avoid the Indian
shore, and men. It will be long ere you will see your
native country and friends again. My fatal hour is
come, and I am henceforth dumb. Here the image
fell in pieces, the graves shut, the lamps in its eyes went
out ; and by the light of the lamp before it they departed full of wonder, and passed through another
door which led to a long passage, at the end of which
they found themselves on the other side the hill, in an
open country ; there they saw the open sea, and on the
coast a small stone building, which coming nearer to,
they found to be a house. At the door of it stood a
venerable man in a Persian dress : he observed them as
one amazed ; when they came near, he came to meet
them, and speaking Spanish, asked whence they came,
and who they were ? Don Lopez informed him. He
embraced him, saying, Welcome, Christians, in God's
name ; enter, and refresh yourselves. They came in
and found a house neat, and well furnished, with car-
pets, porcelane, quilts, painting, screens, and such
furniture as the Persians of distinction use ; with three
well dressed slaves, who brought wine, sherbet, and
fowl,

fowl, and boiled rice. Being seated with muck cere-mony, the Persian staid not to be intreated, but said, Eat, gentlemen, and I will tell you how I came to this place; and why I dwell here. They bowed, and re-spectfully kept silence, much desiring to know who he was? Which he thus informed them of.

CHAP. IV.

I WAS born in Persia, my father was a general in the emperor's service. I was made a captain of his guard at twenty years of age, much esteemed by him, and in great favour, and knew no greater happiness than to be great, or religion but Mahometism : I had a noble house and a seraglio, where five women of great beauty served my pleasures, and sweetened all those hours that I dedicated to my diversions. It happened that a Turkish captain brought some slaves to sell at Ispahan ; amongst which was a Spanish girl, a virgin of but thirteen years of age, fair as nature ever made : her complexion exceeded art, her eyes were dark blue, her hair light brown, her features soft and charming; she had an air so innocent, so modest, so engaging, that she attracted the eyes of all that past along: it was my fortune to be going to the palace that way: I saw her, and stopping to admire her beauty, I presently asked the price of that sweet girl ; the captain asked me a hundred crowns : I paid him down the money, and sent one of my slaves home with her. It is im-possible to describe to you how uneasy I was to go home ; my impatience was so great, that I thought each hour a year whilst the emperor detained me. He was going to ride in the Almaidan, which would have obliged me to stay with him all day ; I therefore feigned a sudden
indis-

indiſpoſition, and begged leave to retire ; he conſented, and I flew to my charming ſlave : the eunuch that kept my women had placed her in a chamber to wait my commands. I haſtily aſked for her ; they told me dinner waited : but I neglected eating, and entering the chamber, found the charming Maria, for that was her name, ſeated upon a couch, pale as death, her head gently reclining on her lovely hand, her face all bathed in tears. She roſe at my coming up to her ; I took her in my arms with a tranſport I had never known before, and bid the eunuch bring in wine and meat, and I would eat here. He withdrew : I kiſſed, embraced, and ſhewed her all the moſt tender marks of eſteem : ſhe trembled, wept, looked down, and ſighed as if her heart would break. Dinner brought in, I courted her to eat and drink ; but ſhe refuſed. Unable to delay my bliſs, I took her by the hand, led her into the bed-chamber ; but then ſhe fell upon her knees, ſtill ſilent, not anſwering one word, and ſhewed ſuch fear and grief, that I was ſhocked ; my blood cooled, and I reſolved to court her to my arms, and ſtay till ſhe would make me happy. I took her up, wiped away her tears, and aſked her in Spaniſh, why ſhe treated me ſo cruelly ? having aſked what nation ſhe was of when I bought her. You are, ſaid ſhe, an odious Mahometan, and I a Chriſtian : I am your ſlave by Heaven's permiſſion ; but my ſoul is free, and cannot conſent to ſuch a hateful deed. Leave me or kill me ; for I prefer death to a diſgraceful life. Force me, and I will hate you, loath you, ruin your joys, and fly you with ſcorn and coldneſs : but ſpare my virtue. Oh! ſpare my ſhame, and I will adore you, do any thing that you command. In ſhort, ſhe melted my ſoul ; I treated her as if I had been her ſlave, and uſed her ſo, that ſhe promiſed if I would turn Chriſtian, ſhe would yield to be my wife. In few days the emperor was informed what a beautiful virgin I had purchaſed : he aſked me gently, Tanganor, may I not ſee the fair Spaniſh girl you have at home ? Pray

bring

bring her to me this day: I have heard much of her.—— I remained silent, as one thunderstruck for some time; at last recovering, My mighty lord, said I, she is not what fame reports, but I will fetch her to you. I departed from court that moment so distracted, I knew not what course to take; I acquainted Maria with what happened, who appeared as disordered as I: I resolved not to part with her, yet dared not keep her; the emperor was not to be trifled withal: if he were disobliged, death and ruin must follow. Whilst we were debating, my eunuch entered the room trembling; My lord, said he, the emperor has sent Bendarius, his chief eunuch, with a guard to demand the fair slave. Ere he had finished, the eunuch entered, and taking her by the hand, who was all in tears, Weep not, fair virgin, said he, for such I hope you are, an emperor's bed courts your acceptance; you are too fair for any subject to possess. He gave her no time to reply, but took her away in a sedan, leaving me in the utmost distraction and despair.

I knew my ruin was decreed, and was too well satisfied of Maria's virtue, to believe that she would yield to the emperor, without such reluctance as would inform him she loved me; and then my death was certain: I therefore resolved to convey into some secret place what money, jewels, and plate I could; and disguising myself, retire to some place, where I might lye concealed. Achmet, my eunuch, generously offered to attend, and conduct me to his mother's house, which was far from Ispahan, near mount Taurus. I accepted willingly his offer, and loading two horses with what was most valuable, departed that night; and travelling all night and the next day, got clear of all pursuit.

So soon as I was arrived at mount Taurus, I blacked my face and hands, and changed my dress for that of a slave; buried my treasure, and resolved to continue here till Achmet returned to Ispahan, and learned what

Maria's

Maria's fate was ; charging him to procure a fight of her, if poffible, and to return and tell me ; refolving if fhe had yielded, and was content, to crofs the mountain, and retire to the defarts, and there fpend my days.

Achmet departed, **and** it was many days before he returned ; during which you may imagine the anxious thoughts that poffeffed my foul : but, juft God ! how great was my furprize when I faw him enter the houfe with Maria in his hand ? She had a veil on, which I throwing up to falute her, faw that fhe was blind. **My** Lord, faid fhe, ftart not at the fight, my eyes are facrificed to virtue, with the lofs of them I have procured your happinefs ; I would have done more, had Chriftianity permitted, and would have died ; but I have cheaply bought my repofe with the lofs of one fenfe.——Thou glorious woman ! faid I, clafping her in my arms, what words can exprefs my wonder and affection ? Thy virtues fhine more than thy lovely eyes did, and fhall procure thee an immortal name. I led her to my homely chamber, refrefhed her with wine and food, and there fhe told me what had befallen her. I was, faid fhe, brought to a noble apartment, which you, no doubt, have feen in the palace : there the eunuch brought two female flaves to me, with a habit fuiting a queen, and departed. The maids dreffed me, whilft my foul was tortured with a thoufand apprehenfions. I fancied myfelf preparing to be facrificed, and almoft wifhed I had not been a Chriftian. When they had decked me as they pleafed, they withdrew ; and foon after the emperor came in, a man whofe perfon and mein was noble and agreeable. He gazed upon me fome time, then took a ring of great price from his finger, put it upon mine, and faid in Spanifh, Fair Maria, you are worthy a monarch's bed : fame has done you wrong, and Tanganor was a villain to his prince and you. I'll make you miftrefs of queens, and fhew you what a Perfian monarch can beftow on her he loves.

loves. Come to my arms, and let your soul welcome
mine! Here he embraced, and almost stifled me with
kisses; I gently strove to loose myself, and, falling
down at his feet with tears, begged to be heard: My
mighty lord, said I, look not upon me with desire, I
am unworthy you, I am a wretched maid, torn from
my friends and country by a villain, a robber, and
by his means now made a slave; but I am a Christian,
and a virgin, and ere I will yield to your desires I
will die. Tanganor is by promise my husband, he has
vowed to be a Christian, and to marry me; Oh! let
your bounty give me back and make me happy, or resolve to see me die here at your feet: I will be only his,
and never yield to gratify another.----Fond maid, said he,
I have heard too much; all that my slaves possess is
mine, and you are, and shall be so; your virtue charms
me more than your eyes. Now I am resolved never to
part with you: force must, I find, procure me now what
your consent shall afterwards secure me of.----Here he
took me in his arms, and carried me to a rich bed, on
which he threw me. My soul was shocked at this, and
so surprized, I soon resolved what to do; My eyes shall
never see my shame, said I, nor more inflame mankind:
these I offer up to virtue, and they shall weep no more
in aught but blood. At these words I tore my eye balls
out, and threw them at him. I saw no more, but
heard him say, Ah cruel maid, what have you done?
Tanganor, you are happy: had I been so fortunate to
be beloved like you, I had been more than mortal.
Maria, I would give all Persia to restore your sight:
by Mahomet you are more than woman, and I will
never presume to sue again for what you must deny.
Tell me what I shall do to expiate my crime.----Restore
me to my lord, I beg only that grace, said I, and I
will pray for you with my last breath.----He answered,
I will resign you to my rival; but it is hard. Blind as
you are, you charm me, and to keep my word I must
not view your face again; go, and take care I never
                                                    see

see you nor Tanganor more, left I forget my promise, and relapse.---Here he called Bendarius, kissed my hands, on which I felt his falling tears, and left me. I was carried strait back to your house, where Achmet found me sick of a fever, which recovering I came with him; and now am happy, if you keep your faith with me. Thus Maria finished her sad story; and after this I need not tell you I adored her, and there sought, and found a Christian monk who first baptized me, and then married us. I then considered what course it was best for us to steer; and resolved to retire with her into this island on this side where the Japanese vessels often call for fresh water. I carried her through the Great Mogul's dominions down to Goa, and there we took ship for this island, where my slaves, which I brought with me, repaired and fitted up this house. Here I have now lived fifteen years, and have three children by my dear Maria, who keeps much in her chamber, because of her being blind. Once a year we receive letters from my friends, and returns from my estate of fruits, spices, clothes, and what is wanting. The emperor never enquired more after me, nor molested my house or friends; my brother manages, and lives upon my estate. And thus, gentlemen, I have related to you my unfortunate life: and if I can assist you, command me. The ship we expect soon, it shall carry you where you please. They returned him many thanks, and he desired them to bring the ladies. I have, said he, a priest, my chaplain in the house, whom I brought from Goa with me, he shall supply your spiritual wants, and my dear Maria shall with joy entertain the ladies. My house is large enough to receive you all, and it will be a great happiness for us to be all together. I have often wondered there were no inhabitants to be seen when I have walked over the hill, but never thought it worth while to search farther. Don Lopez and the count de Hautville took leave, being impatient to inform Teresa and Emilia of the strange discoveries they had made, and
promised

promifed to return to the noble Tanganor's the next morning.

CHAP. V.

IT was noon before Don Lopez and the count reached the cottage, where they found the ladies, to whom they related all the furprizing adventures they had met with. And now, my charming Terefa, faid Don Lopez, we may quit this difmal place; Providence has directed us to a better, where we fhall have company and entertainment fuiting our defires and wants. And you, faid he to the poor Indians, our generous hofts, fhall be received, and if you like of it, entertained at eafe, or return to your own country in that fhip that will, I hope, carry you to Japan, and us to Mexico. An univerfal joy now fpread itfelf through this little family; dinner was got ready, and nothing fpared of what profions they had got. The poor Indian got out his canoe in the evening, to put aboard it what wine, brandy, and falt meat they had left. They lay down at night to fleep, but Don Lopez flept not at all; his foul was tranfported, having nothing in view but the poffeffion of his dear Terefa: he knew a Chriftian prieft was at Tanganor's, and refolved to prefs her to make him happy. At break of day they all rofe, and fet out for Tanganor's: the poor Indian and her children followed, loaden with the mean furniture their cottage afforded; which they could not confent to leave behind them. Don Lopez and the count emptied the rich cheft that belonged to Don Lopez, and fearing to venture it in the canoe, carried all the plate, money, and clothes that were in it with them, the ladies affifting. In fome hours, refting often in the way, they arrived at Tanganor's

Tanganor's, who received them courteously, with father Augustine, his chaplain, a man whose humble appearance and affable behaviour spoke his virtues; he embraced, and welcomed them with great tenderness, and taking the ladies by the hand, said, Come, my children, I will lead you to a lady, who though blind, shall welcome you; and one whose virtues you may be proud to imitate.----Tanganor conducted the gentlemen; they all went to his lady's apartment, whom they found sitting in a chair with her three children seated on little stools by her: Her son, who was then about eight years old, was reading a holy meditation for the morning; whilst the two little girls, Maria and Leonora, were at work. Tanganor informed her of the ladies being there whose story he had told her the night before. She rose to salute them, saying, Ladies, excuse me if I pay respect to the younger first, since I cannot see you. My soul rejoices at the arrival of such company; though I cannot see the light, yet I can relish the charms of conversation. Here Teresa and Emilia embraced her, admiring her beauty, which could not be altogether eclipsed by the black ribbon that covered her eyelids; her shape, her features and complexion were incomparable. Madam, said Teresa, I wonder not that an eastern monarch adored you; you are still so lovely, that your lord may justly account himself supremely happy in the possession of such a wife. The want of sight adds to your charms, and causes us to love and admire you, even before we converse with you. Emilia joined in her praises; and, in fine, the lady put an end to the discourse, by begging them to accept of a breakfast with her, which was brought in. They passed the day with much pleasure: in the evening, Don Lopez, who had privately acquainted father Augustine with his design, taking Teresa by the hand, led her aside into a room, where he thus addressed himself to her: Charming Teresa, God has been pleased to preserve and bring us together in a wonderful manner; I know that you are not insensible or ignorant of my passion for you,

nay, I even hope that you love me; do not longer,
charming maid, defer to make me happy. Here is a
priest to join us; give to my arms and care, that person that my soul adores and loves above all earthly
things. It is I must guard and carry you to Mexico
again. Though you are very young, yet you are of
years to marry. Fate has decreed you mine; keep me
no longer languishing, but crown my hopes, and yield
to Heaven's will, who brought me safely to you. Here
he embraced her tenderly; she blushed and answered,
Don Lopez, you shall be happy. Though with much
confusion I consent to make you master of Teresa's
heart and hand, do as you please: if we must perish on
the sea, or wander in strange lands, it is better we
should be married, and my honour so secured, than to
be still but friends. I own your merit, and confess I
love you. He clasped her in his arms transported, led
her to the priest, who that joyful night performed the
ceremony, making Don Lopez blessed as man could be.
And now for some days they past the time in pleasure;
Tanganor diverted them with hunting, fishing, and
shewed them many curious Caves, and Pagan oratories
which yet remained on the island. At last the ship arrived from Japan, bringing much goods, as rich Persia
silks, cotton, linen, spices, fruit, sugar, tea, chocolate, liquors, live fowls of several kinds for breed, tame
beasts, and all things wanting. Tanganor with these
treated and made presents to his guests of what they
wanted: and the ship being to return to Japan, he proposed to them what to do. They resolved to go for
Mexico with the ship, which being now unloaded,
might easily go thither before it returned to Japan; so
taking their leaves, the count and Don Lopez, with
their wives, departed, leaving the poor Indians, who
chose to live with Tanganor. The wind fitting fair
they soon arrived at Mexico, where they found the
governor, Don Lopez's father, gone for Spain, being
recalled, and Don Sancho de Avilla, Teresa's father,

ther, they found very fick; her lofs having thrown him into a deep melancholy, and lingering fever, of which he never perfectly recovered, but in lefs than a year's time died, leaving a vaft eftate to his daughter Terefa. In a fhort time after, the governor being gone, his fon Don Lopez refolved to go home to Spain; in order to which he fold off all his effects and lands, taking bills on merchants at Barcelona; and with Terefa, the count de Hautville and Emilia, who defired to accompany him, defigning to go to France from Spain, went on board a Spanifh fhip with much riches, and fet fail for Spain. They had good weather and a profperous voyage many days, but when they came near the entrance of the Streights of Gibraltar, the wind began to blow hard, and drove them on the coaft of Barbary. Here two pirates of Algiers came up with them, and foon gave them to underftand who they were, by firing at them, and fummoning them to furrender; they made all the defence they were able, but, alas! the fhip was heavy laden, their hands and guns few: howfoever, the captain was very brave, and Don Lopez and the count de Hautville affifting, they refifted the Turks, till fuch time as the grappling irons having hold of the veffel, the cruel infidels boarded it, and entered in fuch numbers as obliged the poor Chriftians to retire into the great cabin, which the Turks broke into fword in hand. The captain was killed before upon the deck, both the young lords wounded, the feamen moftly dead, or dying, fo that none were left but the two helplefs ladies, and their wounded hufbands, whom they held bleeding in their arms, and a poor boy who ftood weeping by. The poor affrighted ladies fell on their knees, imploring the infidels pity: Their beauty pleaded more than all they could fay in their favour. The Turkifh captains raifed them from the ground, gazing on their charming faces; and having given orders to their men to plunder the fhip of what was moft valuable, and bring her into

Algiers,

Algiers, they ordered them and their husbands to be brought on board one of their ships, where Achmet Barbarosa, who commanded the biggest, received them, ordering the lords wounds to be dressed by his surgeon; and entertained the ladies with much civility and seeming compassion. Teresa was big with child, and so disordered with the fright, that Don Lopez was in the utmost concern for her.

In a few hours they landed at Algiers, and were conducted to Barbarosa's house together, and lodged in an apartment, where he left them to go to the governor of Algiers, to acquaint him with the rich prize he had taken, and to offer him what share he pleased of the slaves and plunder. Our unfortunate travellers thus left alone, Don Lopez was the first who broke the melancholy silence that till then reigned amongst them. Charming Teresa! said he, my joy, my love, my all, soon shall we be parted; all my hopes of happiness are ended; your youth and beauty now will cost my life and your repose; you will be ravished from me by some powerful infidel, who will adore your charms, and force you to his cursed embraces. Teresa, drowned in tears, fell on his neck, and could not speak. Then the count, whom loss of blood had rendered faint, and scarce able to speak, looked on Emilia: My dear, said he, do you hear this unmoved, what may your wretched husband hope? Can you consent to live another's?---No, my dear lord, said she, you know me better; my soul is prepared for all events, and I will die rather than live a vassal to a vile Mahometan's unlawful lust.---And so will I, answered the reviving Teresa. Fear nothing, brave Emilia, we will go together, trusting in that God who is able to preserve our souls and bodies. Slaves we are doubtless doomed to be, but our minds cannot be confined; our lives we must not end with our own hands, but may resist all sinful acts till life and sense be lost.

At

At these words a servant entered the room, a renegado Spaniard, wicked as hell, and one who, by renouncing Christianity, and had endeared himself to the governor of Algiers, and was by him made rich; he told the ladies in Spanish, they must go with him to the governor; And you, gentlemen, said he, must prepare to go in a litter that will presently be here, to carry you to his country seat, where you may recover your health, and write to your friends to send what ransom shall be required for you. At these words, the brave Don López rose, and clasping Teresa in his arms, replied, Vile slave! depart before these hands stop your voice, and rend you in pieces: I will die, apostate villain, before I will part with her; my arms shall grasp her even in death, and bless the hand that kills us together. The count de Hautville stood before Emilia; they had no swords or arms of any kind to defend themselves. The slave, as if amazed, departed the room, shutting the door fast after him, but soon returned with a band of soldiers, who rushing in seized the ladies and lords, giving them no time to speak to one another. They led, or rather dragged Teresa and Emilia through the streets to the governor's palace, and there secured them; their arms pinioned, they tied them to two pillars in the hall, and so retired to the gate. Mean time the lords were bound hand and foot, thrown into a cart, and drove to a country house of the governor's, forty miles from the city; there they were carried into a spacious room, and chained to the floor by the leg; a matrass and quilts lay there upon the boards, on which they might lye down. Here they had food and wine brought them, for the Turks guessed by the vast treasure they found in the ship, and their habit, that they were persons of quality, and therefore feared to lose their ransoms if they killed or starved them. They refused to eat two days; but the third, hunger compelled them to it. Thus they remained some days, in the most disconsolate condition that ever men were in;

where

where we muſt leave them, to enquire what became of Tereſa and Emilia.

The renegado Roderigo giving an account to the governor of what was paſt, and of the ladies arrival, he ſoon entered the hall with captain Barbaroſa, to whom he had promiſed to give her he leaſt liked ; but he beheld them with admiration, ſeemed divided in himſelf, not knowing which to chooſe. He was a man of an excellent ſhape and ſtature, his mien great and majeſtic, his veſt and tunick were made of cloth of gold, his turbant glittered with jewels, diamonds, rubies, and emeralds, which ſeemed to emulate each other ; in fine, he was not much above thirty, and was one of the moſt beautiful and accompliſhed men of his nation, which I mention out of reſpect to thoſe unfortunate ladies, whoſe virtues are to be the more admired in reſiſting the paſſionate ſolicitations of ſuch a man. Tereſa's youth, and the charming innocence that blooms in virgins faces at fourteen, which ſhe had not loſt by being a wife, wonderfully ſtruck him ; grief added to her charms, her downcaſt eyes received new fires when lifted up. He gazed upon her with ſuch tranſport, that had not the captain, who was inflamed with her beauty, reminded him of Emilia, he had fixed on Tereſa ; but turning to the other, he was doubly wounded : her riper charms, with the heroick ſoul that ſparkled in her eyes, a ſecond time inflamed his ſoul, and he could part with neither. Barbaroſa, ſaid he, I muſt have both theſe lovely women ; name the price, and make ſome other choice, theſe muſt be mine. The captain murmured, but ſeeing he was obſtinate, he dared not tempt his fate, but told him they were at his ſervice. The governor pleaſed, ſtrait ordered him two hundred pieces of gold ; ſo he departed horribly vexed, and meditating revenge. Then the governor ordered the ladies to be unbound, and placed in two different chambers, with ſlaves to watch and attend them. Here the trunks of rich cloaths they had brought from Mexico, were, to their

great

great surprize, brought and presented to them; nothing
being taken from them by the governor's order.

Nothing was more dreadful to these ladies than this
separation; they both refused to eat or drink, and by
night were so faint, that they were scarce able to stand.
About ten o'clock in the evening a supper was brought
into Teresa's chamber; and soon after the governor entered the renegado waiting on him retired to the door,
which he shut, and stood without: the governor seeing
her look pale as death, sitting unmoved, approached
her with much tenderness, fearing she had taken some
fatal resolution to destroy herself: he kissed her hands,
kneeled at her feet, and intreated her to rise and eat.
He courted her with all the eloquence love can inspire,
to which she gave no answer but sighs and tears; at last
she looked upon him earnestly: Governor, said she, you
plead in vain; I am deaf to all intreaties, and can
never yield to gratify you. I am married, and with
child by a noble husband, whom I am bound to love,
and for whom I will preserve my person, nor will I ever
consent to your desires; nor will I ever eat again, till
you have freed me from this place: resolve therefore to
see me die, or generously set me at liberty. Do not
attempt to force me, lest I do some dreadful deed,
and fill your soul with endless remorse. Here she fell
at his feet, and let fall a shower of tears, then fainted.
This touched his soul, and made him relent; though a
Mahometan, he was generous and compassionate. He
took her in his arms, poured wine into her mouth, and
with much difficulty brought her to life again. Then
she renewed her complaints; to which he replied,
Charming, matchless woman, where virtue, beauty,
wit, and every grace conspire to captivate my soul! too
happy he who calls you his. Fly not from me to death;
but give me leave to wait upon you, and merit your
esteem, by all a lover can perform. I will never use base
force, but prayers and sighs shall thaw your breast, and
Selim will be your eternal slave. To prove I am so,

E 4   this

this night I will leave you to repose, and not presume to urge you farther. He kissed her hand, and, opening a door, withdrew into another room. Then a black-a-more maid entered, and folding down the bed, made signs to her to undress; which she fearing to do, though in great want of sleep, refused, and only lay down upon it. The maid left a candle burning, and withdrew, shutting the door after her. Soon after Teresa heard Emilia's voice in the next room with Selim; and hearkening, heard him say, Are you then cruel like Teresa? Come, come, trifle not with me; I am resolved to possess you, and will not be denied. She heard a noise, and then Emilia said, Villain, I fear you not, I will sacrifice you to preserve my virtue; die, infidel! and tell your prophet, when you come to hell, a Christian spilt your blood. Then she heard a dismal groan, and soon after Emilia entered the chamber, with a look that spoke the terrors of her mind, and the strange deed her hands had done. She had Selim's habit on, and in her hand the dress of a woman slave; Disguise yourself in this, said she, my dear Teresa, and follow me; with this I will free us both, or die. Here she drew forth a bloody dagger Selim wore. Teresa, trembling, put the habit on, and followed her: they passed through the chamber Emilia came out of, for Teresa's chamber door was locked, and there she saw Selim lying on the bed, weltering in his blood. They found another door; opening which, they descended a pair of back-stairs, and entered a garden, in which the renegado Roderigo was diverting himself with one of his master's fair slaves: he started, and came boldly up to them, doubtless suspecting something; but Emilia stabbing him, prevented any noise; the woman he was sporting with, having retired the moment they appeared. They forced open the garden-gate, and not knowing where to go, hasted out of the town, nor stopped till they had reached the fields. Here they wandered, ready to die for want of food and rest. At last, unable to go farther, they sat

down

down under a tree in a wood, and confulted what to do; they fuppofed they fhould be purfued, and if taken, furely put to death. Terefa, whofe courage was not equal to Emilia's, was almoft ready to defpair; and fhe feemed fo difpirited, that Emilia ufed all her eloquence to comfort her. My dear friend, faid fhe, look up to Heaven, that never fails to fuccour the diftreffed: the God that this day ftrengthened my feeble arm to deliver us, will, I doubt not, fend us help. Death is the worft that can befal us, and that is only what we are born to fuffer, and what no human power can fhield us from; nay, what we ought to meet with joy, fince we have an eternal ftate in view, that fhall compenfate for all the miferies we fuffer here. Since no guilt wounds our confciences, we need not fear to die, or dread all our inhuman enemies can inflict upon us. Come, chear up, and ftrive to go yet farther from that hateful city which we are fled from; perhaps fome hofpitable cottage may receive and fhelter us. At thefe words Terefa caft a-dying look upon her. Alas! faid fhe, my dear, my faith is ftronger than my body, though not fo great as yours; I cannot rife, my trembling limbs are now un-able to bear my weight; and if no help be fent us foon, then I muft lay down the tedious burthen of life in this fad place, and leave you. Here fhe fainted. At this inftant Emilia heard a ruftling among the trees, and looking behind her, faw a young man about twenty years of age, whofe handfome face and fhape furprifed her; he had on the habit of a flave; he came down from the tree they were fitting under; he accofted her with much refpect, and in French, which he had heard them converfe in. He was by birth a Venetian, as the fequel of this hiftory will inform us, and addreffed himfelf to her in this manner: Madam, be not fur-prifed that I have overheard you: I am joyful to tell you, it is in my power to ferve you. I am fervant to a widow woman who lives not far from this place, to whofe hufband it was my good fortune to be fold; fhe

by

by my means has embraced the Christian faith, though
we keep it a secret: she gets her living, and mine, by
making turbans and embroidery, which I carry home
to our customers, and the shops. We live very comfortably, and I am certain, if you will give me leave to
conduct you to her, she will receive you kindly, for she
is a person of great goodness. Emilia gladly accepted
his offer, and they lifting up Teresa, who was scarce
alive, led her along to the widow's house, which was
just behind the wood. The slave, whose name was Antonio, gave his mistress a brief account of their condition:
she embraced and welcomed them, bringing out meat
and drink, with which being much refreshed, they related to her the cause and manner of their escape from
the city; upon which she advised them to change their
clothes, since they would surely discover them: but
when Emilia came to pull off her turban and vest, she
was amazed to see the rich jewels it was adorned with:
in the pocket of the vest she found 100 sultanas of gold,
the buttons were diamonds. They blessed God for this
treasure, which would enable them to live here, and
procure them means to escape hence together. They
immediately cut the clothes in pieces, which served to
make the caps of the turbans; and the jewels they
ripped off, and hid in a box in the ground, resolving
Antonio should dispose of a few of them at a time, as
they had occasion, to the Jews, many of whom the
widow woman worked for in embroidery, particularly
in rich belts which they traded with to Spain and other
parts of Europe. The good widow, whose name was
Saraja, brought them mean Turkish habits, such as she
wore, saying, Ladies, you must now conceal your quality and beauty with this homely dressing, and pass for
young maids whom I have bought to assist me in my
work.---Teresa, who was much joyed at this unexpected
good fortune, replied, embracing her, I will assist you,
said she, in working with all my heart; we both know
how to use our needles. A bed was laid for them in

Saraja's chamber after the Turkish manner, that is, a carpet was spread upon the floor, on which were laid a quilt, blankets, sheets, and coverlids: and now had they known what was become of their lords, they had been tolerably easy. Antonio set out for the city the next morning, to learn what news he could, and returned at night with this account: I am, said he, acquainted with a Christian boy, who is slave to the governor: I walked two or three times before the house to watch his coming out; at last I saw him come sweating up the street with a surgeon; I winked upon him as he passed by; he returned the sign and entered: I waited not long, before he came out again; Lorenzo, said I, cannot we drink a dish of coffee together this morning? I am obliged to wait for some money one of my mistress's customers owes her, and therefore have an hour to spare; which if you can, we will pass together.—Lord, said he, our house is all in confusion; my master bought two Christian women yesterday, one of whom has this night wounded him cruelly, and left him weltering in his blood upon the bed; our renegado Roderigo they have likewise killed, as we suppose, for we found him dead in the garden, and they are escaped. Hearing some dismal groans in the night, I entered the room, and found my master in this condition; so I raised my fellow-servants, and we have brought him to life, and the surgeon has some hopes of his recovery. We informed him the women were fled; but he commanded us to make no search after them. He praised their virtue, and seemed to pity them, saying, he wished their happiness, and commended their courage. I asked Lorenzo whom these women belonged to? He said, he did not know. So I suppose none but Roderigo knew any thing of your lords. Thus ended Antonio.

Here the ladies remained undisturbed seven months, never stirring abroad but in the dusk of the evenings, when they walked only into the wood. Mean time Antonio often enquired of Lorenzo for news, but heard hope. Several ships sailed for Europe in this time; but the ladies resolved not to leave Barbary till they heard of their husbands. We shall therefore leave them at the widow's, and proceed to give an account of what befel the unfortunate Don Lopez, and the Count de Hautville.

CHAP. VI.

THE two lords being chained, as has been before recited, had no hopes of getting their liberty: they had writ, the one to France, the other to Spain, to their friends, of whom they knew not who might be living: but alas! the sum demanded was very great; and the time they must wait, before it was possible for them to receive any answer from either of those places, so long, that there were but little hopes of their living to receive it. But these considerations were nothing grievous to them, in respect of those relating to Emilia and Teresa; their ignorance of their condition, and distracting apprehensions of their ruin, almost overcame their reason and Christianity: they were both sick with grief, and incapable of comforting one another. But Providence, that saw their wrongs, at length provided a way for their deliverance: a fair virgin, who was a slave to the governor, waited on a mistress of his, whom he having enjoyed slighted, and had sent to this his country-house, where she had now been two years. This girl, who was then but twelve years old, often came into the chamber where these poor gentlemen were confined, to bring them tea and coffee from her lady; who, having had a sight of them, admired Don Lopez, and therefore ventured to do something to oblige him. This pretty girl they asked some questions of; as what country she was of, what religion? She told them, she was a Venetian; that her mistress was the same; that

they

they both were brought there by misfortunes, but seemed shy of saying more. One evening she entered the room, followed by a lady, in a Turkish dress exceeding rich; she was about five-and-twenty; her shape and mien was enchanting; her face so lovely, that it would have charmed the most insensible: a cloud of blushes overspread her face, and her disorder was such for some minutes, that she could not speak. The Count and Don Lopez, whose weakness and chains hindered them from rising, to pay her the civilities due to her sex, bowed their heads and kept silence also, expecting her to tell the business that brought her there. At last she spoke to them thus in French: Is it possible, that the cruel governor can be so void of humanity to treat you thus barbarously? Can he see such noble persons as you appear to be, perish in chains, and not relent? Though I risque my life to do it, noble strangers, I will free you. But, continued she, addressing herself to Don Lopez, may I hope to find you grateful? Will you give her a place in your heart, who gives you life and liberty? Will you preserve her life, who is determined to save yours? With you I am resolved to live or die. Speak then, for time is precious, and deserve my love, or hate. Don Lopez was too well skilled in the fair-sex, not to understand this lady's meaning; and since no other means but this was left to free them, wisely concealed his being pre-engaged. Nay, doubtless he was not altogether insensible of Eleonora's charms, for so was the lady named. He bowed with a look full of love and gratitude, saying, Liberty, which in itself is the greatest blessing man can possess, joined with so great a good as your favour, who would refuse? Your charms would even render confinement supportable; a dungeon with such a companion would be pleasant: shew me the **way** to freedom, and it shall be the study of my life to make you happy: I will defend you to the last drop of my blood. At these words, he grasped her knees and sighed. Poor Eleonora suffered herself to be deceived,

and

and thought of nothing but being happy with the man she loved. The Count de Hautville was amazed at Don Lopez's proceedings; his soul was constant and noble, and would have refused a life offered on so hard terms as the breach of his faith to his lovely Emilia. But his years were more than his friend's, and his temper more sedate. The sweet girl Anna fetched wine and sweet-meats to them. Eleonora sat down by them, eat, and suffered Don Lopez to kiss her hands, and say a hundred tender things to her. They appointed midnight for their escape, when she promised to bring them files to take off their fetters, and disguises to put on to prevent all discovery. She had provided a place for them to retire to also, near the sea-side: she had by this means, when she was first a darling mistress to the governor, prevailed with him to free a slave whom she fancied; it was a young Black whom her father had purchased when a child, of a captain, and given her, and being taken with her in the ship she was taken in, by an Algerine pirate, lived some time with her at the governor's; his name was Attabala. The governor at her request gave him a little house and garden, which he used in the summer to repair to for his pleasure, to fish on the sea-coast, and take the evening air on the water with his pleasure-boat. This place he gave to Attabala to live in, and take care of, and it being now winter, there was no fear of his going thither. In this slave she could confide; to him she had declared her design the day before, when he came, as he often did, to see his dear mistress, bringing her little presents of fish and fruits, as grateful acknowledgments of the favour she had done him. From this place it would be no difficult matter for them to escape to some Christian ship or port. Having staid with them two hours, she retired; and then the Count entered into talk with Don Lopez in this manner: My dear friend, Heaven seems now to smile upon us, a gleam of hope appears to comfort us; but, tell me, was it well done to dissemble?

Are

Are you changed? Is your wife forgot? and the sacred
matrimonial vows no longer valued? Excuse me if I
blame you; let nothing make you buy our liberty by
a crime; it is better to die here, than live with Heaven's
displeasure.----Don Lopez blushing, replied, Forgive
my weakness; I do not mean to proceed farther than
an innocent deceit. Teresa is always present with me:
but had I refused this lady's offer rudely, we had, perhaps, been here detained and murdered; and then
Teresa and Emilia never can be rescued from the villain
that robbed us of them. Be satisfied, therefore, that I
have acted prudently, and not designed amiss. The
Count was then contented; and now the joyful hour
approached when darkness and sleep had lulled the busy
world to rest; Eleonora came with Anna loaded with
jewels, gold, and clothes; they quickly filed their fetters off, and found the faithful Attabala at some distance from the house, with three horses, swift Barba-
ries, that run fleet as the wind; on two of these the
lords mounted, Don Lopez taking the lady, and the
Count the girl behind him; the Black riding the other
horse led the way, with which he was perfectly acquainted: in few hours, just at day-break, they reached the house, and being safely lodged, began to taste
the pleasures of liberty. Next day the governor, who
was recovered, was informed by the servants that remained in the country-house, of the lords flight: but
he had that night received an order from the Emperor
to repair to Fez, to take a command in the army, to
which he was determined to send him. This took up
all his thoughts, so that he took little notice of their
escape; and, as they afterwards learned, he never returned to Algiers, but died in the army of a fever.
And now Don Lopez had an opportunity to enquire
who Eleonora was, and the fatal accident that brought
her to this place. He treated her with such respect and
affection, that he could ask nothing of her, but what
she was ready to grant. One morning as the Count
and

and Anna, whom Eleonora now treated as a friend,
as became a person who was indeed her equal, were
conversing together, Don Lopez intreated her to relate
the adventures of her life.---Yes, my lord, said she, I
will, provided Anna, and you, gentlemen, will do the
same; for she would never let me know who she is,
though a Venetian as well as I. Anna replied: Madam,
whilst I was a slave I was not willing to be known: now
I shall take pleasure to entertain you with a story full
of strange adventures. Then Eleonora began in this
manner.

CHAP VI.

I Was born at Friuli, a place situate on the Adriatick
sea, in the Venetian dominions; my father was a
wealthy merchant in the city of Aquilegia; he had no
child but me by my mother, who was his second wife,
and the daughter of a noble Venetian. He had two
sons by a former wife, who loved me not, because my
father seemed to prefer me in his affection before them;
all his ambition was to see me well disposed of during
his life. I was also very apprehensive that my brothers,
if he died before I was married, would put me in a convent, to get my fortune, and be revenged upon me.
The great portion he offered with me, with that tolerable person the world thought me, procured me many
admirers, as soon, or indeed before I was of an age to
marry. Amongst these there was a kinsman of my
mother, the eldest son of a Venetian senator, whom the
custom and laws of that state will not permit to marry
out of a noble family, became much enamoured with
me: his name Seignior Andrea Zantonio. He secretly
courted me, my mother and father giving encourage-
ment; my heart soon yielded, and I gave him the preference above all others. I was now almost fourteen,

and it was refolved that we fhould be privately married
at a country-feat of my father's. Thefe proceedings
could not be kept fo fecret, but that the fervants were
fome of them privy to them. Amongft my lovers, there
was a rich captain of a fhip, who had caft his eyes upon
me in my infancy, and was one of the firft that entertained me with difcourfes of love; he was in years, and
I treated him with ill-nature, and indeed could not
endure him: yet he perfifted, till at length I ufed
him fo ill, that he concluded I had made choice
of another, and made it his bufinefs to find out
who was the fortunate man: in order to which, he
gained my maid, who waited upon me, by bribes to
difcover all to him. She informed him from time to
time of Seignior Andrea Zantonio's courting me, and
all that paffed. His bufinefs obliged him to be often
abfent on voyages to Spain, and elfewhere; and he arrived but the day before my intended wedding, of which
being informed, he refolved to prevent, it if poffible.
He therefore went to Seignior Andrea's father, and
acquainted him with the ill news, promifing if he would
affift him, he would prevent it; which he foon agreed
to do, being much enraged at his fon. The captain
defired three or four men to aid him, which he immediately procured him, fending four ruffians difguifed
along with him; with thefe he lay in ambufcade, in the
way which we were to pafs to my father's country-
houfe, where Seignior Andrea was to come to us the
next morning, not thinking it proper to go with us.
There were none in the coach but my father, mother,
and me; two men-fervants rid before the coach, and
my poor Black was behind it: as we paft by a wood,
the captain and his crew bolted out upon us, with
vizards upon their faces, and piftols in their hands;
they ftopped the coach, and tore me out of it, whilft
my mother fhrieked, my father ftormed, and one of the
fervants going to lay hold of me, was fhot dead. They
fled with me into the thickeft part of the wood, where
they

they bound and gagged me. The poor Black, Attabala, who has now helped to deliver you, being very nimble of foot, pursued me, and running after them, came up crying, just as they were binding my hands. They seized and bound him also; then they placed us before two of them on horseback, and made for the sea-side; where being soon arrived, we found a boat ready, into which one of them entered; we were next lifted in by the seamen that rowed it, and then the four villains that assisted in taking us, cried, Farewel! and rode off. The captain taking off his vizard so soon as we were put from the shore, discovered to me the author of my misfortune.---Madam, said he, I have, you see, done a bold deed to manifest my love, and secure you to my-self; fear nothing more, you are now in the hands of a man that adores you, and it is your own fault if you are not happy.---I could not answer, being gagged; but the disorder of my mind cannot be expressed. I saw myself in the hands of a man whom I hated, and no way left to escape. I was ten times more sensible of the loss of him I loved, than I could have before imagined. My soul shivered at the thoughts of what was to follow. I could no more hope to see my country and friends, for thither it was not to be supposed this villain would ever venture to bring me again, at least not in some years. I was tortured with a thousand dismal appre-hensions, when I saw the ship which lay by to receive us. He took me up in his loathed arms, and with the seamen's assistance, though I struggled, put me on board. Attabala and I were presently unbound: and now I be-gan to expostulate with Alphonso, for that was the cap-tain's name. What do you propose, said I, in taking me thus by force? Do you vainly imagine to be happy with me, whilst I hate and detest you, and view you as the only cause of my being wretched? Never will I pardon or love you, unless you carry me back to my father's. I will make you as miserable as myself, and never suffer you to rest whilst I am with you. I always

disliked

disliked you, but now my aversion is confirmed, and I
would prefer the most vile wretch on earth before you.
---Rage on, said he, fond girl you shall be mine, and
only death can free you from me. Here he suddenly
kissed and embraced me. You shall, said he, this night
marry me, that I may have a lawful title to you, and
you have nothing to reproach me. I will not be a
ravisher, but having secured your person and your
honour, take what will be then my due.---No, villain,
I replied; my tongue shall never call you husband; I
would sooner suffer hot pincers to rend it from the root
than speak those words, or answer to such a question.---
Silence, said he, gives consent, and I shall not want
witnesses to prove our marriage. Here he went out of
the cabin, and left me in the extremest grief and despair.
Poor Attabala comforted me the best he could, offering
to risque his life to kill him; but I regarded nothing
he said to me.

It was now night, and very dark; I heard the winds
blow, and a mighty disorder and noise upon the deck;
the captain stormed and called loudly to the seamen in
terms I did not understand; he came twice down into
the cabin, kissed me, and said, Madam, it is a rough
night, but fear nothing: yet I read a concern in his
face that spoke our danger. I cannot say that I was
much terrified with the thoughts of death, because at
that instant I was apprehensive of something worse. I
recommended myself to God, and calmly expected the
event of his good pleasure. Before day the ship had lost
her masts, and most part of her rigging; she was so
shattered, that nothing but getting to some shore, or
meeting with some ship, could save us. We were now
drove in sight of Barbary, when a ship coming up, our
ships crew hailed her. She soon came near, and lay
by, hoisting French colours. The captain sent his boat
aboard, but to their surprize they were all clapped under
hatches, it proving a pirate ship of Algiers. The
captain wondered the boat staid, but at last, seeing the

ship

ship bear up to us, he suspected the truth. He would
have made some defence, but the ship was disabled;
so he hastily catched up his sword, and mounting the
deck was there met by a crowd of the pirates, who had
boarded the ship: he was soon dispatched, and his men
all killed, or taken. I remained with poor Attabala
in the cabin all this while, and was so lost in thought,
I was scarce apprehensive of my danger: when the
Algerine captain entered the cabin with his men, they
took me, and conveyed me into the pirate ship, rifled
ours, and then set her adrift. They put me into the
great cabin with Attabala, and in few hours we came
to Barbary, landed at Algiers, and the next morning
Ibrahim the captain presented me to the governor.
What my thoughts were, and how I expressed my sorrows under all these misfortunes, would be too tedious
to tell you: In fine, the governor treated me kindly,
pretended to love me passionately, and forced me to his
bed; after which he denied me nothing, purchased and
freed Attabala at my request, and for eight years, though
he had many other new mistresses, gave me the preference, and loved me with the same ardour as at first.
He reproached me often that I brought him no child,
which Providence no doubt did not think fit to give us:
at last a French lady, of incomparable beauty, was
presented him, and she brought him a son the first year
of their acquaintance. This caused him to grow cold to
me, which I resenting, we quarrelled; so he sent me
away to the place you found me in. There I mourned
my misfortunes with a Christian sorrow, and never
thought to see the world again. Here I and my dear
Anna came together; she was purchased by him a month
before I left him, and I begged her of him to keep me
company. Thus have I given you a true narrative of
my misfortunes; and now Don Lopez, if we reach a
Christian shore again, and you prove grateful, I may
yet live to be happy.---Madam, said he, it shall be my
study to make you so.---Fair Anna, said the Count, we
will

will refer your story to the afternoon, it being now dinner-time; and I doubt not but we shall hear something as extraordinary as what Eleonora has related to us. They rose, and Don Lopez led Eleonora to the table; they dined, and then returned to her chamber, which was a pleasant room, having the prospect of the sea. Here they sat down, whilst Attabala made their coffee, and then they importuned Anna to keep her word; which she with a sigh consented to do, saying, My story is little worth hearing, and were it not to oblige Eleonora, I would beg to be excused.

CHAP. VIII.

I AM the daughter of an unfortunate prince, who was once a lieutenant-general in the Venetian army. My mother was a lady of great birth; but the family being ruined, had no fortune; my grandfather, being one of those who headed the Hugonot party against his sovereign Lewis XIV. lost both his life and estate. My mother, then an infant, was bred up by an Hugonot sister of my grandfather, who spared no cost upon her education, but could give her no fortune proportionable to her quality. She had beauty, wit, and was certainly a very charming person. My father, who was the eldest son of one of the noblest families in France, saw and loved her; he visited her in secret, often made her large presents; and knowing his father and family would never consent to his marrying her, he resolved if possible to debauch her; but her virtue made her resist him, though she loved him: so that he was forced to have recourse to stratagems to accomplish his desires. He used to walk with her often in her aunt's garden alone, she thinking herself secure from all attempts there. He

had

had procured a key to the garden-gate, pretending it was
more convenient for him to come in that way, becauſe
it was moſt private; and therefore her aunt gave him one
ſhe had uſed to carry in her pocket, to let her niece and
her in when they thought fit. He ſent three of his
ſervants in the night, who going in, hid themſelves in
this garden. His page, who conducted them where he
ordered, brought back the key to him. In the morning the prince comes himſelf in a travelling coach to
the garden-gate; there alighting, he enters the houſe,
calls for my mother, and pretends he was going in haſte
on a journey on ſome extraordinary buſineſs for the
king. After ſome talk with her aunt, he takes her into
the garden, to ſay ſome little tender things to her alone,
as ſhe ſuppoſed. As they were walking in a cloſe walk,
his ſervants diſguiſed ſtarted out upon her, and ſtopping
her mouth, bore her to the coach, into which he entered, drawing up the canvaſſes; and the coach driving
ſwiftly, he carried her thirty miles off to a remote old
caſtle which belonged to his father, but had not been
inhabited by any thing but ſervants a long time. When
he entered, the gardener and his wife, who had lived
there to look after the furniture and gardens many years,
made haſte to open the rooms, and aſked no queſtions.
Here he accompliſhed his ungenerous deſign, and here
he kept my diſconſolate mother ſome years: her aunt
concealed her loſs, and, as ſhe thought, her own diſ-
honour, as much as was poſſible, concluding ſhe was
gone with him by her own conſent; ſhe therefore pretended ſhe was retired farther into the country to ſome
relations: yet it reached the ear of my grandfather, who
only laughed at it, and called it a piece of galantry in
his ſon to receive a lady who fled to his arms. He often
preſſed my father to marry, but his affection to my mother, and conſcience, which now began to awaken him,
made him always decline it. The lady her aunt loved
her ſo tenderly, that ſhe ſoon after the loſs of her, fell
ſick with grief, and died. And now the war being

broke

broke out between the Turks and Venetians, my father resolving to marry my mother, who was young with child, and with her charming affable behaviour and tears had entirely gained his heart, he proposed to the duke his father to go to Venice a volunteer, with an equipage suiting his quality, to make a campaign or two. To this his father readily agreed: all things were got ready, and my mother, disguised in men's clothes, went with him. As soon as they arrived at Venice, the doge presented him with the command of a regiment of horse. Here he acquainted a bishop with the engagements that were betwixt my mother and him, together with the reasons why it must be a secret: the good bishop married them, and placed my mother with a widow lady of great quality and worth, who was his own relation. Here my mother was brought to bed of me, and unfortunately died in child-bed; so that my father returning from the army at the end of the campaign, found my mother just dead, and me at nurse. His grief was very great, and his fondness of me so extreme, he begged the bishop and lady to take all the care imaginable of me. The next campaign he was made a lieutenant-general, and was killed, dying in the bed of honour, leaving me a helpless orphan, whose greatest happiness at that time was, that I was too young to be sensible of my loss. My father had deposited in the lady's hands a great sum of money, as a provision for me in case of his death. The generous Angelina, for that was her name, bred me up with as much care and tenderness as if I had been her own child. She had a lovely youth, her only son, who was seven years older than me; for him she declared she designed me, provided we loved one another: his name was Carolus Antonio Barbarini: we lived together, and his name was one of the first things she taught my infant tongue to pronounce. At seven years of age I found how dear he was to me, and he being fourteen, began to feel the glowing passion he had for me warm his

5   breast.

breaſt. I was careſſed and loved by all his family, and had a proſpect of being one of the happieſt women in the world. The Turks gaining many unfortunate victories over the Venetians, I was not thought ſafe at home, but ſent with ſome young ladies of Angelina's family to a monaſtery. There, with many others, I was taken captive by the cruel infidels, and carried to Conſtantinople, where my tender years preſerved my virtue. A ſea captain bonght me, and carrying me to Algiers, made a preſent of me to the governor, whom he uſed to ſupply with miſtreſſes, for which he was doubtleſs well rewarded. This is my unhappy ſtory. I ſuppoſe the governor reſerved me for his uſe, when I was older; but God has beeen pleaſed to deliver me out of his hands, for which I bleſs his name, and I hope to ſee Venice once again with his aſſiſtance. Here ſhe finiſhed; and Eleonora riſing up, embraced her, ſhedding ſome tears. Are you then, ſaid ſhe, the charming girl the noble Angelina bred up? Fair Anna, forgive my ignorance that made me treat you as a ſervant; my mother was Angelina's ſiſter; you are dear to me by the ties of blood, and far my better in your noble father. May Providence reſtore you to my kinſman, and bring us ſafe to Venice again! Here the two lords related part of their adventures; Don Lopez concealing that part only that related to Tereſa, whom he mentioned as his ſiſter: they related the manner of their being caſt on the diſmal iſland, their eſcape thence, and unfortunate meeting with the Algerine pirate, with the ladies being raviſhed from them for the governor. At laſt they declared they would not leave Barbary till they were found and reſcued. Attabala undertook to go to the governor's, and learn what was become of them, which he faithfully performed in a few days after. He went to enquire after his maſter's health as uſual, found none but ſervants, who informed him of the ladies eſcape thence, and how the governor had been wounded by one of them, and that Roderigo was likewiſe killed;

in

in fine, of all they knew, but where the ladies were
retired to, that they could not tell. So Attabala returned with this account; upon which the lords refolved
to difguife themfelves, and go together in fearch of
them in all the villages near the city, to one of which
they fuppofed they muft have fled for fhelter. They
dreffed themfelves in the habit of Grecian merchants,
which habits Attabala bought for them at the city, and
both fpeaking Greek, they doubted not to pafs for fuch,
if queftioned. Thus metamorphofed they went daily
out, and ventured to enquire if any ladies in European
dreffes were arrived in that town or village which they
paffed through. Thus they did in every place they
could think of; but finding all their fearch in vain,
they began to imagine they were hid in fome wood or
cave, and therefore concluded to vifit all lonely woods
and places leaft frequented: this they did for feveral
days alfo, but without fuccefs. One evening as they
were returning home, they paffed by a fmall wood, into
which it was difficult to find an entrance: they ftopped,
and having viewed it well, they perceived fome foot-
fteps and beaten ways over the grafs. They entered
into the thickeft part of it by this path, and there found
a difmal fort of a hut made only with boughs of trees,
and a piece of fail-cloth; under which, upon fome
ftraw, lay a woman, whofe face, though very beautiful,
expreffed the greateft want and mifery. She had a
canvas waiftcoat and petticoat on, was barefoot, had a
filk handkerchief tied about her head, and a piece of
flannel wrapped about her fhoulders; fhe was young,
fair, and finely limbed, but her eyes were funk: fhe
was meagre, pale, fick, and fo weak fhe could not rife.
The lords viewed her with fuch compaffion, that they
were ready to weep. In the name of God, faid the
count de Hautville in French, what are you? And how
came you to be left in this difmal place? I am not able,
faid fhe, to tell you; if you are Chriftians, give me
fomething to eat or drink for our Saviour's fake. They

had nothing with them; but Attabala, who went with them as a guide, hasted to the next village, and soon brought some bread and wine, with some of which they a little revived her. She drank a good draught of the wine, but had not strength to chew or swallow the bread. As they were assisting her, a man came up, whose face, shape, and mien engaged their attention: he was dressed in a jacket and drawers of canvas, a red cloth cap upon his head with fur, barefooted, and so pale and lean, that he appeared the very image of death; in a ragged handkerchief he held in his hands, he had nuts and wild sour grapes with a few dirty bones, such as seemed to have been flung out into the streets for dogs. He retired back when he saw the lords; at which the woman called to him in a sort of extasy: Come here, my dear lord, God sends us friends and food! He then bowing, approached them. Their surprize was such, when they saw him nearer, they could not speak. His feet bled, his sinews and nerves were all open, his bones stared upon one another; in fine, he was the most miserable object their eyes ever saw. They put the bottle of wine and bread into his hands, at which a flood of tears poured from his eyes; and going to lift the bottle to his mouth, he staggered and fell down; at which the woman shrieked, and fell into strange convulsions. Don Lopez, who caught the bottle when the man fell, endeavoured with his friend's assistance to get some wine down his throat; but his teeth being set fast, it was very difficult. Mean time Attabala was employed to hold the woman, who beat her breast, gnashed her teeth, rolled her eyes, and appeared to be in the agonies of death. In some time both recovered a little; and Don Lopez ordered Attabala to run back to the town, and hire horses to carry them to Attabala's house. This was soon done, and the lords mounting, took the man and woman up before them, and so posted heme; where being arrived, they put them into warm beds, not being certain they were

man and wife, Attabala having firſt waſhed their feet.
This, with ſome burnt wine, and bread ſopped in it,
threw them into a profound ſleep till the next morning;
when Eleonora, Anna, and the lords viſited them to
enquire who they were, and how they did: they firſt
entered the man's chamber, who no ſooner ſaw them,
but he raiſed himſelf up in the bed, and lifting up his
hands broke out in theſe paſſionate expreſſions: To thee,
firſt, my merciful Creator! I return my thanks; it is to
thee I owe this great deliverance, and all the good
things I have received in my whole life. I bleſs thee for
the miſeries I have ſuffered: it is moſt juſt, my God,
that I ſhould be puniſhed with cold, hunger and thirſt,
who broke my faith with thee, and fled thy altar for a
ſenſual ſatisfaction. It was I ſeduced the virtuous Clarinda from her bleſſed retirement, for which ſhe ſuffers
both in mind and body; but no more will I offend my
God. Now pardon us, and as thou haſt delivered us
from death, ſo grant peace to our ſouls. Then bowing
to the lords: To you, bleſſed inſtruments of Heaven's
bounty! ſaid he, who have ſaved the life of her whoſe
life is dearer to me than my own, you who ſaved both
from certain death, I return unfeigned thanks, and will
make all the grateful returns my preſent circumſtances
will permit. They embraced, and congratulated him
with much tenderneſs, and promiſed to return to him as
ſoon as they had viſited the lady. To her they went,
and found her waking. She was very faint, and the ladies welcoming of her, deſired ſhe would drink chocolate
with them, and not ſpend her ſpirits by talking; yet
ſhe uttered many affectionate thanks and acknowledgments to God and them. The breakfaſt was brought
in, and ſoon after the gentleman being riſen and dreſſed
in a ſhirt, a thing he had not on before, waiſtcoat,
breeches, cap, night-gown, ſtockings, and ſlippers of
one of the lords, entered the room, and appeared like
what he really was, a man of quality, of excellent parts
and perſon. Anna had likewiſe ſupplied the lady with a

ſhift

shift and night-clothes; she appeared to be about two-and-twenty, and the gentleman upwards of thirty. Being refreshed with eating, the gentleman, without being asked, addressed himself to the company thus: Gentlemen and ladies, said he, I am positive you are very desirous to know who this lady and I are, and what strange misfortunes reduced us to the deplorable condition you found us in; I will therefore as briefly as I can satisfy your curiosity, and you must excuse me, if I do not relate every particular with exactness, since my strength is but little at present. They assured him they would rather deny themselves that pleasure than trouble him; and begged that he would proceed.

CHAP. IX.

THIS lady and I, said he, were both born in France, in the same province; Dauphiny gave us birth. My father (whom it is necessary I should mention first, because I am ten years older than she, which occasioned my misfortune, in being destined to the church, before she was grown up to inspire my soul with that fatal passion that has undone us) was the king's lieutenant for that province, and marquis of Harcourt. I was his third son, and therefore designed for the church, in which I could not miss of preferment, being descended of so great a family; nor did I want the qualifications requisite to render me capable of that noble profession. I was not inclined to any vice; nor, I thank God, wanted sense to learn, and retain, all that was taught me: In fine, I was very dear to my father, and much esteemed by my friends and family. I passed through my study, and was ordained a secular priest at twenty. I was soon dignified with being made a canon of the

royal

3

royal cathedral of Cambray. My brothers were greatly preferred in the army, and we were all very great and very happy; but Providence did not think fit I should continue fo. I got an ague and fever, which rendered me very weak; the phyficians advifed me to the country air. Upon which I retired to a village, where my father had a little fummer feat. In this town was a monaftery of Benedictine nuns; this place I vifited, having two young ladies my relations there. Here I faw the charming Clarinda, who was then about fifteen; fhe was daughter to the count de Villeroy, who having ten children, four fons and fix daughters, fent three of his youngeft daughters to this monaftery, of which the lady abbefs was his fifter. He gave a thoufand pounds fterling with them, and all poffible perfuafions and means were ufed to perfuade them to embrace this holy way of living, as is cuftomary in France, becaufe great fortunes and families fhould not be impaired and ruined by portioning many children; therefore they commonly dedicate fome of them to the church, which prevents their impoverifhing eftates, and too greatly increafing the family. Thus they were enabled to give fuch great portions with their eldeft daughter, and to make fettlements on the fecond fons, as may marry them into noble and rich families fuitable to their own. But though this be an excellent piece of policy, yet it often caufes the children to be very unhappy, and the church crowded with thofe whofe inclinations do not fuit the habits they wear, but tend to the world, and figh after the pleafures of it; nay, too often do, as I have done, forget the facred vows they have made, and follow the dictates of their paffions. Clarinda was fair as an angel, witty, free, affable, and in all things fo engaging, that I foon loft my heart to her; I ftruggled with the growing paffion, fometimes refolved to fee her face no more; but love overcame all my refolutions, and I at laft refolved to poffefs her or die. I foon found means to reveal my paffion to her, and fhe in a fhort time yielded

F 3 to

to fly with me to any part of the world, for in France
we could not stay. I had a great deal of money by me,
and now I thought only of amassing such a sum as might
provide handsomely for us in Holland or England, to
one of which places we were determined to go : in order to this, I made bold with some very rich jewels,
which were laid up in a reliquary, of which I kept the
keys; to prevent discovery I employed a Hugonot jew-
eller to set false stones in the room of the true, which I
picked out before he saw them, pretending to him that
I was desirous to repair and beautify those sacred things;
and that time having reduced them to this condition, I
could not bestow diamonds and rubies, and was willing
to make them decent, at my own expence : and indeed
I thought there was but little use for diamonds to adorn
dry bones and relicks, which we were not certain belonged to those holy persons whose they were pretended
to be ; and that the money bestowed on the poor would
have been much better employed. Though in me this
was sacrilege, and a great crime, yet having given the
reins to my passion, I ran headlong to destruction. All
things being ready, I provided a boat to carry us down
the river Rhosne to Arles, from whence I doubted not
to get passage to England, in some ship from Marseilles
that was going home through the Straits. Clarinda
failed not to be ready at the appointed hour, which was
midnight. I brought a ladder of ropes, which throwing over the wall of the garden, which was not very
high, she mounted, and turning it over on the other
side descended. I received her with open arms, and all
the transport a man may be supposed to feel, who has
rigorously lived to his duty, denied himself all the pleasures of sense, and gives a loose to his desires. The
sad prisoner, who has lived long confined in a dark
loathsome vault, feels not a greater joy at the sight of
day and liberty than I did then. I hastened with her to
the boat, into which I had already conveyed disguises
for us both, with all things necessary. The jewels I
                                                    had

had hid about me in a purse, and my pockets were
stuffed with gold, besides all I had put into the trunk I
had got aboard with our clothes and linen. As soon as
we were come aboard, and alone in the cabin, we dressed
both in gentlemen's habits. I threw our others into the
river. And now it is needless to tell you that I enjoyed
the maid I so much languished for, promising to marry
her so soon as we were arrived in a place of safety.
When we came to Marseilles, which we soon did, we
discharged the bark, and went ashore with our things
and lodged at an inn. And now growing distractedly
fond of Clarinda, I longed to perform my promise of
marrying her; and in few days after, having purchased
some woman's apparel for her, we stepped out one
morning early, and going to a country village two miles
from Marseilles, were lawfully joined by the parish
priest: and had I not been before engaged to live single,
I had been one of the happiest men on earth. We
waited not long before an English ship arrived homeward
bound. I agreed for our passage; we went aboard, and
soon after set sail. And now my fears were all over, I
fancied myself going to a country where I should rather
be applauded than condemned for what I had done,
where I should be free in all respects; and though I
never had a thought to change my religion, yet I fancied
I should be extremely happy in a place where I should
live free from all constraint: but God, whom I had
offended, soon convinced me of my folly. An Algerine pirate met us, and after a sharp dispute took the
ship, and made us all prisoners, carrying us into Tunis,
where he sold us for slaves. It was Clarinda's fortune
and mine to be bought by a merchant's widow, who
sent her steward to market to buy a man and a maid
servant. When he brought us home the lady viewed
us, and seemed pleased with his choice of us. She asked
me many questions, as what nation I was of, what I
could do, who Clarinda was, and such like; to which
I answered, that she was my sister, that we were born

in

in France; that I could write, cast accounts, play upon
several forts of mufic, but neither of us had been bred
to work: I faid my fifter could work finely at her needle.
She told me it was our own faults if we lived uneafy,
and that she would ufe us kindly. In short she liked my
person, and in few days gave me to understand what
she expected. She was old, and very difagreeable; yet
having given the reins to paffion, the fear of being
parted from, or of Clarinda's being ill ufed, made me
refolve to oblige the hag, which I accordingly did.
And now I was treated as the mafter of all, I fat at table
with her, and Clarinda with us; I was denied nothing,
but managed her affairs and fortune as I pleafed. I
had ftill left my own purfe of jewels, which I had
hung about my neck with a ftring; and when the pirates took us, they ftaid not to ftrip us of our shirts,
fo they found not what was concealed next my fkin.
This I always kept about me; but I wanted two things
which are the greateft bleffings of life, liberty and a good
confcience. I continued to pleafe Admela the widow
fome time; but one fatal evening she having walked
into the garden, I ftole to Clarinda's room, where she
was working, as I often did undifcovered, and taking
the privilege of a hufband to enjoy my virtuous wife,
was by a malicious flave watched, and betrayed: he
envied my good fortune in being beloved by his miftrefs.
He thought he had now a good opportunity to ruin me,
and infinuate himfelf into her favour. He gave her an
account of what he had feen; and when I came into
the garden fome time after, and gave her my hand, she
looked upon me with fuch rage and difborder in her face,
that I quickly apprehended what was to follow. I entertained her as ufual with pleafant talk; ye fupped,
and I went into her chamber, when her fervants withdrew, as I was accuftomed to do; but when we were
alone, she explained herfelf in this manner. Malherb,
faid she, for under that name I concealed myfelf, Clarinda is more than a fifter to you, and I have nurfed a
                                                    viper

viper in my bosom, that steals your affection from me.
You adore her, and doubtless care not for me. I
thought to have provided nobly for her and you; but
since she makes me wretched, I will remove her from my
sight and yours for ever. Here she wept. What different passions rent my divided soul at this dreadful
moment, words cannot express. I stood for some minutes
immoveable as a statue: at last I endeavoured to pacify
her, begging her not to credit what a villain said, who
conspired my ruin, envying my good fortune. At last
I gained so far upon her, that she received me to her
arms; and then I made her promise to put the villain
away that abused us, which the next morning she performed, ordering him to be sent to a country house she
had near the sea-side, twenty miles distant, to look
after the gardens. He uttered a hundred curses and
imprecations against me; but they did not hurt me, or
serve him. And now I was obliged to caress Admela
in an extraordinary manner, and be more circumspect
than ever with Clarinda, on whom she kept a watchful
eye. We continued thus some time; but Admela observed the tender regard we had for each other so well,
that she was convinced I had imposed upon her: and
being very cunning, she took no notice to me; but taking Clarinda with her into the garden one morning,
when I was gone out to receive some money of the merchants for her, she had her seized, and put bound into a
cart; where being covered over with some sacks, she was
drove to the country house, where the Irish villain was,
and there locked into a chamber, where they chained
her by the leg, and only one old hag, who had been
Admela's nurse, left with her. Here she remained a
long time: at my return home I missed her, and asking
where she was, none answered; at last my devil-mistress
told me, she was where I should never see her more. I
raged and stormed in vain; nay, I used tears and prayers, but jealousy had rendered her soul obdurate and inflexible; in fine, none would inform me what was be,

come

come of her. From this hour I refolved to fhun Admela's arms and bed; at laft fhe threatened me with Clarinda's death if I treated her fo ill. Thus I lived two whole years in perpetual torment and anxiety of mind; my health decayed, and I was no longer the fame man. Admela grieved, and being old, fell into a lingering illnefs that at laft ended her days, but not my forrows. And now having got much riches of the widow's into my power, I refolved to find out where Clarinda was, though I fpent it all; but all my defigns were vain. Muftapha, a Mahometan captain that was nephew to Admela's hufband, and his heir, comes home, and feizing upon all, caft me into prifon, where I lay three months, and then was turned out to be ufed as a flave, with a clog chained to my leg, to prevent my efcaping. I was forced to carry burdens, as a porter, about the city, to earn a morfel of bread. Whilft thefe things paffed, my dear Clarinda remained a prifoner very fick; the Irifh villain and old woman lived rarely, and grew great friends; he meditating how to revenge himfelf upon me, and having always viewed Clarinda with defire, prevailed on Dimas, the old hag, to let him fometimes vifit her. He always brought her fomething, as fruit, coffee or wine, to revive her poor decayed fpirits; and though grief had much altered her face, yet her beauty charmed the villain. One day when Dimas was gone to Tunis for money for their falary, which Admela allowed them, he thus addreffed Clarinda: Madam, faid he, I am touched to the very foul with a tender fenfe of your fufferings. I adore and love you equal with him you are parted from; grant me the enjoyment of your perfon, and I will free you. Malherb is dead, the revengeful Admela poifoned him three days after you were brought here. Dimas has orders to poifon you, but I keep her from it. I am an European and a Chriftian; give yourfelf to me, and I will procure a fafe paffage for us to Ireland, where I will marry you. At thefe words fhe lifted up her eyes,

and

and with a flood of tears replied ; Is my dear husband
dead then ? Can I no more hope to see him ? Then why
do I live ? At these words she swooned. Macdonald, for
that was the villain's name, held her up in his arms, till
she recovering, poured forth the most passionate expressions of grief. He then departed, fearing to hear her
reproaches, and subtilly considering, that after the first
efforts of her passion were over, reason would take place,
and she would reflect upon the misery of her present condition, and the impossibility of being freed from it by
any other means but by him ; and so concluded, she
would at last comply and fly with him, which was the
thing he desired to compass, by this invented story of
my death. Dimas returning, wondered to find her so
afflicted, and asked her the reason of her grief ; but
Clarinda fearing to tell her, and discover what had
passed betwixt her and Macdonald, gave her no answer.
And now Heaven kindly inspired her with a thought
that this story might not be true : Why, said she, am
I kept here if he is dead ? Admela has no need to fear
me, if the man we love is dead ; if she would have taken
my life away, she might have done it long since ; no,
doubtless, this villain tells me this to make me despair
of any help but his. My God! continued she, who can
bring good out of evil, direct me what to do. Thus
she passed the sleepless night, and at last resolved to dif-
semble with Macdonald, and if possible, get her liberty,
without injuring her virtue. The next time he came
to her alone, when Dimas, who was jealous of him,
was absent, she pretended to hearken to his proposals,
and told him, if he would contrive a way for them to
escape, she would gladly go with him. He seemed
transported ; and the next night, whilst Dimas slept,
whom he had given a large potion of opium to, in some
coffee they had drank together, he rises, and packing
up what money and clothes he could get in the house,
he came into Clarinda's chamber, filed off her fetters,
and they hasted to a neighbouring wood, where they

sat

sat down, fearing to lose themselves, it being a very
dark night; resolving to stay till the day-break, and
then he proposed to go down to the sea-side, in hopes
to find some ship's boat to go off to sea in; if not, he
had made an acquaintance with a poor fisherman, of
whom he used to buy fish, in whose cottage he doubted
not they might safely stay. And now the villain began
rudely to press her to yield to him. Macdonald, that
you are a villain, said she, I am sensible; I have used
you to obtain my liberty, I never design to gratify you;
therefore desist, or expect to die by my hand, or kill me,
for I prefer death a thousand times before a life of in-
famy. If my husband still lives, I may be happy; if
he be dead, I have no more business with the world,
and shall gladly die: but this be assured of, I will resist to death. Macdonald's surprize was very great,
yet he persisted in his wicked design, and when he found
persuasions would not do, proceeded to use force, saying, Clarinda, it is in vain you strive; the happy
Malherb ruined me, and I will revenge myself by rob-
bing him of you. At these words, she caught a bayonet
from his side, and stabbed him, before he suspected her
design. And now guess the terror of her mind, alone
in a dismal wood, she knew not where to go, a dying
man lying by her. She withdrew some little distance
from the place, and there falling upon her knees, begged of God to deliver her from the miseries of life by a
speedy death. At last, day breaking, she looked round
her, and rising walked through the wood in a path-way
which led to a hill. This she ascended with much pain,
being very weak. In a shady valley, on the other side
the hill, she saw an antient man of a venerable aspect;
his beard reached to his waist, his habit was a coarse
grey cloth, very old, his feet were bare; he had a
little pitcher in his hand, and was going to fill it with
water at a small spring that rose at the bottom of the hill.
She approached him trembling, and fell at his feet,
crossing her breast. He lifted her up, saying in French,

God

God save you, woman! what would you have?—A
place to conceal myself, father, said she; I am a Christian, fled from those that sought to ruin me; I am
faint, sick, and friendless: Oh, assist me in what you
can: if not, I must perish, for I cannot go much farther.
He led her down the valley, and brought her to a poor
cottage, there he gave her some bread and boiled roots,
which was what he lived on; and here she recounted to
him how she was with her husband taken and made
slaves, with the cause of her confinement at the country
house; how she escaped thence, and had killed, as she
supposed, the villain that would have forced her. Then
the old man, she having finished her story, began thus:
Daughter, I am a man who have long since retired
from the world; I am a priest, born in France; I was
chaplain to an India ship; and being desirous to see
the world, chose that way to travel, in hopes to be useful
to the ignorant. We were taken by the Algerines, as
you have been, and I was seven years a slave to a
merchant at Fez, where I learned to live hard; he at
last freed me, and being well acquainted with the place
and people, I resolved to live here the remainder of my
days. I never eat flesh, nor drink wine, but content
myself with bread and roots, to which you are welcome.
I get my living by practising physick among these poor
barbarians, and so have frequent opportunities of bap-
tizing infants, unperceived by them, and sometimes
converting poor souls to the Christian faith. Sometimes
I paint small pictures of holy persons, for which they
give me bread and roots. Thus have I lived these forty
years, daily visiting the sick in the adjacent towns and
villages: and now, daughter, if you can content yourself to work, I will procure you a cottage and business,
for with me it would be indecent for you to stay. You
say you have killed a man, a thing you ought to mourn
for all the days of your life. Alas! could you find no
way to touch his soul, but to cut him off in that dreadful
moment when he was least prepared for his eternal state?

Why

Why did you not rather call earnestly to God to deliver
you? Are you certain he is dead?---No, father, said she,
but I believe so. He rose hastily, saying, Stay here,
and I will go and see if God has mercifully spared him
to repent. He run to a cupboard, took out a bottle of
cordial, and with his staff in his hand departed, going
as nimbly as if he had been young, though he was old
and feeble. This sight filled her soul with an unusual
strain of devotion: My God! said she, what a lively
devotion glowed in the face of that good man? How
vigorously he performs his duty, and how careless have
I been of mine? How have I distrusted God, how lamented for a mortal man, and how little for his and my
sins? I will henceforth resolve courageously to support
all adversity. Why did I imbrue my hands in blood, and
rashly ruin the soul of him whose hands gave me liberty
but some few hours before? I should have strove, and
reasoned with him; God would have strengthened me,
no doubt, and touched his heart. Well might the
Psalmist cry out to be delivered from the guilt of shed-
ding innocent blood. Here she melted into tears, and
truly repented her rashness. Not long after, as she sat
pensive, the good father Clementine returned, for that
was his name, and with much joy told her, Macdonald
was sitting under a tree when he came, so weak with
the loss of blood, he could not rise. I viewed his
wound, said he, after giving him some cordial; it is
in his thigh, deep, but not mortal. I mentioned nothing of you to him, but admonished him seriously to
prepare for death, not letting him know that I thought
his wound not dangerous. He viewed me earnestly,
and at last said, Are you a Christian Priest? I assured
him I was; he seemed overjoyed, made his confession to
me, expressing great sorrow for his sins. I went to a
poor man's house, and we have got him thither. There
have I left him in bed; at night I have promised to return: he says your husband is living at Tunis. Poor
Clarinda blessed God and him for this good news. He

conducted

conducted her to a widow woman's house where she was
to live till news could be got of me; there she helped to
embroider belts with this good woman, who maintained
herself with that work. It was a great way from Tunis
to this place, and it was some time before any body
could be found to go thither with her, which the good
Clementine could not do himself, because he could not
leave his sick patient. Poor Macdonald died, before
her departure, of a fever, occasioned by his great loss
of blood, and was very penitent. The clothes and
money he had were by the priest taken care of; who,
having paid the countryman for lodging and diet for
Macdonald, gave the rest to Clarinda. She took
leave of the generous father with tears, promising to
return to him soon with me; he said he would provide
for us to live. The good widow loved her much, and
invited her to live there again: the woman's son went
with her; they came safe to Tunis, and lodged at a poor
woman's who was kin to the widow. Here they learned
the news of Admela's death, my imprisonment and poor
condition. Clarinda got the young man to enquire
me out; at last he found and brought me to her, but
when she saw me in so miserable a plight, a clog chained to my leg, my beggarly habit and altered face, no
words can express her concern; yet our souls leaped for
joy. We kissed, embraced, and wept; so moving was
the scene, the poor countryman and woman of the house
could not refrain from tears. She told me what a retreat was provided us; but I feared being pursued, and
thought it was better for me to stay at Tunis. We took
a lodging in this woman's house, she promising to procure needle-work for Clarinda, to help to maintain us.
In few days the honest countryman went home, carrying a letter from us to the good father, full of our
acknowledgments. And thus we lived for ten months,
in which time Clarinda found herself with child. We
lived very poorly; and no hopes of freedom appearing,
at last I resolved, she importuning me, to file off my

fetter,

fetter, and steal away to the widow's house, where she could lie-in more conveniently, and with Clementine the pious priest's assistance, be better supplied with necessaries. We had little money, no guide, and travelled on foot mostly in the night, fearing to be observed and questioned in the day. We soon lost our way, and wandering about, came to the wood where you found us. Here poor Clarinda fell into the pains of childbirth, and was delivered of a dead child, which was doubtless lost for want of help. I did all I was able to assist and comfort her, but she was now in so weak a condition as rendered her unable to go from this dismal place. All I could do was to wander in the neighbouring villages to seek for food to sustain our lives. In this condition God sent you to us; and now if he assists us to get safe to France again, Clarinda and I are determined to do penance for our past sins, and if a dispensation cannot be granted, part for ever: I will return to serve my God at the altar, and she to her peaceful convent, to wash away our stains and oversights with tears, to obtain a happy death, and rise again to everlasting peace and glory.----Thus he ended his moving relation, which drew tears from every eye. The lords and ladies caressed them both in an extraordinary manner, and the praises of the good father Clementine were confirmed by every tongue. And now the count de Hautville called for wine to refresh the gentleman, whose name they now knew to be monsieur de Chateau-Roial. Soon after, dinner being ready, they repaired to the parlour, and the ladies, charmed with Clarinda, strove to entertain her as well as they were able, and to recover her health, she being very weak, and much indisposed. We must now take leave of them for some time, and return to Emilia and Teresa, whom we left at the widow's.

CHAP.

CHAP X.

TERESA was a month after her arrival at Seraja's delivered of a dead son, and lay some time sick; but recovering, and both the ladies working with their needles all day, gained a great deal of money, whilst Antonio went frequently abroad, to make inquiry after Don Lopez and the count de Hautville. At last going to the city with work, he met Lorenzo, who told him how the lords were escaped with a lady and girl from the country house; but he knew not whither, and that the governor was gone for the army, from which he had sent him two days before on business. This was all Antonio could learn, and enough to fill the ladies with new hopes of seeing them again. Sometimes they imagined they were got to some ship, and returned home; yet it seemed not very probable they would leave Barbary without having found them: then they concluded they lay somewhere concealed, and would not fail to enquire them out. This, with the knowledge of the governor's being gone for the army, made them more venturous than before, and they walked out sometimes into the adjacent towns, and often in the open fields, in hopes of meeting their husbands. But it so happened, that Muley Arab, youngest son to the emperor of Fez and Morocco, who was used to hunt often near this place, it being now winter, riding by one evening with few attendants, saw these unfortunate ladies, attended by Antonio, walking home to the widow's. Their beauty surprized him, though their appearance was mean; he ordered one of his slaves to follow them, which he did, and returned to the prince, who the next morning sent one of his chief favourites to the house. He talked with the woman in the Turkish language, asking her who these women were. She told them they were poor maids, captives, whom she had bought to work with her in embroidery. He presently demanded what

price

price she would part with them at, saying he would purchase them.   At these words the poor woman was confounded.   She replied, trembling, I love them so dearly
I cannot part with them.—Then, said he, you shall
go along with them ; my master, the prince of Fez, will
provide nobly both for you and them ; he will be here
this night.   He instantly departed, and left the widow
and ladies, to whom she explained what the Mahometan
had said, in the utmost distraction : whither to fly they
knew not, and to stay there was certain ruin.   They
therefore resolved immediately to pack up their money,
clothes, and jewels, and be gone towards the sea-side.
Whilst they were doing this, Antonio enters the house
quite out of breath.   He had been out that morning
with some goods to a merchant's near Attabala's house,
and returning, saw the two lords and Attabala walking
in a field near it.   He concluded it was them by the
description Emilia and Teresa had given of them, and
therefore hasted to bring the good news, having never
rested in the way, though it was ten miles from the
good widow Seraja's.   Ladies, said he, I have fortunately found your husbands ; now we shall be happy,
and only Antonio will remain wretched.   Teresa and
Emilia transported, replied, Blessed be our God, who
ever helps us when distressed ! Let us go hence, with them
we shall be secure ; and though you, our good angel,
have not yet informed us who you are, yet I doubt not
but we, or our husbands, may be instrumental to make
you happy also.   Here they informed him of Muly
Arab's message, and the necessity of their removing
thence.   I will then, said he, return to the house where
they are, and give your lords notice of your coming :
mean time, delay not to haste to us, we will meet you
on the way ; but if you meet any company on the road,
conceal yourselves behind some trees, or stay in the
great wood till we come to you.   Teresa put the box of
jewels into Antonio's hand, saying, Take you these
in your care, and give them to our lords to secure, before

fore they come to us: we will follow your directions,
and be foon with you. He drank fomething to refresh
him, and departed; it was not long ere they followed,
making what hafte they were able to get to the place
appointed; but, alas! Fate has otherwife decreed. The
Moorish lord returning to his prince, related to him the
diforder Seraja was in at his propofal, and advifed him
to be quick in fecuring the women. My lord, faid he,
they are the faireft creatures my eyes ever faw, and, if
I miflake not, Chriftians, and of noble birth. The
prince, more inflamed with this relation, gave orders to
fome of his attendants to follow him; and mounting a
fwift Arabian horfe, fet out for the widow's, Ifmael the
Moorish lord leading the way. They found the houfe
empty; and all things being left in diforder, fhewed
the inhabitants were fled in the utmoft hafte and confufion. The prince raged, commanding his vaffals to
divide themfelves into parties, and purfue them with all
diligence. The cunning Ifmael advifed him to make
for the fea-coaft: They are doubtlefs, faid he, fled
thither, in hopes to get off in fome fhip or boat to fome
of the European forts or confuls, to Tripoli or Ceuta.
Muley Arab followed his counfel, and foon overtook
the unfortunate travellers, who being loaded, unufed to
walk faft, and afraid of every paffenger they met, were
not got half way to Attabala's. The Moors feized upon them; and it was needlefs to afk who they were, for
their charming faces betrayed them. The prince viewed them with tranfport, defcended from his horfe,
and fpeaking to the affrighted widow, who fpoke his
language, bid her tell them they fhould not fear, he
was paffionately in love with them, would make them
great, they fhould live in his palace, and fmile in his
arms. To all which fhe anfwered not, but with low
curtfeys, and down-caft eyes, at laft fhe too well explained his meaning to the almoft defpairing ladies,
whofe profpect of approaching happinefs rendered this
cruel difappoinment infupportable: nor was their terror

lefs that their lords fhould come up to them at this fatal
juncture, and be expofed to the cruel infidel's fury.
This is the uncertain condition of man's life, that we
fcarce know what to wifh for, or to fear. Thefe poor
ladies but a few moments before impatiently longed to
fee their dear hufbands, and now they dreaded their prefence worfe than death. Thus the fruition of our wifhes
is oft our punifhment; and we ought to defire nothing
earneftly, but leave all to Providence. Emilia, Terefa,
and the widow, were placed in the middle of the band
of Moors, and led by three of them, who quitted their
horfes, to take care of thefe unfortunate ladies. It
was with much difficulty they got them to the next
village, where the prince ordered they fhould ftay to
reft, till one of his coaches came to carry them to his
fummer palace, which was not many miles diftant.
Here he entered the houfe of a Baffa, who was much
overjoyed at this fortunate opportunity of obliging his
prince. Here the ladies and widow were conducted to a
chamber, where two eunuchs waiting on them, hindered their converfing together; for they dared not to difcover their thoughts to each other, for fear of being
underftood, and betraying their lords. They fat looking dejectedly, tears and fighs only expreffed the ftate of
their minds: wine, fherbet, fweet-meats, cold-meats,
and the moft delicious things that pleafe the tafte, were
prefented to them; but they refpectfully refufed to eat
or drink. Muley Arab was magnificently treated by
the Baffa, and his coach being come, departed, the Baffa
waiting on him, with many of his flaves, to guard the
coach into which he entered, with the two ladies, out
of refpect to whom the rich curtains of the coach were
drawn. Seraja was prefented with a horfe to ride on,
which a flave leading, fhe went next the coach; for the
prince ufed her very kindly, defigning to make her affift
him in gaining the ladies affections. And now he had
an opportunity of viewing the charming Terefa and
Emilia at leifure: the firft having lain-in but fome

months before, and been long fick, looked pale and
thin; but her youth, and the innocent fweetnefs that
bloomed in her face, rivalled Emilia's majeftic charms,
where the heroine appeared, and every look drew admiration and refpect.   Muley Arab gazed, and burned;
his eyes fparkled with defire, and he languifhed to poffefs both: he was divided in his choice, yet gave Terefa
the preference; he longed to fpeak his paffion; and
having learned the Spanifh tongue, addreffed himfelf
in that to them, afking, if either underftood it. Terefa
replied, I do, my lord. He was tranfported that fhe
underftood him, and began to fpeak the moft tender and
paffionate things to her that love could dictate; for the
Moorifh nobility, and indeed the whole nation, are
much inclined to love, very amorous and galant.   At
length cafting down her lovely eyes, with a modeft blufh,
a look, where virtue, fear, and refolution were all
blended together, Prince, faid fhe, being fo greatly
born as you are, and fo generous in your deportment
to us ftrangers, I prefume to implore your pity, and
promife myfelf fuccefs, fince you appear fo humane and
princely in your fpeech and mien; we are both Chriftians of noble birth, already difpofed of to two gentlemen, who were unfortunately brought to this place by
pirates, and made flaves. None ought to have the
honour of fleeping in your arms but virgins, whofe hearts
and perfons have not been fullied with another's embraces, or love. We are already pre-engaged, and
cannot oblige you without horror and diflike, or meet
your love with mutual warmth and fatisfaction; nay,
we muft rather choofe to merit your utmoft difpleafure
and die, than yield to gratify your lawlefs love. While
fhe fpoke, the prince liftened as if he had heard fome
Syren fing, and grew more mad in love. Her wifdom
charmed him, every look, each motion fired his blood,
and he thought every moment was an hour till he reached home. He anfwered with a bow, and faid, If
man can make you happy, Muley Arab will: by
Mahomet

Mahomet I fwear, you fhall command my very foul, and I will make you bleffed as woman can be. This he fpoke to make her eafy, and in myfterious words concealed his meaning, which was never to part with her; nor did he think Emilia lefs worthy of his favour, though he did not love her equal with the other.

They at laft arrived at his palace, where he took Terefa by the hand, the Moorifh lord Ifmael leading Emilia. They were conducted to a noble apartment on the top of the houfe, where the prince took leave of them, leaving a female flave to attend them. Terefa begged him to permit Seraja to come to them, which he immediately granted: fo faluting both with paffion, he retired. The reafon of which was this: he had received from the emperor his father's hands, fix months before, a wife, who was the daughter of an Arabian prince, who had affifted him in reducing a powerful rebel and his party who had rebelled againft him, and dethroned him, had not Abdela the brave Arab come to his affiftance. This lady was very handfome, and of a haughty difpofition, very proud and revengeful; fhe loved him paffionately, and was fo jealous of all women that he but feemed to like, that fhe had poifoned feveral of thofe fair unfortunate creatures fhe found in his feraglios, whom he had purchafed or received as prefents. He therefore dreaded fhe would ferve thefe ladies fo, if he omitted to vifit her immediately upon his return home, left them, and going to her apartment, appeared very pleafant and obliging, fat down to dinner with her, a particular favour in that nation; and after dinner propofed to her to return that night to Fez, to the royal palace, becaufe he fhould go forth very early next morning to hunt, and fhould difturb her, and defigned to return to Fez in the evening: to this fhe willingly confented. And now he thought he had fecured himfelf one happy night, in which he purpofed to enjoy one of the lovelieft women in the world: but the prayers and tears of the virtuous Terefa and Emilia had reached Heaven;

God

God who difappoints the wicked, and preferves in a
wonderful manner thofe that fear and love him, had
otherwife decreed. Ximene the haughty princefs was
quickly informed, by a flave whom fhe favoured, that
the prince had brought home two European wome fair
as angels, in the purfuit of whom he had fpent that day;
that his hunting was but a pretence to procure her abfence. In fine, this officious woman told her all that
could excite both her curiofity and revenge; which fhe
was fpurred on to do by a fecret reafon, which was,
that fhe had been in her youth vitiated by the prince,
and afterwards neglected: this made her diftracted
whenever fhe faw him fond of any other, and ftudy to
make him wretched, which fhe could no other way
bring about but to continually incenfe Ximene againft
him, who always rewarded her for thefe cruel, malicious
fervices. The prince, who had been thofe unlucky
moments abfent, whilft the treacherous Dalinda had
whifpered this fatal fecret to her lady, returned to give
her his hand to the coach, which was then ready with
her attendant to fet out for Fez, but found her much
difordered: I am not well, faid fhe, and I cannot go
to-night. At thefe words fhe pretended to faint, and
fell down on her bed. The prince was fufficiently vexed
at this crofs accident, but did not fufpect his fecret
defigns were betrayed to her. He feemed much
concerned (as no doubt he was), kiffed, embraced, and
ufed all poffible means to pleafe her. She feemed to
recover, faid fhe would lye alone that night; though
fhe had a fecret defign, and not ficknefs, made her
choofe to do fo. In fome time he afked her to take the
air in the gardens; but fhe refufed, and chofe to let him
go alone, for that was what fhe wanted. He longed to
confult Ifmael, having perceived a change in Ximene's
face and humour, that made him fear fomebody had told
her of the ladies. Whilft the prince and his favourite
walked in the garden, Ximene conjures the flave to fhew
her Terefa and Emilia: fhe leads her lady to the room;

5   Ximene

Ximene only passed through it, and returning to her chamber, was so surprized at their beauty, and fired with jealousy, that she resolved to poison them that night, and commanded Dalinda to make a China bowl of delicate sherbet mixed with a deadly poison, which she always kept ready prepared for such wicked purposes. Dalinda failed not to execute her mistress's orders, and having mixed the deadly potion, left the bowl upon a table in the next room, designing to carry it up to the ladies as a present from the prince, whilst Ximene detained him with her, which she resolved to do that night, knowing the ladies would not live till the next morning after drinking that fatal draught. No sooner had Dalinda left the room, but the prince returning from the garden enters it, and being very dry takes up the bowl, concluding it was sherbet made for the princess; and going into her chamber drinks to her. She, not imagining Dalinda had been so indiscreet to leave the poisoned sherbet there, refused not to pledge him, taking a good draught of it. She seemed very obliging to the prince, to engage him to stay with her, asking him to drink tea with her. They sat down together, and Dalinda being called for, soon missed the bowl, and perceived the fatal error, yet dared not speak. In less than an hour the prince and princess began to fall into strange convulsions; which Dalinda perceiving, and fearing to be tortured and put to death, for being the fatal cause of theirs, packed up what she could, as jewels and gold, and fled to the woods, where she was seen to enter, but never came forth again, being (doubtless) that night devoured by the wild beasts, of which Barbary is very full. A great distraction reigned in the palace; the physicians were called, and used all their endeavours to save them, but in vain. Dalinda was believed the author of this mischief, but none could guess the reason why. Before five in the morning Muley Arab and Ximene expired, she confessing what she designed, and acknowledging God's

justice

justice in her end. And now the slaves and favourites
of the dead prince walked like silent ghosts, looking
upon one another. A messenger was sent to acquaint
the emperor with this dismal news of his son's death,
whom he was very fond of: Ismael the Moorish lord
bare the fatal message, and soon returned with a troop
of soldiers, who by the emperor's order discharged such
of the attendants as he thought fit; took all the women
in his seraglio, and conducted them in coaches, being
all veiled, to an old seraglio where the wives and con-
cubines of the deceased princes are kept, some all their
lives, and others are disposed of to the favourites of the
emperor, or prince who succeeds the prince to whom
they belonged. To this dismal place were Teresa and
Emilia carried; yet they in their hearts praised God for
their deliverance from Muley Arab, whose surprizing
death, and the manner of it, they looked on as an
earnest of God's favour, and were the more encouraged
to confide in his merciful Providence. The good widow
was offered her liberty to return to her home; but she
chose to attend the ladies. They had in this decayed
palace the liberty of walking in the gardens, lying together, and hoped soon to find an opportunity to escape,
resolving to fly to Attabala's, if it were possible to find
the way: but, alas! it was more than sixty miles thence,
and almost impossible for them to reach it without
falling into new misfortunes: the widow advised them
rather to make to the sea-side, and endeavour to get a
passage to Spain or France, promising to go herself to
Attabala's, which she could do safely. This counsel
they approved of; and though they were very unwilling
to part with her, yet they at last consented to her going;
she easily obtained leave of the governess of the seraglio,
and chief eunuch, and so left them, setting out for her
own home, where she doubted not to find news of Antonio and the lords. And here we shall leave the ladies
for a time, and relate what happened to Don Lopez,
the count de Hautville, and the rest of Attabala's

guests, since Antonio parted from the ladies, and the
good Seraja's house.

CHAP. XI.

ANTONIO soon reached Attabala's house, and
found the two lords, monsieur de Chateau-Roial,
Clarinda, Eleonora, and Anna, at dinner: he asked
for Attabala, who coming to him, he desired to know
if two gentlemen were not there, whose names were
Don Lopez and count de Hautville: I come, said he,
from their ladies, Emilia and Teresa, who are now on
the road coming to them. Attabala ran into the parlour, and told this good news: all the company rose
from the table. Antonio was called in; but what
words can express the transport he and Anna were in,
when she knew him to be her lover Carolus Antonio
Barbarini, the generous Angelina's son, that noble
Venetian lady who had bred her up? They flew to one
another's arms. He gazed upon her, wept for joy, at
length swooned upon her bosom; joy so disordered his
soul, that every faculty stood still, and his heart and
pulse forgot to move. Don Lopez held him up, and all
the company stood looking on surprized. At last
awaking, as it were from a long sleep, he lifted up his
eyes, and cried, Anna, thou dearest thing on earth!
behold the man that has followed you to this barbarous
place, and for your sake ventured to brave both death
and slavery: we will part no more whilst we live; I will
perish by your side, or carry you safe to Venice again.
And now, gentlemen, said he, arm yourselves, and
set out this moment to meet your wives; as we are on
the way I will tell you more: we must not delay one
moment to go to them; here is a box of jewels of great
value

value which they gave me for you, and I will give to Anna's care till we return. At these words Eleonora casting her eyes upon Don Lopez, cried, Ah! faithless Spaniard, you then are married, and another claims your heart; you have deceived me cruelly. He was too much in haste to answer more than in these few words: Forgive me, madam, I dared not tell you truth, nor did I know whether Teresa were still living; had she been dead, the charming Eleonora had a juster title to my heart than any woman: yet you shall be happy; I will esteem, respect and love you next Teresa, keep you still near me, and make your interest always mine. They hastened him to depart, and the three gentlemen, Attabala and Antonio, set out well armed to meet the ladies. They came to the wood, hallooed, called, and ran to every corner of it, but in vain: at last they went quite to Seraja's house, and finding all in disorder, concluded they were fallen into Muley Arab's hands; in which opinion they were confirmed by the report of some passengers whom they inquired of. Nothing could be more afflicted than the count and Don Lopez; they were even inconsolable, and monsieur de Chateau-Roial and Antonio had much ado to prevail with them to return home. They would have pursued the Moorish prince; but Antonio told them the attendants he had with him were so numerous and well armed, that it would be the action of madmen to attempt an encounter with them. The lords seemed quite abandoned to grief, and returning home, appeared so cast down, that at last the charming Clarinda spake to them in this manner: My lords, are you men and Christians? Have you been both delivered from perishing in the merciless seas by God's Providence, from a desolate island, where he supplied you not only with bread, but with friends, and a ship to carry you thence in safety, and land you at the port you desired? Has he preserved your lives from the pirates sword, and freed you miraculously from chains and slavery? preserved your wives from the vici-

ous

ous governor? and have you now forgot his mercies, and doubt his power? Is there one of us here who are not living monuments of the Almighty's goodness, and shall we despair? Suffer not then your reason to be silenced by passion; but call to mind the great things God has already done for you, and put your confidence in him, who will never leave nor forsake us, whilst we trust in and love him. He will give his angels charge of the virtuous women you so mourn for, and restore them safely to you, if he thinks fit; if not, by your submission to his divine pleasure, endeavour to obtain his favour, an happy end in this world, and eternal joy and repose in the next, where your wives will be restored to you; and all your sufferings here converted into joy and glory. Here she ended her admirable discourse; and the count de Hautville returned her this answer: Madam, your advice is good, and I will endeavour to take it. Come, my friend, said he to Don Lopez, shake off your weakness, and let us leave all to God; this life is short, and full of disappointments, let us behave ourselves like men and Christians. He that made us and our wives, will preserve them. Here fair Anna interrupted them, saying, My lords, look upon this young gentleman and me, and learn to trust in Providence. I have not yet had time to ask him how he came here, nor by what miracle conducted to this place. ---Charming Anna, said Antonio, I will with pleasure satisfy both you and the company; but first my advice is, that Attabala should go to Seraja's house, and see if any person be there, and leave word in the village, which she and the ladies, if they escape, will probably go to, to enquire after me: and let Attabala leave word with Johanna Benduker, her dear friend, that her slave Antonio waits for her and her friends at the place they were to come to, when he left them. Attabala may likewise enquire after the prince, and what else he can. In the mean time let us continue quiet; for should we remove hence before we hear from them, they would

never

never be able to find us, nor can we be so safe elsewhere. They all approved of this advice, and Attabala went to Seraja's that afternoon. And now the company sitting together, Anna fetching the box of jewels, gave them to the lords, saying, Here is the rich treasure given to my charge, which I deliver to you, to whom it belongs : upon my word, it would sell for a sum great enough to provide for us all handsomely. The lords were amazed at the number and richness of the diamonds, and Antonio told them how the ladies came by them. Don Lopez said, Since Providence gave them thus, they shall serve us all, and provide for all our necessities : since God has made us companions in adversity, we will mutually strive to make one another happy. Now Anna proposed the hearing Antonio's story since he and she parted, and he related it in the manner following :

GENTLEMEN and Ladies, said he, my name and birth I find fair Anna has already informed you of, and how our affections grew with our years, and the manner in which she was ravished from me. I must then begin my narrative from the most unfortunate hour of my life. The day that we were parted, I was with my dear mother Angelina, at our house in the city, to which we were retired for safety, when the dismal news was brought that the Turks had landed, and ravaged all the coast, and entered the monasteries, and carried away a great number of the nuns and inhabitants round about, destroying and plundering the most sacred places ; and that Anna was amongst those the infidels had carried away captives. This news filled all the city with grief, and nothing but sighs and lamentations were heard in the streets ; ladies of the first quality ran about distracted, tearing their hair, and wringing their hands, for the loss of their daughters, and death of their sons, killed by the cruel infidels : every family had lost one or more out of it, and every tongue was employed

ployed in aggravating the public calamity. But though my grief was not so clamorous, yet I believe none more severely felt the loss of those they loved than I; when I heard Anna was gone, my soul was shocked, and all my faculties failed me; I could neither eat nor sleep; in few days I resolved to follow her, and rather chose to die in slavery, than live free and without her. I concealed my desperate design from my mother, who was highly afflicted at Anna's loss and my melancholy, and pretended I would go to travel only to Rome, Spain, and France. She was very unwilling to let me go, telling me with tears, My dear child, said she, God has been pleased to take your noble father from me, and my sweet Anna, whom next you I loved; you are all that are left me, in you are all my hopes placed; do not leave me then alone. Touched to the soul with her tender expressions, I delayed to go, and confined myself to her presence. But seeing me every day decay and pine away, she resolved to send me abroad, in hopes to divert me; and commanded me to go. I yielded, and all things being prepared, as horses and servants, with bills for money at the places I passed through, I took leave of my dear mother and friends; and with her blessing departed, promising to return soon. My reason for going to Spain was, because had I gone from Venice, which was then at war with the Turks, I should have been liable to be taken, and made a prisoner of war; but if I went from Spain or France, in a vessel belonging to either of those nations, I might be safe, and have the protection of their consuls at Constantinople, by whom I might procure Anna's freedom, paying her ransom. And I resolved, though she had been sold or presented to the seraglio of some villain, for that her beauty would doubtless occasion her to be, yet I would take her to my arms, with as much joy and affection as if she had been ever mine: yet this her tender years made me hope to prevent. In fine, I passed through Italy, and arriving at Barcelona in Spain, I

sent

fent back my fervants with a letter to my mother of my
true intention; got a letter to the Spanifh conful at Conftantinople, from a great Spanifh merchant, to whom
I declared my defign, and who had money in his hands
for my ufe remitted to him from Venice; and with his
affiftance got my paffage in a Spanifh fhip, with the
fleet arrived fafe at Conftantinople, and was well received by the Spanifh conful, who foon got me information that Anna was bought by a Barbary captain,
who was bound to Algiers, to which he ufed to carry
flaves and rich goods. I prefently refolved to go
thither, from which he endeavoured to diffuade me
all he was able; but in vain. I left fome money in
his hands, and the next fhip that was going to Algiers, I went on board as a paffenger, paying for my
paffage before-hand; but the villainous Mahometan,
fo foon as he came into the port, chained and fold me
at the common market for a flave. I was bought by an
old Jewifh merchant; and in one year, keeping his
accounts, for he put me to no drudgery or fervile employments, became his chief favourite. I endeavoured
all I was able to learn news of Anna, but could get
none. And now another misfortune befel me; my
mafter's wife, a handfome Portugueze woman, whom
he had married, and extremely doated upon, caft an
amorous eye upon me; but I conftantly avoided her,
and feemed to be ignorant of her meaning: this fo
highly provoked her, that one day, when I was alone
in the counting-houfe, and my mafter abroad, fhe came
in, and fhutting the door, faid, Antonio, muft I be
forced to tell you I love you to diftraction? Are you
blind to your own intereft, and determined to refufe
me? Am not I fair, and cannot I reward you? See
here. At thefe words fhe threw down a great purfe full
of gold: Take this, faid fhe, and take to your arms a
woman who loves, and can make you happy. At thefe
words fhe clafped me round the neck, and almoft ftifled
me with kiffes; I put her gently from me in great
confufion. At this moment **my** mafter entered the

room; some officious slave who sought my ruin, had observed my mistress and me, and given him intimation of her love to me; and he had thus contrived to surprize us, having only pretended to go out, and staid concealed in the house. She swooned; I stood confounded, though guiltless: he took me by the hair, beat and kicked me unmercifully, and swore he would poison her, and sell me the next day. He had so bruised me I could scarce crawl to a hole under the stairs, and there I laid me down, expecting to rise no more. I too late repented my rashness in leaving Venice; yet would have died contented, had I but once seen my dear Anna safe and free. In the evening of this unpleasant day, the good Tomaso, Seraja's husband, came to the house with embroidered caps and belts, as usual; he staid in an outer room, and as Providence decreed, espied me in this sad condition; my face was bloody, and my clothes all torn: he seemed much surprized, having always seen me well dressed, and caressed by my master; he asked me what was the matter; I told him the truth: he said, he would willingly buy me. I had catched up the purse of gold when my master entered the counting-house; I put some of it into his hand to purchase me, when my master called him into the counting-house, to pay for the embroidery: he asked him for me, to give me something, as he pretended, and sometimes used to do, when my master paid him: my master exclaimed against me: the good Tomaso persuaded him that his wife and I might be innocent, at least that I was very young, and might be seduced. In short, he asked to buy me, and my Jew master, glad to be rid of me, sold me for a trifle. With him I went, and he hired a horse for me to get home to his house, where I was maintained, and looked after as if I had been their own child. In a short time the good man died, and since that I have converted Seraja to the Christian faith, and assisted her in all I was able; and getting acquainted with many great bassas, and merchants servants, still

desirous

defirous to find my dear Anna, I continually enquired for her, and never could learn any thing but this: Lorenza the governor's Chriftian flave told me, his mafter had bought a girl much refembling her I defcribed; but he had fent her into the country, and I could not fee her. This kept my hopes alive, but till this fortunate morning I was never affured of my happinefs; but now I regret nothing I have fuffered, and truft in God we fhall be happy together, and return in fafety to our dear mother, whom I long to fee again.

All the company admired the ftrange adventures thefe two young lovers had met with, and they all refolved to go away together from Barbary the firft opportunity after Terefa and Emilia were found; for now fuch an entire friendfhip was contracted betwixt thefe unfortunate perfons, that not one of them would confent to abandon the reft, till all could be happy together. Villainy and bafe defigns often unite men for a time, but end generally in their ruin, and hatred to one another; but when religion and virtuous defigns are the bafis of men's friendfhips, they are lafting and fuccefsful.

CHAP. XII.

ATTABALA returned home at night, and related what he had learned of Muley Arab's carrying away the ladies; he had left the meffage with Johanna Benduker. And now they were obliged to remain in fufpence for fome days, in which the lords paffed their time very unpleafantly; and Eleonora fecretly rejoiced that her rival was more wretched than herfelf: fhe now behaved herfelf with much refervednefs to Don Lopez, who treated her with great refpect and tendernefs.

At

At laft Seraja arrived, and gave them an account of
the ladies wonderful deliverance, by the tragic end of
the prince and princefs; as likewife of their being removed to the old feraglio, from whence fhe faid it would
be no hard matter for them to efcape. This news tranfported the lords, and filled them with new hopes of
happinefs: they entertained Seraja with the ftory of
Antonio's good fortune, at which fhe much rejoiced.
They made her promife to go with them to Venice,
and to live with Anna, who called her mother, and
careffed her extremely for being fo kind to her lover.
Seraja lay there that night, and the next morning they
confulted what to do. They at laft refolved, that the
two lords fhould accompany Seraja back, that fhe fhould
go into the feragiio, and acquaint the ladies where they
ftaid to receive them, they defigning to lye at fome village near: fo putting on their Grecian difguife, like
merchants, they fet out with her, having bought a horfe
for her to ride upon, which Antonio got at the village
where he and Seraja had lived. They took fome money fufficient for the journey, and left the company,
with many good wifhes attending them. Monfieur de
Chateau-Roial and Antonio would have gone with them,
but it was feared it would render them fufpected to be
feen travelling fo many together. It was but threefcore
miles they had to go, and in two days time they reached
the neareft town to the feraglio. Here Seraja advifed
them to ftay and lodge, till fhe returned to them from
the ladies: they did fo. Entering the town they went
to an inn, pretending they came to buy goods, and
took a lodging. Seraja entered the feraglio, but was
told the ladies were not there, but gone. She enquired
whither: they told her Ifmael the Moorifh lord had begged them of the king, and fetched them thence the
night before. The governefs faid, Seraja, they are fortunate, he is a generous lord, and will ufe them nobly;
here are many young virgins in this place would rejoice
to be fo preferred. The widow hid her concern as much

as poffible, and took leave, returning to the expecting lords with this fad news, which they took heavily, and returned to Attabala's houfe, more forrowful than ever.

And now it is neceffary we fhould enquire what befel thefe unfortunate ladies, whofe unhappy beauties occafioned them fuch great misfortunes. Ifmael having been charmed with their perfons when he faw them at Seraja's, ftudied how to obtain them, and afked the emperor for them. He readily beftowed them upon this favourite, who made hafte to fetch them from the feraglio, fearing their being feen by fome perfon more favoured, and greater than himfelf, who might prove a troublefome rival. When he came there, and told his bufinefs, you may imagine how furprifed the ladies were; he immediately put them into a clofe coach, and carried them to his palace, where he locked them into a chamber, which was in the upper floor of the houfe, out of which a door opened upon a lovely terrace walk made on the top of the houfe, to take the evening air upon. Here the two wretched ladies walked a while, ruminating on their fad condition, and confidering what to do. At laft Emilia, whofe prefence of mind was always extraordinary, and was at this time doubtlefs infpired by Providence, looking down into the garden below, faid thus: My dear friend, fhall we fear to tempt death, by venturing fome way or other down this place, into the garden, from whence God may find us fome means to efcape; or fhall we ftay here and meet our ruin? Terefa thought a moment, and then running into the chamber, looked about to fee if fhe could find any cord or ftring to help them: it was juft the clofe of the day; they found no ftrings, but took the window curtains, and fheets, tied them faft together, and faftening one end to the rails on the houfe-top, Emilia flid down firft as low as fhe could, which was fome yards from the ground, which fhe ventured to leap down; Terefa followed, and both efcaped without much hurt. Recovering their legs, they ran down the garden, and finding a door

open,

open, went out, not knowing where to go. They wandered through some fields, and at last coming to a wood, sought a place to hide themselves till morning, resolving at break of day to be gone farther off. Here they sat trembling, full of dreadful apprehensions of being taken again, or devoured by wild beasts. They knew not what part of the country they were now in, nor how far from honest Seraja's house, where they had so long lived secure: at last they resolved, if possible, to climb up into some low tree, which with some diffi-culty they did, and sat there in much fear. Mean time Ismael, who had been engaged by some company who waited to speak with him at his coming home, which occasioned him to leave Emilia and Teresa so soon, hav-ing got quit of his visitors, went up to the chamber, ordering supper to be brought thither, designing to en-joy himself in their company all that night : but when he found the room in such disorder, and the ladies gone, his surprize cannot be expressed : he soon discovered how they had escaped, and calling for his servants, bid them light flambeaux, and search the gardens and fields adjacent, and if possible bring them back. The amazed slaves ran up and down the fields, and some of them entering the wood searched here and there, but saw them not. What concern the poor ladies were in is easily guessed. At last the servants returned home : Ismael fretted and raged, but in vain, and then went to sleep in an old mistress's arms; at which the servants rejoiced, and went to rest.

The ladies passed the night in prayer, and so soon as day broke came down from the tree almost faint, and hasted over a high hill, from whence they saw a lovely river at some distance : they hasted to it, and in a boat that lay there to ferry passengers over, passed safely to the other side; and asking where they were, the poor man told them the river they had passed over was called Omirary, a river that parts the kingdoms of Fez and Morocco; that they were not far from mount Atlas,

which

which if they paſſed over, they would come into Numi-
dia, a country inhabited by Mahometans and Pagans,
governed by no king, but ruled by ſome chief men,
heads of tribes, choſen by the reſt. They are a people,
ſaid he, inclined to thieving, Turks and Pagans in religion, dwelling in tents, living chiefly on dates, feeding
their goats with the ſtones, which make them very fat,
and yield good ſtore of milk; a country but ill inhabited. The ladies thanked the poor man, and went on
towards the mountains, not knowing which way to go,
ready to faint for want of food and reſt. They had no
money, their habits were fine, ſuch as are given in the
ſeraglios to the women in condition; the day was far
ſpent; they had no food. At laſt they came to the foot
of a great ridge of mountains; there, unable to go
farther, they ſat down: Tereſa, who was of the weakeſt
conſtitution, laid her head on Emilia's boſom, and
ſighing, ſaid, Surely now, my dear friend, my unfortunate life draws to a period; if God ſends us no help
ſoon, we muſt periſh here: our huſbands know not
where to find us, nor are we able to go to them. For
my part, I have only this ſatisfaction, that having done
my duty to God, and my dear lord, I have no reaſon
to fear death. You, my dear friend, will, I hope, not
only ſurvive me; but, by ſome Providence preſerved,
live to be happy with your lord. Tell Don Lopez I died
only his, virtuous and chaſte, as when he took me to
his arms, and hope to ſee him with joy in the other
world. Emilia wept over her, and ſtrove to comfort
her.

Now night drew on, and darkneſs rendered the place
more dreadful. About midnight Emilia ſaw a light at
ſome diſtance, in a houſe, as ſhe thought; and looking
ſtedfaſtly, ſhe ſaw a man kneeling at the door, with a
candle in one hand, and a book in the other, as if at
prayer: ſhe ſhewed him to Tereſa. My dear, ſaid ſhe,
let us try to get to that place; perhaps he is ſome Chriſtian; but if not, we muſt venture: to ſtay here is certain

tain death, and therefore it is better to aſk help of infidels.   Tereſa attempted to riſe, but could not ſtand,
the cold and faſting had ſo debilitated her limbs, they
were uſeleſs.   Emilia was unwilling to leave her, but
at laſt was forced to it : ſhe haſted to the place, and approaching near, ſaw a man of a middle age, tall, well
ſhaped, and would have been very handſome, had not
abſtinence, ſickneſs and hardſhips altered his face : he
had a coarſe frize coat, like a Turkiſh dervize or hermit,
a fur cap, ſhort boots like an Arabian.   He was ſo in-
tent at his devotions, he ſaw her not, though now very
near him : ſhe liſtened, and hearing him pray in the
Latin tongue, was encouraged to ſpeak to him.   She
threw herſelf on her knees before him, ſaying, Generous Chriſtian, help two unfortunate women, almoſt
dead with want and travelling, fled from a vile Mahometan's houſe who would have ruined us : my companion lyes yonder on the cold ground ; give us ſhelter
in your houſe, and a little food or drink to ſave our
lives.   The hermit being riſen viewed her with amazement : Lovely creature, ſaid he, you may command
my life ; who would refuſe to receive ſuch a gueſt ? Let
us haſte to your companion, and fear not to live with a
man, in whom you ſhall find a protector and friend.
He fetched a lanthorn, and putting a candle into it,
went with her, carrying a bottle of rum in his hand.
Emilia's care for Tereſa was ſuch, that ſhe ſtaid not to
drink ; but forgetting her own weakneſs, ran to her,
whom they found almoſt ſenſeleſs.   Emilia gave her ſome
of the cordial, and with their help ſhe was got into
the houſe.

And now the hermit ſhutting the door, haſted to
kindle up a fire of leaves and ſticks, ſetting before them
bread, meat, and wine ; of which having eat a little,
they began to revive ; and the hermit, who waited on
them with much ſeeming pleaſure and reſpect, appearing very courtly in all things, ſaid, Ladies, you are
highly welcome to a man who has lived many years in
a manner

a manner fequeftered from the world. I believe we are of one faith, and equals in birth ; my homely cell begins to look pleafant with fuch company : may I ask who you are, and beg to know your misfortune, that I may be the better enabled to ferve you. The ladies had by this time obferved the room and man : the houfe was very poor and mean, containing below two rooms, and (as they fuppofed) no more above : the furniture was fuitable ; but the mafter of the place appeared to be noble, and of great birth and education. Emilia anfwered him Sir, I think it is but reafonable that we fhould firft know who you are, and your adventures, fince our want of ftrength, and diforder of mind and bodies may well excufe us from fo tedious a tafk as the relation of ours. He bowed, faying, Madam, forgive my curiofity, which made me forget my duty, and be too bold in afking fo great a favour as to know you. Reft is fitteft for you ; my poor bed and chamber waits to receive you. Here is the key, I fhall not prefume to wait on you to the door ; this place will ferve me to wait your commands in to-morrow morning, when I will freely and with pleafure tell you all the adventures of my life paft. The ladies were charmed with his behaviour ; he prefented a candle and the key to them, and would not admit their ftaying below any longer. They went up ftairs, and found a bed and chamber neat as thofe in palaces ; there were fome chairs, a carpet on the floor, with quilts, fheets and coverlids neat and good ; in a clofet were many watches, and tools of all forts belonging to the art of watch-making : many pictures of fine painting without frames adorned the walls of the chamber. They fhut the door, undrefled, and having returned thanks to God for this fignal mercy, went to bed, and flept fweetly. At break of day they wakened and rofe ; the hermit heard them, and prepared a fire : they came down, and he received them with a chearful countenance ; he was preparing coffee for their breakfaft : and now they defired to hear his ftory, which he thus related.

C H A P.

CHAP. XIII.

I AM by birth a Venetian, my Father was a nobleman, and I was his eldeſt ſon; my name is Andrea
Zantonio Borgomio. I was related to a lady, who
having married a wealthy merchant had one daughter,
with whom I fell paſſionately in love : but the cuſtom of
my country forbidding me to marry with any woman
whoſe father was inferior to my own in quality, I reſolved to marry her in ſecret. The day was appointed
when I was to meet her at a country-houſe of her father's to eſpouſe her; but the evening before, ſhe
being in her father's coach with her mother and father,
attended by three ſervants, was forcibly taken out of
it, and carried away, with a black boy who followed her.
The raviſher was a captain of a ſhip, who was an old
man, very rich, and had loved her from her infancy.
She was then about fourteen; he carried her aboard
his veſſel, ſet ſail with her, and was taken by an Algerine pirate who carried her to Algiers, as I have ſince
been informed; but how ſhe was diſpoſed of I could
never yet learn. It is almoſt eleven years ſince we
parted. Her father ſent a meſſenger to inform me of
our misfortune the ſame night ſhe was taken away.
We ſoon diſcovered by what means we loſt her, and I
that minute reſolved to hire a veſſel to follow the villain's ſhip. Her mother being my father's relation,
flew to him for redreſs; but his behaviour ſoon informed
me that he was conſenting to the hateful deed : he
treated her very coldly; and when I importuned him to
procure an order from the Senate to arreſt the villain
and his ſhip, offering to go myſelf to execute it, he
looked upon me, and ſaid ironically, I do not doubt
your readineſs to follow him; you are too much concerned about what ought not to concern you at all;
mind your duty; your kinſwoman is fitter to be his
wife

wife than yours; speak no more to me about her. I
underſtood him perfectly, and was ſo enraged, that I
almoſt forgot he was my father. I went out of the
room from him immediately, took a ſum of money with
me, and, attended only with one ſervant, went directly
to the port, where I hired a light brigantine and went
after her. I gueſſed he was gone for Spain or France.
In few hours we met a ſhip bound for Venice, who told
us he met Capt. Alphonſo's ſhip; they ſaluted one
another; Alphonſo came aboard him, drank a bottle
of wine, and ſaid he was bound for Spain, taking ſome
ſweet-meats and wine this captain had brought from
Leghorn. This made us ſteer our courſe that way.
A great ſtorm roſe that night, and ſhipwrecked us upon
this coaſt. I know not what is become of the captain
and his men, but I was ſaved on a piece of the rudder,
and caſt on the coaſt of Barbary near Tunis. Here I
was taken up almoſt dead by a peaſant, who was very
kind to me. So ſoon as I could walk abroad, I began
to enquire where I was, what the manners and cuſtoms
of the country were? But I was ſoon taken notice of,
and ſent for by the Turkiſh governor of Tunis, who
examining me, took a fancy to me, and ſaid, If I would
live with him he would uſe me kindly; if not, I
ſhould be ſold to ſomebody elſe. It was my beſt way I
thought to accept of his offer, by which I might have
an opportunity to get off for Spain. He employed me
in the managing many of his affairs, ſending me with
letters and preſents to ſeveral miniſters of ſtate and
friends: he was very gentle and familiar to me, and,
in fine, clothed and kept me ſo, that I began to apprehend he had an ill deſign upon me. As I ſuſpected, it
proved; one evening he called for me into his cloſet,
and gave me a rich veſt, turbant, and an entire Turkiſh
dreſs of ſattin, embroidered with ſilver and linen ſuit-
able. He bid me take it and go and dreſs me, for I
muſt ceaſe to be a Chriſtian and a ſervant, and live at
eaſe. Then he kiſſed me eagerly; I turned pale, bowed,

ed, took the clothes, and went out trembling, determining in myfelf to fly thence, whatever was the confe-
quence. Whilft I dwelt with this Baffa Solyman, for
that was his name, he had a renegado flave, by birth a
Hollander, who indeed had not more religion than ho-
nefty or confcience. This man's name was Cornelius
Vandunk; he was a watchmaker by profeffion, and having, as he owned to me, been extravagant and run in
debt, he fled his own country, and went with a merchant to Conftantinople, to work there with him. His
unconftant temper made him uneafy there, fo he wanted
to be gone elfewhere, and went aboard a French mer-
chant-fhip, which was taken by an Algerine pirate.
There he was fold to a Jew merchant, who ufed him ill;
coming to Tunis, he refolved to free himfelf by renouncing Chriftianity. He did fo, by which he ingratiated
himfelf with the Baffa Solyman, and became a favourite, working for him in curious work: He was certainly
a great artift at his trade, and of him I learned fo
much, as to be able to put a watch together, and mend
one tolerably; I took much delight in it: and painting
in water-colours I was alfo a tolerable mafter of. Being
now refolved upon quitting my fervice, I was confidering how I could provide for myfelf, and enjoy my religion, the thing I valued far above my life. I thought
now if I had a good fum of money with me, I might
efcape to fome place far diftant from Tunis, and retire
to an obfcure place, where I might work and fell what I
did make, till I could hear fomething of Eleonora, for
that was my adored miftrefs's name; and having learned
from a merchant that arrived from Algiers, who came
to bring a rich prefent to Solyman, that Alphonfo's fhip
had been taken and plundered, and the crew and paf-
fengers brought in and difpofed of there, I was determined to ftay in Barbary, till I got farther news of
her. I had fome money by me, but not fufficient for
fuch an undertaking. I was now perfectly acquainted
with the cuftoms of the country, and under the religious

gious disguise I have now on, I knew I could pass un-
discovered and live safe. I at last resolved to take some
jewels of Solyman's, which I had by his order laid up
in a cabinet: this I did, and at midnight departed,
having provided myself with an excellent Arabian horse
out of his stable. I staid just without the town till
break of day, when I set spurs to my horse, and rid
towards Algiers, where in short time I arrived safe. I
went to a merchant's house, with whom my master was
acquainted, knowing he could not send after me so far,
not knowing which way I went, at least till I had dispatched my affairs; and I designed to stay here no longer than till I had sold the jewels, and made a full enquiry after Eleonora. With the assistance of this merchant, the jewels were sold in three days time; a Jew
gave me five thousand crowns with them. I was informed the Algerine pirate had presented a lady that
was in Alphonso's ship to some Turkish governor, but
it was not known who; and that the captain was dead.
At last despairing to find her, and fearing to be discovered and taken, I left Algiers, and went through Fez,
which being too populous I quitted, and retired to this
lonely place, having worn this holy disguise seven
years, which I have lived in this place. I bought this
poor cottage of a merchant for whom I work; I pass for
a religious man, a hermit; the people reverence me as
I pass. I mend watches for several merchants in the
adjacent towns and cities. I sell my little pictures likewise to Europeans, and live comfortably, bringing
home what I want. I receive no visits but at my door.
I am called Ismael the holy hermit. I give what
alms I am able to the poor; sometimes clothe the
naked, and secretly assist Christians who are in distress. I have made myself a rule to live by; I dedicate every third hour to devotion in the day, and rise
once in the night to prayer, and am now so reconciled to
this retired kind of life, that I am indifferent whether I
ever return to Venice or not, unless I could be so happy

as to have Eleonora with me, or be assured she were dead; and then I would mourn her here, and die in this place.

Here he ended his relation; Emilia said, what was the Black's name who belonged to the fair Eleonora?---He answered, Attabala.---Then, said she, I shall tell you wonders; blessed be our God who has brought us here together! She then began the relation of their adventures, and in conclusion told him of the lords being at Attabala's house, which she had learned from Antonio, but whether the lady is there or not, said she, I cannot tell. The hermit, for so we must call him till he leaves his cottage and habit, was filled with admiration at the things he heard: and they mutually acknowledged God's goodness in preserving them all in such an extraordinary manner. And now they were very chearful, and fell to considering what was best to be done. They were above an hundred miles distant from Attabala's house; and the hermit knew not whom to trust to send thither: at last he proposed that they should stay there whilst he went, though it was dangerous for him to go so far. The ladies were very unwilling to be left behind; but it was altogether unfit for them to go. The hermit said he would buy a good Arabian horse to ride on, and be soon back; to which at last they consented. He gave them money, shewed them where he kept it hid, and counselled them to put on such habits as he wore. He went and bought them such, with food and all things necessary; and having in five days time put all his affairs in order, pretending to his customers some extraordinary business at Algiers, departed, having first taken leave of the fair hermits with much tenderness and many blessings, they praying fervently for his safe return. And here we must leave them till we have learned what is come of the lords and the rest of Attabala's guests.

CHAP. XIV.

THE lords being now at home in Attabala's house
with Antonio and the charming Anna, who wanted
nothing but a safe passage to Venice to be compleatly
happy, as likewise the fair Clarinda and her lord monsieur de Chateau Roial, who were passionately fond of
each other, yet determined to part, if they could not obtain a dispensation for them to live together lawfully;
and the fair Eleonora, who liked Don Lopez so well,
that she thought no more of her first lover, signior Andrea Zantonio Borgomio: all the company began to im-
portune Don Lopez and the count to think of returning
to their homes: Consider, said they, the dangerous
consequences that attend our staying here longer; if
any one of us is discovered, it will be the ruin of the
rest. The good Seraja likewise pleaded for their going: My Lords, said she, Ismael knows my house,
you are sensible; and should he have the least intimation
of your being here or any strangers, he would doubtless
have you all taken and examined. You must submit to
the will of Heaven; if God pleases, he can send your
wives to you into Spain or France; but I am sorry to
tell you, it is very unlikely, for being now in Ismael's
hands, he will probably keep them too safe; force cannot fetch them thence, you are in a strange country,
and have none to assist you. It is now the season of the
year for ships to come and go to Europe: let Attabala
look out for a ship to carry you hence to Venice, or any
part of Europe, from whence you may go to your several countries, and stay not here to be made slaves,
and the poor ladies who have escaped hither torn from
you again. In fine, all arguments were used to persuade them to go hence; but none was so prevailing as
the generous regard they had for their friends, who
could now be happy if they were not detained there by

their

their respect for them.   The lords begged them to go
and leave them to Providence, offering to divide all the
money and jewels amongst them, and desiring to be
left with none but a servant of Attabala's, and in
his house; but Eleonora opposed that strenuously, and
all the rest refused to hear of leaving them alone. But
now an accident happened, that in few days obliged
them to come to a resolution : the incensed Ismael, mad
to be thus disappointed, and revolving in his mind that
Seraja was the only friend the ladies had, and that it
was most probable they would fly to her, resolves to
go to her house with his slaves, and force her to discover where they were. He accordingly comes to the
house, enquires for her, but could learn nothing. He
levels the house with the ground and departs, threat-
ening to return again, and search all the adjacent towns
and villages. He likewise offered a great reward to any
person that should find and discover her or the young
women, or her slave Antonio. No sooner was he departed, but Johanna Benduker, Seraja's friend, runs to
Attabala's, and warns them to be gone: If you are
discovered, said she, as you certainly will, because of the
reward Ismael offers, you are ruined.---This news both
surprized and pleased Don Lopez and the count ; they
were transported that the ladies had escaped Ismael's
hands, yet feared to stay his coming : at last, Seraja persuaded them to leave Johanna the care of the ladies, if
they came; for, said she, the slave here left and she
will conceal, and get them off if they come, with less
trouble than you can, who will be watched and questioned. Attabala hasted to the sea-side, and going off
in the honest fisherman's boat went aboard a Spanish
ship which lay there, and agreed with the captain to carry
them to Venice. Returning home, Attabala hastened
them to get off; they packed up all, leaving with Attabala's servant money for Teresa and Emilia to get home ;
Johanna promising to take care of them. But when the
count and Don Lopez entered the boat, their concern
                                                    appeared ;

appeared; they both turned pale, and the big drops rolled down their cheeks. My God, said Don Lopez, pity me, and preserve Teresa, whom I am now forced to leave behind me! Ye angels, guard her, and conduct her to me safe! The count only lifted up his hands and eyes, and sighed deeply. Thus come on board, they were by the Spanish captain well received. They rewarded the fisherman, and he departed. And now joy filled every face but the two lords, and they were extreme sad. The ship lay that night at an anchor, and the wind being contrary they were obliged to wait its turning. This doubtless Providence ordered; for towards the close of the day Attabala's servant comes in the fisher-boat with the hermit, who, entering the great cabin with him, saw Eleonora, whom he immediately ran to, catching her in his arms with such transport, that she had not time to discover who he was; but his voice soon informed her it was signior Andrea Zantonio. She seemed equally glad; and if she was not so transported, yet she was doubtless pleased to see the man she had once loved so well. After some passionate expressions to her, he turned to the company, saying, I know not which of these gentlemen are the fortunate husbands of the virtuous Emilia and Teresa, for to them my business is. The lords soon informed him; he told them how he had saved and left the ladies safe at his house at the foot of Mount Atlas. The lords embraced him, and made him welcome, with repeated acknowledgments for his generous treatment of their wives, whom they were impatient to see. Eleonora also was curious to know his adventures after they were parted, which he related to her and the company. Then she presented Anna and Antonio to him, telling him who they were. He embraced them tenderly, glad to find some of his own nation there, Antonio being his kinsman. They now deliberated what to do. Venice being the nearest place, they resolved to call there first. Antonio and Anna, Eleonora and signior Andrea Zan-

tonio our hermit, feared not to be welcome to his father, if he was yet living, after so long an absence.
He had always resolved to marry Eleonora, who now
told him, with much confusion, what had passed between her and the governor, which force excused; so
that his passion being sincere as ever, he took her to his
arms with as much joy as if she had been a virgin, and
the chaplain of the ship performed the ceremony that
evening; which gave Antonio an opportunity of pressing the charming Anna to make him likewise happy.
Her youth and innocence made her hard to be persuaded
to yield; but all the company joining, she gave him her
hand, which he received with transport; and the next
morning the whole company, meeting in the great cabin, resolved what to do farther. The two lords determined to go with the hermit to Emilia and Teresa;
the rest of the company were to stay aboard; and it being unsafe for the ship to lie there long, they agreed it
should weigh anchor, and put out to sea for two or
three days, and then return and stay at an anchor till
they came back with the ladies, which could not be
sooner than five or six days, because they could not
travel so fast with them. The lords took a tender fare-
well of the whole company, and so departed, going
ashore in the ship's boat. They staid that night at Attabala's house, where none remained but the faithful
Abra, a Turkish boy Attabala had bred up and made a
Christian of in secret, to whom he had given his house
and effects. The next morning he went and hired
horses for the two lords, on which they set out for the
hermit's house; and travelling thither, we must leave
them, and give an account what befel the ladies in the
hermit's absence.

CHAP.

CHAP. XV.

THE second night after the hermit's departure, Teresa and Emilia, having recommended themselves to God, went to bed, and composed themselves to rest. About midnight they were waked with dismal groans and lamentations, which seemed to proceed from some person near the house. They listened a while, and heard a woman's voice, who expressed her grief in these words, in the French tongue : My God! where shall I find shelter? Who shall assist me in this barbarous place? When shall my sorrows end? Why is my wretched life prolonged? And to what end dost thou preserve me yet on this side the grave, to suffer farther miseries? Has not thy vengeance yet overtaken him that ruined me? And can thy justice suffer me, who am innocent, to be thus miserable? Must I live still to be the slave of cruel infidels? Oh, shew me some hospitable cave or cavern in the rocks to hide myself, and die at peace in! Here she sighed, her voice seemed to decay, and groans succeeded. Teresa and Emilia, whose hearts melted at these moving sounds, were both fearful to propose what both desired to do, which was to open the door, and take the stranger in. They were alone, and in a lonely place, unable to resist whatever violence were offered. It might be some imposture. At length, compassion forced Emilia, whose courage was extraordinary, as she had before manifested, to speak thus to Teresa : Shall we deny that charity to another which we were saved by in this place? Shall we not relieve a Christian, and one of our own sex, in distress?---Teresa answered---Do what you please. Emilia went to the window, and called, but none answered. Then she struck a light, and they went down stairs, and opening the door, saw at a little distance from it a woman fallen down upon her face. They dragged her into the houfe, and faftening the door, fet her in a chair, and poured fome cordial down her throat, upon which fhe revived. She was richly dreffed in an Arabian habit of filk embroidered, her hair was hanging loofe, very fair, and in great quantity. She had a fmall wound in her left breaft, a necklace of brilliant diamonds about her neck, ear-rings of great value, and her face and perfon delicately handfome. She appeared to be about five-and-twenty, and extremely frighted. At laft having recovered her reafon, fhe looked round her, and then perceiving the charming Emilia and Terefa, in their odd hermit's drefs, to be women fpeaking words of comfort, and very earneft to help her, fhe broke out into thefe paffionate words: Am I with Chriftians? Are angels provided to take care of the unhappy Charlot? Has my God heard me at laft, and brought me to a place where virtue and charity refide? And am I freed from impious infidels? Here fhe kiffed Emilia's hands, who was putting balfam to her wound. And now the ladies afked her who fhe was, and her misfortunes that brought her there. She willingly informed them. I will recount to you, faid fhe, a ftory full of wonders, fo moving and fo ftrange, that you will be filled with admiration. They made a fire, and having given her wine and meat, fat down by her, fhe defiring them to put out the light for reafons fhe would tell them.

I am, faid fhe, a native of France, born in Paris: My father was a celebrated painter. He had by my mother, who was the daughter of a French colonel, a woman of great beauty and fortune, no child but me. Our houfe was frequented by a great many of the nobility, who came to have their pictures drawn, or fee my father's curious paintings, he having a collection of the choiceft pictures, both antient and modern, of any painter in Paris. He was very rich, and defigned me a great fortune. I was tolerably handfome, and this caufed me to be extremely courted, both for a miftrefs and a wife; but my father's ambition was fo great, and he

thought

thought fo well of me, that he refufed to give me to
feveral good tradefmen and merchants, hoping to match
me to fome great officer or count: in fine, a young
nobleman coming to have his picture drawn by my father, faw and loved me, courted and vifited me often
in private, fearing his father's difpleafure, who was of
great quality. I was fo foolifh to imagine his defigns
were honourable ; and being charmed with his agreeable perfon, behaviour, and bewitching converfation,
grew infenfibly to love him paffionately. He too well
perceived my weaknefs, and made his advantage of it.
He made me many prefents of value, careffed my father
and mother highly ; fo that they entertained and gave
him all the liberty imaginable with me, fufpecting nothing of his bafe defign, which was to ruin me ; which
he thus effected : he had gained my maid to be his creature, fhe filled my ears with his praifes daily, and increafed my diftemper. One day, when my father and
mother were invited to dine abroad with fome grave
company, where it was not proper for me to go, my
lover, who had information of their being abfent, comes
in a hackney coach, and after fome amorous difcourfes,
as galant and pleafant as ufual, afks me to go abroad
with him, taking Phillis my maid with me. We will
go to a friend's of mine, faid he, whom I can truft,
and be merry. I was proud that he would fhew me to
his friends, and thought myfelf very fafe, having Phillis with me ; nay, I thought him fo noble and fincere,
that I had not the leaft diftruft of him. I dreffed myfelf richly, and went into the coach with him, leaving
my parents and home, which I fear I fhall never fee
again ; he carried me ten miles from Paris ; there we
alighted at a houfe, hired for his fatal purpofe, as I was
too foon fenfible ; I faw none but two fervants, a man
and maid, who received him as their mafter. The
houfe ftood in a garden, and no houfe within call. Here
he gave me wine, and a dinner, which was ready prepared. I began to be much furprized, and appre-

henfive

henfive of what followed. He told me after dinner he
was tired, and muft lye down upon the bed: in fine, I
trembled, and faw too late I was betrayed. And to
dwell no longer on the difmal fubject, here he forced
me to bed; and though I ufed prayers, tears, and
refifted all I was able, he at length overcame me, fwear-
ing he would marry me. Here he ftaid all night, and
left me the next morning in the hands of my betrayer,
Phillis, and his two fervants, who watched me as a
prifoner. I knew not where to go; I loved the villain
that had undone me; was afhamed to be feen, and was
fo well watched, that if I would have gone thence I
could not. He came frequently, kept me nobly, and
ufed me tenderly. My poor father and mother too well
gueffed their misfortune, and mourned for me in fecret.
My lover went no more to vifit them. My father attempted to fpeak with him, but the fervants ufed him
rudely. The neighbours laughed and ridiculed him,
becaufe he had difobliged many of them, whofe fons
and brothers had been refufed when they addreffed me:
in fine, he fell fick, and in lefs than two months died,
leaving my mother a rich, but difconfolate widow. I
was kept no longer fo very ftrictly, being big with child,
and my father dead. I was permitted to vifit my poor
mother, to whom I related my misfortune; we wept together, but could find no remedy. I was kept thus five
years, in which I never appeared abroad, but with a
mafk. I had three children. My dear mother often
came to me privately, and paffed fome days with me;
my two fons died at nurfe, my girl grew, and my betrayer was very fond of me and her. I ftill flattered
myfelf he would at laft marry me; but his father, who
had taken little notice of his keeping a miftrefs, thought
it was time for him to marry, and give an heir to
his family; he propofed a young lady of quality and
fortune fuitable; and having now glutted himfelf
with me, my lover made no difficulty to oblige his father and himfelf with a new difh. He married the lady,

who

who was handsome and a virgin; he grew fond of her, and slighted me. I never saw him, but I reproached him with my wrongs, so that he not only continued to slight me, and came seldom to see me, but used me so unkindly that we never met but we quarrelled. This, with the torments of his conscience, doubtless made him resolve on being rid of me. He comes to me in his own coach as usual, for now he made no secret of our converse, which made him not very easy with his lady; he appears very sad, and treats me with unusual tenderness, sups, and goes to bed with me; and there, with all the marks of affection and penitence, says thus to me: My dear Charlot, I have wronged you cruelly, my conscience is wounded, I have not had a moment's quiet since I married, and now I am resolved to make you reparation; I am yours, and not hers whom I finfully married. I am determined to leave her, and have provided a ship to carry, and money to maintain us in England, whither I mean to fly with you and my dear child. You may imagine, loving him as I did, how easily I was persuaded to credit him: in fine, I agreed to all he proposed with joy; and a few days after he came, took me, and would have had the child, but my mother would not be persuaded to part with it: he carried me to Calais, where we went aboard a merchant ship. I had carried only my clothes and maid, and he pretending he had remitted his money to England, brought only two large portmanteaus on board. He led me into the cabin, where we supped, and lay all night. He left me dressing in the morning to go talk with the captain, I suspecting nothing. In some time I sent Phillis to call him to breakfast, and she staying long, I called, but nobody came: at last I looked out, and saw the ship under sail. The captain came; I asked for my lord and maid; he told me they were gone on shore in the boat. I wrung my hands, and wept; he told me it was all in vain, he had orders for what he did. In short, I fell sick with grief, kept my bed, and was

H 3

brought

brought to Tripoly before I knew where I was. Here
I was brought to shore, carried to a house, robbed of
my clothes and jewels. The portmanteaus brought
aboard by my villainous lord were empty, as I satisfied myself before : in this place I was sold to an Arabian
captain, or chief of a tribe. He carried me with him,
and what became of the Christian that sold me I know
not. Abenbucer the brave Arab used me kindly, loved,
and preferred me before all his women ; but alas ! what
joy could I take in this dismal course of life ? A thousand times I have wished to die. I was carried up and
down with the rest of his women in a covered waggon,
when we moved our habitations, which we did twice in
the sad year. I lived with him three days since we came
near this mountain. A brother of Abenbucer's, great
as himself in power, of a humour different, resolute and
revengeful, some time since saw and liked me, and
studied how to take me from his brother. Yesterday
Abenbucer being gone with his band to forage, Abdelen
comes with his band of soldiers to the tent, and takes
me away: just as he was going off, Abenbucer comes
by ; in short I screamed ; a bloody dispute ensued, in
which I was the victim to their rage, being dragged by
the hair from one side to the other ; here I received my
wound : at last seeing the two brothers sharply engaged,
I ran from them, and escaped over the mountain, where
I wandered the rest of the day, fearing to be pursued,
till darkness, loss of blood and weakness obliged me to
stop ; at last my senses failed, and had not God sent
you to assist me, I had perhaps perished on the cold
ground.

The ladies admired, and wept at the sad story ; and
then lighting a candle, got her to bed, where they
spent the remainder of the night in discourse, telling
her part of their adventures. Towards morning they
slept, and rising late, found Charlot so ill she could not
rise ; and now she expressed her fears to them : Ladies
(said she) I fear it will not be long before the incensed

brothers,

brothers, at leaft he that furvives, will come in fearch
of me over the mountains; it is my advice, therefore,
that we remove to fome town of ftrength for fome days,
left you are difcovered and ruined by protecting me.
Your beauty, which far excels mine, will perhaps caufe
them to bear you hence with me; you are very unfafe
here. This alarmed the poor ladies, who finding but
too much probability in what fhe faid, were now afraid
to remain here; Emilia, therefore, goes to a neighbouring village where the hermit was known, fays they
were his kinfmen whom he had left in the houfe, and
defires a lodging, and fome lad of integrity to ftay in
the houfe for fome days till Ifmael their kinfman returned, becaufe they had been frightened with a band
of robbers, who were roving on this fide the mountain;
which was not very frequent, they not often venturing
to come on that fide. The honeft Moors revereneing
their habit, offered them a houfe to live in till the good
Ifmael came home. Emilia gave the poor of the place
a large alms, which highly increafed their refpect for
her; and fo fhe returned with a lad with her, the fon
of one of the principal men of the village. She had,
before fhe went, packed up their money, and dreffed
the fick lady in an old habit of the hermit's, packing
up her rich cloaths and jewels in a bundle. They led
her betwixt them, and left nothing of much value behind them, ordering the lad to bring the hermit, and
whoever came with him, to them. The boy did not
fear the robbers, when nothing was left in the houfe
worth their taking; but the fourth night of his ftay the
poor lad was murdered by fome robbers, who entered
the houfe in the night, and plundered it, and fearing
difcovery, killed him in the bed as he flept; which
fome days after was difcovered by the thieves being
taken, one of whom being put to death, confeffed this
fact, with many others.

The next morning after the boy was killed, the hermit and the lords arrived, and entering the houfe, were

entertained

entertained with this difmal fpectacle: the door was open, the houfe plundered, and the ftrange lad lying dead, the hermit concluded the ladies were murdered; and now the lords grief cannot be expreffed. The hermit found all the money gone, and believing it to no purpofe to ftay there longer, perfuaded the lords to go back: My friends (faid he) it is in vain to ftay here and mourn, it is Heaven's pleafure: if the fhip fails without you, you will perhaps perifh here alfo. The virtuous ladies are, no doubt, happy and at reft; God has permitted it to be fo, and we as mortals muft fubmit: if we ftay here one night, it may be our fate to be murdered alfo, or carried by the robbers into flavery. They yielded to his advice, and returned in great affliction to Atta-bala's houfe; and the fhip coming again to an anchor, they went aboard, and fet fail for Venice, leaving word with Johanna, if the ladies were ever heard of, to fend them word, and to affift them, if they came, to get to them; refolving to ftay fome time at Venice before Don Lopez and the count went to Spain, where the latter refolved to ftay with Don Lopez the reft of his days, both determining never to marry again: Clarinda and the count de Chateau-Roial having agreed likewife to go with them to Spain, and to ftay there till intereft could be made for them, by their friends in France, for a dif-penfation from Rome, for him and Clarinda to be man and wife, by difcharging him of his vows; he fearing to be punifhed if he returned home without permiffion, and a pardon for the crimes he had committed. They all paffed their time very agreeably in the fhip, except the two lords, who fincerely mourned the lofs of their ladies; and the fhip arrived fafe at Venice the 10th of March, 1715.

CHAP.

CHAP. XVI.

THE ladies waited some days, in expectation of hearing by the lad of the hermit's arrival: at last the father of the boy went to the house, and returned with the melancholy news of his son's death, and the house being plundered; and having enquired of some poor goat herds who were upon the mountain, they informed him, that they had seen three men, two of whom appeared Grecians, and the old hermit, alight at the cottage door and go in; but they staid not long, but mounted their horses, and turned back by the way they came. From this account the ladies concluded, that they finding the house rifled, a strange lad dead, and nobody left to inform them what was become of them, departed, imagining them dead, or fled thence: they therefore resolved to set out immediately for Algiers, and to go to Attabala's house, where they supposed their lords would wait, in hopes to hear of them, at least till they were better informed what was become of them. They took their money, clothes, and jewels; and having given some alms to the village, and a present to the man whose son was killed in their service, departed the town in a covered waggon they hired to carry them, it being the most easy and private way for them to travel, leaving a good name behind them. The poor villagers having conceived a high opinion of their sanctity, accompanied them on the road a great way, praying for the good dervises welfare, as they called them; and in four days time they got safe to Johanna's house, where they first stopped to alight, for they lay in the waggon all the three nights on the road, and went not into any house, only walked sometimes in the lonely places they passed through, to stretch their limbs. Here they discharged the waggon, taking their things out, and sent it back; and here Johanna informed them

of

of their lords being gone for Venice, and advised them
to go early the next morning to Attabala's house, which
she thought more safe than her's. The poor woman
entertained them kindly, and they rejoiced at the good
Seraja's being gone to Venice, hoping to find her well
and happy there. Johanna entertained them with the
adventures their lords had met with, and the fortunate
meeting of the hermit and Eleonora, at which they
were much pleased. This night they rested sweetly,
being in great want of sleep: the next morning early,
they went to Attabala's: there Abra made them very
welcome; they were obliged to stay here till an opportunity of a ship could be found to carry them to
Venice. And now poor Charlot, whose wound was not
perfectly cured, fell very sick; the disorder of this long
journey threw her into a fever, of which she was so
dangerously ill, that her life was despaired of: Emilia
and Teresa used all their endeavours to save her. Whilst
she lay in this condition, Emilia walked frequently
down to the sea-side with Johanna, who came and staid
with them, to wait upon, and keep them company,
till they got off; and as they were musing one evening
on the shore, they saw a man lying upon the sand, who
appeared so miserable that it moved their compassion
and wonder together. They drew near to him; he was
young, but his face was so pale, and disfigured with
dirt and want, that it appeared frightful; his hands
were so lean that the bones and nerves were visible,
the skin being shrivelled and withered; his cloaths
were miserably torn and ragged; he had no shirt on,
only a poor coat and breeches, with shoes and stock-
ings suitable; he had three wounds in his stomach
and breast, which appeared not to be fresh, but foul
and rankled, and not covered with any plaisters.
Emilia was so touched with this dreadful object, that she
wept. The man looked stedfastly upon her, she being
in her hermit's dress, and that made him silent, believing her a Turk. At last he said in French, Why
                                                    do

do you stand staring upon me? Am not I a man? What
do you see to wonder at? If you compassionate my
miserable condition, relieve me, or kill me, for I am
weary of living.----Emilia answered, Are you a native of
France, and a Christian? I am, said he, one, who
being cast on this barbarous shore, am reduced to this
misery. Follow us, said she, and we will relieve you.
He looked eagerly upon her, and scrambling up, made
shift to crawl to the house after them: being entered
the door, she desired Johanna to give him wine and meat,
which he devoured with great greediness; and a few
minutes after fell into strange convulsions; they gave
him some cordial water, and Abra ran and brought a
quilt, coverlid, sheets and bolster, and made a bed:
the lady withdrawing, Johanna and he washed his face
and hands, put him on a shirt, and laid him in bed:
then they put balsam to his wounds. He seemed almost
insensible of all they did to him; but nature, which
struggled hard to digest what he had eat, at last threw
him into a sweat, and then he fell into a slumber; upon
which they retired, leaving him to rest. Emilia going
up to Charlot's chamber, who was now on the mending
hand, related to her and Teresa the strange adventure
she had met with, which drew tears from their eyes also.
The stranger slept all night, as they supposed; for Abra,
who lay in the next room, heard nothing of him, only
sometimes a deep sigh or groan. About eight in the
morning Emilia sent Johanna to ask how he did: when
she entered the room, she was surprized at the change
of his countenance, and concluded he was a person of
quality, and very handsome when in health; he made
the most grateful acknowledgments imaginable, begging to know who the charitable person was, to whom
he owed his life. She answered, that she was commanded by that person to ask his name and quality, if
it were not improper, that they might know how
to treat him. Alas! said he, the gentleman's curiosity
will not be much more satisfied, when I tell you that I

H 6   am

am the fon of a marfhal of France, and that my name
is Victor Amando, count of Frejus ; born to a plentiful
fortune, and by one unfortunate action ruined. I was
going to Rome in a fhip from Marfeilles, and by a ftorm
caft on this fhore : here I have been robbed in a wood,
wounded and left for dead ; and not knowing where to
go, or who to apply to, being unable to go far, I wandered
about the wood for thefe ten days paft, eating nothing
but wild fruits and nuts, which threw me into a bloody
flux. I at laft crept to the fea-fide, and there fat down,
unable to go farther, having no other defign, but to lie
there and die, which God prevented by your generous
mafter's hands. At thefe words Abra entered the room
with a Grecian habit for him, which Don Lopez had left
behind, and waited to drefs him : at which Johanna retired, and went to her ladies with the account of what
he had told her : but who can exprefs the furprize poor
Charlot was in when fhe heard the ftranger's name, and
knew him to be her faithlefs lord, who had ruined, and
bafely fent her here ? My God ! faid fhe, how wondrous
are thy ways, and how miraculous thy power? Has thy
juftice then found him out, and brought him here to fuffer ?
I thank thee, my God ! Being very weak, fhe fainted ;
the ladies were much amazed at her words, and foon
gueffed who the ftranger was : they revived Charlot with
cordials, and begged her to compofe herfelf, left her
fever fhould return with this great diforder of mind,
and confider with them, whether it would be proper for
her to fee him now, or to ftay till they had founded his
inclinations, and learned whether he were fingle, and
inclined to repair the injury he had done her, by an
honourable marriage. Emilia and Terefa went into the
parlour, and fent for him to breakfaft ; they were both
in their hermit's drefs, as men. When the count de
Fréjus entered the room, they gave him a good morning
with great gravity; he returned the compliment: they
treated him now with ceremony : he much admired the
beauty of thefe young men, and foon perceived by their

voices

voices and mien that they were women difguifed. At
laft Emilia entered into a ferious difcourfe with him, in
this manner : My lord, I am no ftranger to you, nor
the actions of your life ; nor am I furprifed at the mif-
fortunes that you have met with, which I hope the Almighty will fanctify to you, and turn to your advantage.
Where is the unhappy Charlot and her child ? Oh!
my lord, how could you expect profperity to attend you,
till you had expiated by repentance the cruel injury you
did that lovely maid ? At thefe words the count was
even thunderftruck, to hear a ftranger in Barbary reproach him for a crime he thought a fecret to the greateft
part of his own acquaintance. He at laft lifted up his
eyes, the big drops rolling down his face. My God!
faid he, I own thy juftice. And falling at the ladies
feet, Bright angels, faid he, for fuch doubtlefs you are,
who pry into the hearts of men, and know our fecret
actions, pray for me to the Almighty ! I have finned fo
greatly that an age of penance cannot expiate my crimes.
Oh! teach me what to do to appeafe Heaven. The
ladies raifed him, faying, Rife, fir, we are frail mortals like yourfelf, and living monuments of the Divine
mercy, preferved in this inhofpitable land by miracles.
But tell us, were Charlot living yet, would you repair
her injuries ? Witnefs, faid he, that God in whom we
truft, he who has feen my tears, and heard my prayers,
that I would marry her that hour I were bleffed with her
dear prefence ; nay, I would choofe to beg with her,
and fuffer every ill, nay death itfelf, rather than wrong
her any more, or marry with a queen : long have I
mourned my fin, nor can I ever deferve fo great a
bleffing as to fee her face again. Are you then fingle ?
faid Terefa : Is your lady dead ? And may we credit
what you fay ?---Oh! what a wretch am I! faid he,
that cannot be believed. Here Charlot, who had
liftened, entered the room. I would believe you, my
lord, faid fhe, but have fo fuffered for my credulity
already, that I hardly dare truft you. He fell at her

feet

feet tranſported, all he ſaid was confuſed, he embraced
her knees, gazed on her face, and at length fainted,
falling down on his face. Her tenderneſs for him revived; ſhe ſtrove to raiſe him, but through weakneſs
and ſurprize ſwooned, falling by him. This ſight was
extremely moving: the ladies calling, the ſervants entered, and took them up; in ſome time they recovered,
and were laid together on the bed the count had lain on.
And now looking tenderly upon her, he ſaid, Charming,
much injured Charlot, can you forgive me? I am now
ſingle, our dear child is well, and is my heir; God has
caſt me on this ſhore to bring me to myſelf and you;
this happy place has brought me peace of conſcience.
Do you but pardon me; and conſent to marry me, I
will bring you home to France with triumph, with God's
leave. She gave him her hand: Tell me, ſaid ſhe,
what has befallen you ſince the fatal day you left me.
I will, ſaid he. The ladies being ſeated, he thus
began.

CHAP. XVII.

THE unhappy day, ſaid he, when I baſely left you,
a day I ever muſt repent of, I went aſhore with the
treacherous Phillis, whom God has already puniſhed,
having ſtruck her ſoon after with madneſs, in which
ſhe died inſenſible, and I fear unrepenting. I returned to Paris to my wife, and thought myſelf happy,
vainly fancying I had ſecured my peace for the future.
Your mother inveighed againſt me, ſaying, I had tre-
panned you: but I diſſembled with her, pretended you
had by misfortune fallen over-board, and was drowned,
to my inexpreſſible grief, which I was forced to ſtifie, for
fear of my father and my wife's reproaches. This
Phillis

Phillis justified to be true; and my great fondness of our child, and the large presents I made your mother, prevailed with her to credit this story; so I remained quiet from all clamours but my conscience, which hourly reproached me: I had no rest, my soul was on the rack; I grew surly and morose to all the world; my wife grew to hate me, and we lived miserably. A thousand times I wished for you again. At last I discovered that she did me justice, in dishonouring my bed with one of my pages: I exposed her to the world; we parted, and in a short time after she died in childbed of a child, which I did not believe mine: and that dying with her, put an end to all disputes. And now being little esteemed by my friends, and conscious to myself of my wickedness and shame, I left France in that cursed vessel which brought you here, being forced to be civil, and keep a correspondence with the villain who commanded it. We were bound to Italy, where I designed to see Rome, and pay my devotions at all the holy places there. I asked him when he came in sight of this coast, if he thought it was possible to find you, resolving to purchase your freedom with all I was worth; but he told me it was in vain to attempt it. Soon after this discourse a tempest arose that tore our ship in pieces, and cast me on this shore; the captain perished in my sight. I was half dead when I reached the shore; and was scarce able to walk: I saw a small coffer on the sands, and taking hold of it, I made shift to drag it to the wood. Considering I was in a strange place, I thought it must contain something that would be useful to me, having neither clothes, food, nor money. I sat down, and rested that night, having nothing to eat to refresh me. At break of day I found my limbs stiff, and a great faintness over all my body; I broke open the coffer, and found money, clothes, and many rich things in it, by which I judged it belonged to the villain captain. As I was looking into it, three Moors appeared, who coming up to me, one struck me over the head with

a sabre,

a fabre, which stunned me quite; they gave me three stabs in the stomach and breast with a knife; and emptying the chest, fled, leaving me for dead. It was long before I came to myself; but when I did, you may guess my condition: I bled much, I fought for some dust to stench the blood, and that performed it; but being unable to walk far, and not knowing where to go, I remained there destitute of food and help. Here I examined myself as I ought, prepared to die, and, I hope, made my peace with God, whose mercy has been signally manifested in my deliverance, and our wonderful meeting.

The ladies admired, and blessed God for their good fortune, and his conversion; and wished nothing more than to see them married, which they could not accomplish till a Christian ship arrived, which was in less than a month's time; when a French ship came to them, sent from Venice, to enquire after them; which no sooner arrived, but Abra went aboard in the fisherboat: monsieur Robinet the captain welcomed him. When the ship was ready to depart, he gave notice, and they came aboard, bringing their money, clothes, and jewels; and taking leave, with much affection, of the good Johanna, whom Emilia and Teresa offered to take with them; but Abra and she had agreed to marry, fo she chose to stay in Barbary. The captain entertained them nobly, as became the generosity and good breeding of a Frenchman, and a Christian. They related to him all their adventures, excepting the occasion of Charlot's misfortunes, which they concealed in respect to the count de Frejus. And here he and Charlot were married by the chaplain, a good Carmelite, who made them an excellent discourse upon the subject of their deliverances they had all met with in that barbarous place, from whence God had been now pleased to free them. They were bound for Venice, where they expected to find their lords.

It will now be proper that I should inform you what reception the lords and the rest of our travellers met with at Venice. Antonio and his fair bride invited all the company, at their landing, to go home with them to his mother, the noble Angelina's. At their arrival, the servants seeing their lord and the beautiful Anna, were so transported, they scarce knew what they did: they wept for joy, and so great a noise was made in the house, that Angelina, who had been long sick in her chamber, imagined the house was on fire, and crept out to the stair-head, to see what was the matter: but when she saw her son and Anna coming up to her, she was scarce able to express her joy. They threw themselves at her feet; she blessed and raised them, clasping them in her arms and weeping on their bosoms. They informed her, that they had brought other persons of worth and quality with them, whom they would recommend to her favour. She composed herself a little, and her son led her down, where she received them with demonstrations of respect: but when she saw her niece and seignior Andrea Zantonio, she was amazed: Just Heavens, said she, kinsman! who thought to have seen you together?---God had decreed it so, madam, said he; and therefore seas and Barbarians could not prevent it. Angelina called for supper, saluting Clarinda, welcoming the lords, the count de Chateau-Roial, and the good Seraja at supper, which was splendid, as the company and occasion merited. Great part of the company's adventures were related, and Angelina informed seignior Andrea, that his father was dead, very much afflicted for his son's loss: But my brother and sister, niece, said she to Eleonora, are well, and to-morrow we will go and see them. Beds were made for all the company, and no excuse would pass but the lords, Clarinda and her lord, must all stay there while they continued at Venice. The next day the whole city rang of this strange story, and all the noblemen and ladies, who were friends or related to Angelina, crowded thither

to

to see, and welcome Antonio and his charming lady to
Venice. A meffenger was difpatched early in the morning
to Eleonora's father, who by noon arrived at Angelina's, with her mother. Poor Attabala was likewife much
careffed for his faithful fervice to his lady. In fine, a
month was paft in nothing but feafts, balls, and entertainments, to welcome thefe noble Venetians home ; in
all which the Spanifh and French lords fhared. Yet
Don Lopez and count de Hautville were deeply melancholy : they had related the ftory of their misfortunes,
and Emilia's and Terefa's lofs ; and a French fhip lying
in the harbour, Angelina propofed to them to fend for
the captain, and agree with him to caft anchor and call
at Attabala's houfe, to which they fhould direct him,
and make enquiry after thefe unfortunate ladies. They
did fo ; and this was the fhip that Abra went aboard of
at his coming to an anchor. And in this veffel they
came fafe to Venice, but not before the lords had left it ;
for Don Lopez, defirous to fee his father and native
country again, having little hopes of Terefa's being
found, or efcaping if alive, growing uneafy at the
multitude of company he was obliged to be engaged in
every day, and wanting to be alone with his friend,
whofe melancholy humour fuited beft with him at that
time ; he therefore propofed to the count de Hautville
to go thence foon : however, they were detained two
months longer ; in which time monfieur de Chateau-
Roial fell fick of a fever ; and though all poffible means
were ufed to fave him, yet all proved ineffectual, and
the phyficians gave him over. He behaved himfelf in
this his laft fcene of life fo like a Chriftian and a hero,
that it charmed all that attended him. At laft the pangs
of death being on him, he took a folemn leave of every
one there prefent, but particularly of the two lords who
had preferved him and Clarinda from perifhing. He
at laft having received the laft facraments, concluded all
with taking leave of the difconfolate Clarinda, who had
not for many days gone into a bed, or left his bed-fide :

he

he grafped her hand, and fixing his dying eyes upon
her, faid, My dear Clarinda, the hour is now come
when we muft be parted, though not for a long time;
God does not think fit to continue us longer together. I
have unfortunately occafioned you many misfortunes;
we have known little fatisfaction in the enjoyment of
one another; now human paffions will ceafe to fire my
foul, and my reafon will govern. Believe me, fenfual
pleafures are bitter in reflection, and in death afford no
confolation; I hope my peace is made above. I am
glad to leave the world, and can advife you **but two**
things: the firft is, to be contented with our feparation,
fubmit to God, and acquiefce in all things he decrees;
nor murmur at misfortunes, which are the holy fires
that muft purge our fouls of vice, and make us fit for
glory. And next, I beg that you would quit the world,
and in a convent fpend the remainder of your life,
where you may be no more in danger of being again
unhappy; nor give that lovely perfon to another, who
may involve you in worldly cares. Alas! my dear,
life is well fpent in learning how to die; live fo that
we may meet again to part no more.——Yes, my dear
lord, faid fhe, I will obey you, and never venture into
the world again. Here his agonies increafing, his
confeffor began the prayers, and in few hours he departed. Clarinda, after he was handfomely interred in
the Benedictines church near the altar, was invited into
the convent of nuns adjoining; to which fhe went, attended by Angelina, Antonio, Anna, Eleonora, feignior Andrea, the two lords, Seraja, and all Angelina's
relations and friends, who loved her much, and left
her there to enjoy uninterrupted peace, where no
worldly cares can enter to difturb her.

After this Seraja choofing to ftay at Angelina's, the
lords took leave, and went for Spain in a Spanifh veffel.
They arrived fafe at Barcelona, from whence they went
to Madrid; and there at his feat near that city found
Don Lopez's father, Don Manuel de Mendoza, who
was

was aftonifhed to fee him. He and the count de Hautville entertained him with a faithful account of all the
ftrange adventures they had met with, which filled him,
and all his friends to whom their ftory was related, with
admiration. But no part of their hiftory was more
wondered at than that of Tanganor and Maria; the
heroic action fhe did, in pulling out her eyes to fave
her virtue, charmed all that heard it related.

And now Don Lopez was worfe fatigued than ever,
being obliged to receive vifits from all his, till then,
unknown relations, and all the Spanifh nobility that
heard of him; fo that he had fcarce an hour to himfelf,
or to give to his friend alone. At laft he retired to a
feat of his father's in the country, where he paffed a
few days to the fatisfaction of his mind, but the prejudice of his body; for here he and the count talked
and thought of nothing but Emilia and Terefa, and
that melancholy, which company and noife before diverted, feized their fpirits; fo that in few days they
both grew altered; forgot to eat or fleep as nature required; and nothing but leaving the world, and retiring to a convent was thought of.

One morning about ten o'clock, a coach ftopped at
the gate, with an elderly lady in it, who much defired
to fpeak with Don Lopez. The fervants brought her
in; and Don Lopez being informed of her being there,
readily came to her, hoping to hear fomething of the
ladies; but it proved otherwife: My lord, faid fhe, I
have heard with amazement your adventures, and your
noble Venetian friends; it is the fubject of all the people's difcourfe in this province: but there is one ftory in
particular, in which I am nearly concerned, which re-
lates to a lady whofe name was Maria, loft from her
country, and me her afflicted mother, long fince. I beg
to hear from your own mouth what I have heard from
others, that being informed of each particular circumftance, I may be able to judge whether the lady you
have feen be my dear child or not. Don Lopez fitting

down by her, related all the story of Tanganor and his lady, and then begged to know how this excellent lady came into the hands of the Turks. The lady much tranſported, being now poſitive that it was her daughter he had ſeen, wiping away the tears, which joy had filled her eyes withal, proceeded to ſatisfy his requeſt in this manner: My lord, my huſband Don Fernando Valada was a merchant at Barcelona; it had pleaſed God to give us a very handſome fortune; but it was many years before he bleſſed us with a child, which was the only thing we wanted to make us completely happy. At laſt I proved with child, and was delivered of this lovely girl, which we bred up with the utmoſt care and tenderneſs. When ſhe was turned of twelve years old, my huſband having a ſhip very richly laden returned from Goa, which lay at anchor in the road, invited a great many of his relations and friends on board to give them a treat: I was at that time unfortunately indiſpoſed, and therefore ſent my daughter with her father to ſupply my place. It was Autumn, and late at night before the company broke up: the pinnace carrying part of them aſhore, and returning to fetch my huſband, Maria, and the reſt, it grew dark, the wind roſe, and my huſband was afraid to let her venture to go ſo late, and apprehending a ſtorm, thought it beſt to ſtay aboard till morning: but alas! the ſtorm increaſed, and about two o'clock the ſhip was drove to ſea, having loſt her anchors, and running before the wind, was drove on the coaſt of Barbary: there the ſhip was beſet with three Algerine pirates, and after a ſharp fight, in which my dear huſband was killed, the ſhip was taken and carried into Algiers. A Turkiſh captain, who was come there to purchaſe fair ſlaves for his villainous maſters to make ſale of, bought my dear child; but where he carried, or how he diſpoſed of her, I could never be informed till now. What I tell you, I got information of by means of a friar, who was chaplain to my huſband's ſhip, and being a very ſickly

I

man, and unfit for flavery, the pirate captain difmiffed him, and put him on board a French fhip they made prize of in their way to Algiers; and having plundered it, put on board it all the wounded and difabled perfons, and fome provifions, and bid them go home. But alas! they were unable to manage the fhip, and had not God fent an Englifh fhip, who met them at fea, they had perifhed: the Englifh captain putting fome hands aboard, brought the fhip to Barcelona, to which place he was bound. Thus, my lord, faid fhe, I have informed you what you defired to know; and now I only beg one favour more of you, which is, to direct me how I may fend to my dear Maria, whofe virtues have now made her ten times dearer to me than fhe was by the ties of nature. Don Lopez told her the only way was to fend by fome Eaft-India fhip, as he would direct. After many thanks fhe took leave, and having a brother who was captain of a merchant fhip, got him to go to that ifland, and had the fatisfaction of having a meffage from Maria's own mouth, with a letter from Tanganor, promifing to come to Spain the next year, fo foon as he had got another return from Perfia. In the mean time he fent her his eldeft daughter, the lovely Eleonora, whom fhe received with the greateft joy imaginable. This was a year after fhe was with Don Lopez, whom we fhall now leave at his country feat, and return to enquire after the ladies.

CHAP XVIII.

THREE months after Don Lopez and the count de Hautville's departure from Venice, the charming Emilia and Terefa arrived, with the count de Frejus and his lady, the now happy Charlot, and were by

monfieur

monfieur Robinet conducted to Angelina's houfe, where they were received with great joy and civility : and here they put on habits fuiting their fex and quality, and were obliged to ftay fome days both to refrefh themfelves, and in compliance with the importunities of their friends, feignior Antonio Borgomio and the engaging Anna, and feignior Andrea and Eleonora his lady, whom utually ftrove to divert them ; rivalling each other in the magnificence of their feafts and balls : and all their relations vifited and invited them to entertainments ; fo that a month was paft before they could handfomely take leave. They forgot not to pay a vifit to Clarinda, whom they dearly loved and honoured, lamenting monfieur de Chateau-Roial's death, whom they much pitied whilft living ; fearing no difpenfation would be granted him to live with Clarinda. And now monfieur Robinet, who obligingly ftaid for them, prepared for their departure, taking aboard wine and frefh provifions of all kinds, to accommodate them in the way. And now taking leave, though with fome uneafinefs, being much preffed to ftay longer, they went on board, accompanied by all their generous friends, who waited on them to the fhip. The good Seraja, who was overjoyed at their arrival, gladly went with them, being amazed and charmed with the treatment, and fine things fhe met with, and faw in Europe. Abundance of fine prefents were made to Emilia and Terefa by the Venetian ladies, of rich Venetian brocades and fome jewels, to be the monitors to remind them of their abfent friends ; rich wines, lace, perfumed gloves, fweet-meats, and all forts of things ufeful and ornamental. Nor did Emilia and Terefa omit to make fuch returns as became them to do, promifing the noble Angelina and Anna never to neglect an opportunity of writing to them, and to keep their friendfhip alive with frequent converfe of letters. And thus embracing one another they parted, and the fhip fetting fail, arrived at Barcelona. The captain took a lodging for

the

the three ladies and the count de Frejus at their landing, and then making inquiry for Seignior Don Manuel de Mendoza, Don Lopez's father, was soon informed where he was; and going the next morning to his seat, which he rid to in few hours, he informed that noble lord who was arrived in his ship. He received the news with much joy; and curious to see his daughter-in-law and Emilia, of whom he had heard so much; as likewise desirous to bring the lady, and good news to his son himself; he ordered his coach and six to be got ready against the next morning, when he set out with the captain for Barcelona, where he found the expecting Emilia and Teresa, whom he tenderly embraced, and welcomed the count de Frejus and his lady, admiring the ladies youth and beauty, especially Teresa's, which he had expected to see much changed. He carried them to his seat the next day, having entertained them at a relation's house the day of his arrival at Barcelona, and the night of his stay there: then he paid captain Robinet nobly, making him promise to call on him at his next return from France. He treated his daughter and company in such a manner at his seat, as even amazed them; and then set out for the country seat, where those they most longed to see were. When the coach came near the gate, he begged the ladies to abide in it, till he went in and prepared his son and the count to see them, Lest, said he, the surprize of seeing you on a sudden may hurt them. They consented. Ladies, said he, I assure you your husbands are much changed for the worse; that is, they are pale, lean, and dispirited, but you will be the best cordial to revive them. He quitted the coach, and, attended with two servants only, entered the gate, and asking for his son, was informed the count and he were in the gardens. Thither he went, and found them sitting together in a deep discourse: they started at his coming up to them, like men lost in thought. Gentlemen, said he, why do you pass life thus in solitude, unactive, and lost to

the

the world? Son, I blush to think the loss of a woman, though a wife, should rob you of your reason, make you forget your duty to your prince and country. Come, wake, shake off this lethargy, rouse at the call of glory and honour, and let your ancestors souls no longer mourn, to see you waste your youth in pining for a woman, which should be employed in doing deeds worthy your birth, and to perpetuate her name.--Alas! my honoured lord (said he) you cannot comprehend what I have lost: consider the amazing proofs Teresa gave me of her virtue, and the sad condition I have left her in. See here, my friend, a man brave as the world can shew, he droops like me, for such another woman. Why should we be censured if we leave the world, and live retired? Are not our convents filled with such, and do not they merit our esteem?---My son (replied the old lord), they leave the world by choice, you only because you are disgusted; suppose your wives are dead, must you rebel and murmur against Providence?---(Ha! said the count de Hautville starting) dead! what are you going to prepare us for? If they are so, tell us at once, our resolutions are already made, a cloister shall secure us from all future mischief; we will not make a second choice. Let glory, and the idle ambition that deludes mankind, tempt them to venture in a crowd, and end life in a tumult; we will study how to die, and wait our Maker's pleasure, till he rids us of a tedious life, and calls us to eternal rest. Here the cold sweat trickled down his face; and the old lord, admiring their constancy and affection, took him by the hand, and said, Come, friends! revive, God has heard you; I have some good news to tell you; I have heard, from your wives, they are not far off; follow me. Here turning **about, he** went to the gate, they following in such disorder they scarce knew what they did: but when they saw the ladies, they forgot all ceremony, and rushing into the coach, regardless of Charlot the stranger, they fell on their knees before their wives, embracing them,

who were so transported, the tears flowed from their
eyes, and they mutually blessed God, and said so many
passionate things, that the old lord, Charlot, and the
count de Frejus wept.   In some time they began to remember who waited ; and Don Lopez recovering himself, begged pardon of his father.   My son, (said he)
it is a laudable error ; you have a wife worthy the
affection you bear her, she merits all your care, and
God has blessed me beyond my desert in such children.
The ladies alighting, entered the house.   And now
an universal joy spread itself through all the family, and
ten days were past in nothing but balls and entertainments.

They departed thence for Madrid, where Fame had
spread the news of their adventures before their arrival ; and there they saw the splendor of their glorious
monarch king Philip's court, where the French galantry
has taken place of the Spanish gravity, and wisdom
and good manners seem to walk hand in hand ; where
solid sense and generosity, greatness and goodness, appear united ; where men are statesmen and courtiers together.

For six months they passed the time agreeably, and
then the count de Hautville having received news from
France, that his father was dead long since, and the
title and estate his due ; though his supposed death had
consigned it to another, who was ready to resign it to
him with pleasure ; communicated this news to the
company : but Teresa and Emilia knew not how to
think of parting, they being both with child.   At last it
was resolved the Count de Hautville, now marquis de
Ventadore, should go to France, settle his affairs, and
return to them ; Teresa begging Emilia might lye-in
with her.

The count de Frejus and the marquis, with Charlot,
who longed to see her mother and child, went together
to France over the Alps, Emilia making her lord promise never more to go upon the faithless seas.   They
arrived

arrived fafe in France, where they were greatly welcomed, and Charlot's lovely daughter received by her
parents with great tranfport.

The marquis de Ventadore quickly returned to Spain,
and was, not long after, bleffed with a fon, which Emilia
brought him on the 10th of Auguft, 1719; and the
charming Terefa made her tranfported lord father to
a fon and daughter, on the 13th of September the fame
year: the two lords ftood godfathers to each other's fons,
and Don Lopez's father and Emilia to Terefa's daughter,
who bare Terefa's name; and Don Lopez, in perform-
ance of his vow, built a church, and dedicated it to St.
Terefa.

And now one would fuppofe, that having paft feven
years in an almoft continued fcene of misfortunes, and
thus fortunately arrived in their native country, the
happy Don Lopez and his charming wife might expect
to pafs the remainder of their days in peace. It is true,
the fair Terefa was but nineteen, and that fatal beauty
that had occafioned her fo much forrow, was rather
improved than diminifhed: but her known virtue would
have awed any bold admirer from once daring to difclofe
his flame, and fecured her from all attempts of love,
one would have imagined. But alas! it was otherwife
decreed. A young nobleman of Spain, fon of a duke, and
favourite of his young prince, the prince of Afturias,
whom he was bred up with, nephew to Don Manuel
father of Don Lopez, coming frequently to vifit him
and Terefa, who was now up again, and feemed to
rife like the glorious fun, to blefs the world with new
charms in her face, and fire in her eyes, content adding
fmiles to her natural fweetnefs; the unfortunate Don
Fernando de Medina gazed away his liberty, and grew
fo mad in love, that he forgot all ties of blood, honour,
and chriftianity; and refolved to poffefs her, or die in
the attempt. He knew her virtue rendered all means
but force impracticable, defpairing to gain her any

I 2

other

other way; and therefore fubtilly contrived how to effect it, without her being aware of it, or her hufband able to find out where fhe was, or who had ftolen her. In order to this, he hires four defperate Catalonian gentlemen, fons of fortune, who had been employed before in fuch, or as bad undertakings: thefe he promifed a great reward to. One of thefe hired a houfe next a wood, about five miles from Fernando's country feat, and placed in it two old hags, proper for fuch a wicked defign. Here they made a chamber ftrong as a prifon, furnifhed it with a bed, and all neceffary things. Thus prepared he goes to his kinfman's, invites him and the marquis to a hunting-match, with the ladies. They willingly confented to go, and the next morning went to his houfe, where after being magnificently treated, they went into the field; and purfued the frighted ftag, till the heat of the day made them retire to this fatal wood, where Don Fernando had prepared a treat for them. Here they dined in a tent pitched for that purpofe: and then he propofed to the lords, to leave the ladies there to repofe, whilft they hunted another deer, and fo return to conduct them home in the evening. Two fervants were left to attend the ladies. About an hour after their lords were gone, the four villains who lay in ambufh, with vizards on their faces, and piftols in their hands, rufhed into the tent, and feizing upon Terefa, carried her away before the fervants, who were fallen afleep upon the grafs behind the tent, awaked with the alarm of Emilia's cries. Fernando kept the lords fome hours, and then returning to the tent, they found Emilia almoft diftracted with grief, and the fervants ftanding mute as ftatues: the cunning Fernando fhewed a mighty concern for his kinfman's misfortune. Don Lopez raved, and ftormed like a man in defpair; but all in vain. They fearched all the wood, and paffing by the lonely houfe, faw one of the old hags, who ftood at the door on purpofe. The lords enquired of her, if fhe had feen any man with a lady pafs by that way: fhe told them yes; about two hours before, fhe

faw

saw four men ride by, with a lady bound hand and foot
before one of them, and suppofing them thieves, fhut
the door. They turned to that road (faid fhe), fhew-
ing a contrary way to that they had really taken; Emilia and the lords went on that road the woman directed,
but to no purpofe. At laft night approaching, they
went home. Don Lopez was inconfolable, and the dif-
fembling Fernando, who inwardly triumphed at the
good fuccefs of his curfed plot, ftaid with him all night.
Next morning he took leave, pretending he would
make it his endeavour to find Terefa, and bring the
villains to juftice: but alas! he burned to poffefs **her,**
and flew with the utmoft fpeed to the place, where he
knew fhe was. And now I muft inform my reader,
that the villains did not carry her directly to the houfe
by the wood; but rid twenty miles farther through un-
frequented places, having put her, bound hand and
foot, into a horfe-litter, which they had placed juft beyond the houfe. Here they ftopped till it was dark;
then lighting torches they had brought in the litter,
they returned by the fame ways to the houfe, and left
her in the horrid room where the old hags attended to
watch her. Here they laid her bound upon the bed,
ungagged her, and ftrove to pacify her, but in vain:
fhe wept, and lamented her misfortune in terms fo moving, it would have melted the hearts of Barbarians: but
thefe vile, relentlefs women derided her, afking, what
fhe feared from a man who paffionately loved her? Thus
poor Terefa paffed the remainder of the fleeplefs night
and morning, taking no fuftenance; but refufing to eat
or drink, they feared to unbind her. About noon the
bafe Fernando arrived fo difguifed, it was almoft impoffible to know him; he put a vizard upon his face before he entered the chamber, then fhutting the door,
he came to the bed-fide, and ufed all his rhetorick to
perfuade her to yield fairly to him. Then he proceeded to threats; yet fhe remained inflexible, ufed prayers
and tears to diffuade him from fo horrid a crime:

L 3   Heaven

Heaven (said she) will find you out, and pour its vengeance on your head; my lord will discover you, or
some thunder-bolt dispatch you, and bring your soul
to the dreadful tribunal, where your sentence will be
given. He seemed deaf to all she said, rudely kissing
and embracing her. At last summoning all her reason,
she changed her behaviour: Well then (said she), since
love makes you deaf to all entreaties to dissuade you
from this dreadful deed, unbind me, give me something to drink, and let me find some humanity in the
treatment you give me; if I must be yours, shew that
you love me. Fernando transported at her seeming so consenting, readily called for wine, unbound
her hands and feet. Having first locked the door, she
drank, and watching an opportunity, threw a glass of
wine in his eyes, then flew to the door, broke the lock,
and attempting to run down the stairs, her foot slipt,
and she fell down, and unfortunately broke her right
leg short at the instep, so that she could not rise. By
this time he had recovered himself, and hearing her
groan, ran down stairs, where he found the old hags
standing as amazed. He took her up in his arms, carried her up to the bed, and seeing the blood running
on the floor, soon discovered what had happened; she
swooned, and the shin-bone was shivered, so that it had
cut through the skin and sinews, and appeared. This
sight dashed his amorous fires, and awaked his care to
preserve her. He ran down, took his horse, and went
to a village for a surgeon; who came, and was doubtless surprised to see so fine a woman in such a dismal
place. But Fernando had told him it was his wife,
who was lunatick, and had broke loose, and endeavoured to escape, and so came by this sad accident; pretending himself to be a gentleman who belonged
to the court, and could not keep her in his own
apartment there. The surgeon dressed her, not re-
garding her complaints; and Fernando, who was
obliged to unmask, lest the surgeon should suspect
something, took care to hide his face from Teresa.

No

No fooner was the furgeon gone, but he put on his
vizard, and approaching the bed-fide, faid many kind
and tender things, to which fhe gave no anfwer: ex-
ceffive pain, and the fright, with the fatigues of the
foregoing night, having made her almoft unable to
complain.   At laft he left her, it being neceffary for
him to appear in fight, to prevent his being fufpected of
the villainy he was guilty of.   One of the old hags
watched by her that night, and in the morning, when
the honeft furgeon returned, he found her light-headed,
with a ftrong fever which had feized her, in which fhe
talked of Don Lopez, Emilia, her child, and of being
ftolen.   This made him begin to fufpect fomething.
She remaining dangeroufly ill for fome days, in which
time Fernando came often to fee her, he was much concerned, and took care to let nothing be wanting but a
phyfician, whom he durft not fend for, for fear of difcovery.   In this time great inquiry being made after
Terefa, the furgeon heard of it, and immediately took
horfe, and went to the lords, informing them of what
he knew.   Don Lopez and the marquis defired much
to know who the villain was; but that the furgeon was
ignorant of.   They took horfe immediately, attended
by five fervants well armed, and conducted by the furgeon, went to the houfe; it being midnight before they
reached it, the door was made faft, a horfe being tied
near it, and a light in the Chamber: they confulted
what to do, fearing if they knocked, it might alarm
the old hags, and the ravifher, who might by fome
back-door or window efcape; fo they concluded to wait
till he came down to take horfe.   They did fo, and towards day-break one of the old hags opened the door.
The lords, who were difmounted, and ftood ready,
rufhed in, and running up ftairs, found Fernando in the
room mafked.   Don Lopez ftaid not a moment to deli-
berate, but fhot him through the head: he fell dead at
his feet, not uttering one word.

I 4

Thus

Thus he perished in a moment, unprepared for death, and got a just reward for his villainy. Teresa, who was almost dying, and delirous, looked up, and knew her lord; she strove to rise to reach him, but fell back: he laid his cheek to hers, and strove to stifle his tumultuous joy, and hush her to repose. The hags were seized, and some of the servants dispatched for a horse-litter, in which Teresa was carried home to her lord's, and the vile women sent to prison. Fernando's body being known, was sent home: and though Don Lopez had received so great an injury, yet he feared a trial, or private injury, from Fernando's family, revenge being very natural to the Spaniards; he therefore absconded, resolving to retire to France with the marquis de Venta-dore. And now able physicians being sent for, in some days Teresa got rid of her fever, and began to recover: at last she got up again, but went lame, and never expects to do otherwise whilst she lives: she rewarded the honest surgeon nobly.

Don Lopez got safe to France first, and the marquis, with the ladies, children, and servants, followed; Don Lopez's father having taken care to make a noble provision for his son to live in France. They travelled gently, and arrived safely at Poictou, where they are all happily seated together.

And now it is fit that we make some reflections for our own improvement, on the wonderful Providence of God, in the preservation and signal deliverances of these excellent persons in this narrative.

A great number of Christian slaves are at this time expected to return to Europe, redeemed from the hands of those cruel infidels, amongst whom our noble slaves suffered so much, and lived so long; and no doubt but amongst these, if we enquire, we shall find some whose misfortunes, if not their virtues, equal these lords and ladies. It is in adversity that men are known: he is only worthy the name of a Christian who can despise death, and support even slavery and chains with patience;

whom

whom neither tortures nor intereſt can ſhake, or make renounce his God and faith. How frequent is it for us, who boaſt ſo much of religion, to ſacrifice our conſciences to intereſt ? How impatient are men for ſmall injuries or diſappointments ?

.But now, to ſum up all my reflections in a few words, let us ſeriouſly conſider, that religion is no jeſt, death and a future ſtate certain; let us ſtrive to improve the noble ſentiments ſuch hiſtories as theſe will inſpire in us; avoid the looſe writings which debauch the mind ; and ſince our heroes and heroines have done nothing here but what is poſſible, let us ſtrive to act like them ; make virtue the rule of all our actions, and eternal happineſs our only aim.

THE

HISTORY

OF THE

COUNT DE BELFLOR

AND

LEONORA DE CESPEDES.

CHARACTER OF THE

COUNT DE BELFLOR

AND

LEONORA DE CESPEDES.

BY THE EDITOR.

THIS fhort, but entertaining Novel, was written originally in French *. There was fomething fo pleafing and natural in the incidents of it, that Monfieur de Beaumarchais has founded a comedy upon the ftory, called Eugenie ; in which he has deviated very little from the copy, except in fhifting the fcene from Madrid to London.

Mr. Garrick was fo kind as to recommend the fame fubject to me, to be accommodated to the Englifh theatre: upon which hint I wrote *The School for Rakes*; in which I introduced fome new characters, namely, Frampton, Loyd and Willis; befides the additions made to thofe of Mrs. Winifred, and Lord Euftace. This piece was performed at Drury Lane in the year fixty-nine, and very favourably received by the Public. But I muft here take this fecond occafion of moft gratefully acknowledging, that both the merit of the compofition, and the fuccefs of its reprefentation, were principally owing to the friendly affiftance and patronage of Mr. Garrick.

* The Author unknown.

THE
HISTORY
OF THE
COUNT DE BELFLOR
AND
LEONORA DE CESPEDES.

THE Count de Belflor was one of the principal noblemen in the court of Spain; he fell desperately in love with Leonora de Cespedes, a young lady of extraordinary beauty, but had no intention of marrying her; the daughter of a common gentleman not seeming a proportionable match; and therefore he designed only to make her his mistress. In this view he followed her continually, and omitted no opportunity of expressing his love by his looks and actions; but to speak or write to her was impossible, because she was perpetually guarded by a vigilant, austere duenna, called the lady Marcella. He was at his wits end; and finding his desires enraged by the difficulties which opposed them, was always contriving means to deceive the

she-

she-Argus who watched his Io. Leonora, **on the other hand**, observing the inclination the count had for her, was not able to avoid having some regard for him; and this infensibly improved itself in her unwary breast, into a passion which became at length extreme.

Things **were** in this situation, **when Leonora and her** unsleeping governante going out one morning **to church**, met an old woman in the street with the largest rope **of beads on her hand that** hypocrisy ever wore. She came up **to** them with a very smooth and smiling air, and address-ing herself to the duenna, God save! cries she, holy peace be with you! Suffer me **to ask**, if you are not the lady Marcella, the chaste **widow of** the late Signior Martin Rosette. The governante answering, Yes;—I have met you then, said the old devotee, very luckily, for my business was to let you know, I have a relation at my lodging who wants mightily to speak with **you.** He arrived a few days ago from Flanders; he knew your husband, Madam, particularly well, and **has matters to acquaint you with** of the highest im-portance. He would have waited on you at your house, but the poor man was **taken ill**, and lyes now at the point of death. I live **not above two** yards off; will you be so kind as to follow me?

The governante, who had sense and prudence enough, being afraid of taking a wrong step, was at a loss what to resolve: when the beads-bearer, imagining the reason of her embarrassment, immediately added, My lady Marcella, you may trust me with all the safety in the world, my name is la Chichona; the licen-ciate Marcos de Figueros, and the bachelor Mira de Mesqua will answer for me, as soon as for their own grand-mothers. Though I invite you to my house, it is only for your good; my cousin is willing to restore you a sum of money he borrowed formerly of your hus-band. At the sound of the word restitution madam Marcella yielded; Come child, said she to Leonora, let us go and see this good woman's kinsman; it is an action of charity to visit the sick.

They were at la Chichona's lodging in a minute; she led them into a ground-room, where they found a man in bed, with a venerable white beard, and who, if he was not ill, seemed at least to be so. Cousin, said the grandam, presenting the governante to him, here is the worthy lady Marcella whom you were wishing to speak with, the widow of your bosom friend, Signior Rosette. The antient gentleman, raising up his head a little at these words, saluted the duenna, and having made signs for her to draw near; when she was by the bed-side, I thank Heaven! said he, with a feeble voice, My dear madam Marcella, for sparing my life till now; it was the only thing I desired; I was afraid I should have died without the satisfaction of seeing you, and putting into your own hand the two hundred ducats your late husband, my intimate friend, lent me, to bring me off in a certain point of honour I was embroiled in some time since at Bruges. Pray, did you never hear him speak of this adventure?---Alas, Sir! answered Marcella, he never uttered a syllable about it to me. Heaven rest his soul! he was so generous that he forgot the services he did his friends; and was so far from resembling those vain-glorious pretenders, who boast of the good they never did, that he never let me know he had obliged any one.----He had certainly a noble soul, replied the aged gentleman, and I have more cause to think so than any man: to convince you of it, I must relate to you the affair, from which I was so happily rescued by his assistance. But as I have several things to say, which are of the utmost consequence to the memory of the deceased, I should be glad to mention them only to this discreet lady his widow.

Why then, said la Chichona, you may tell the story to her in private; and in the mean time this young lady and myself will step into my closet. Thus saying, she left the duenna with the sick person, and carried Leonora into another chamber, where, without any preamble, she thus began; Lovely Leonora, the moments are too precious to be trifled with ; you know the Count de Belflor by fight ; he has loved you long, and almost died with impatience to tell you fo ; but the vigilance and strictness of your governante would never allow him fo great a pleasure. In this despair he had recourse to my industry, and I have exerted it in his behalf. The old man you saw is a young valet of the Count's, and the whole affair is a fiction we have invented, to deceive your governante, and draw you hither.

As she ended these words, the Count, who was concealed behind the tapestry, appeared, and ran to throw himself at Leonora's feet: Madam, said he, forgive the stratagem of a lover, who could live no longer without speaking to you. If this kind-natured gentlewoman had not found a way to procure me this opportunity, I should have abandoned myself to despair. These words, pronounced with a moving air by a man who was not displeasing, affected Leonora ; she stood in doubt a while, what answer she ought to make ; but recovering at last from her perplexity, and looking angrily on the count, Perhaps you think yourself, said she, wonderfully obliged to this officious lady, who has served you fo well; but know, you shall receive very little advantage from the service she has done you. Thus saying, she advanced several paces to go back into the other room. The Count stopped her ; Stay, said he, adorable Leonora ! vouchsafe to hear me a moment: my passion is fo pure, that it ought not to alarm you. You have reason, I confess, to disapprove the artifice I have used to obtain the happiness of speaking to you : but have I not, till this very day, attempted it in vain ? For six months have I followed you to the churches, to the walks, and to the plays ; and have ineffectually fought a lucky hour to tell you, that you have charmed me. Your cruel, your unrelenting governante has always had the cunning to defeat my desires. Alas! instead

ſtead of making the ſtratagem I have been forced to employ, a crime in me, pity me, beautiful Leonora! for
having ſuffered ſo tedious an expectation, and judge by
your charms of the pains I have endured.

Belſlor was not wanting to animate his ſpeech
with all the arts of perſuaſion, which graceful men underſtand to practiſe ſo ſuccefsfully: he let fall ſome tears.
Leonera was moved with them; and began, in ſpite of
herſelf, to admit into her breaſt impreſſions of tendernefs
and pity; but far from giving way to them, the more
ſhe felt herſelf affected, the more earneſt ſhe was to leave
the room. Count, ſaid ſhe, you ſpend your breath in
vain; I will not hear you; do not hold me; let me be-
gone out of a houſe where my virtue is in danger; or
by my outcry I will bring in the whole neighbourhood,
and make your audaciouſnefs publick. She ſpoke this
with ſo high a tone, that la Chichona, who had reaſons
enough to avoid coming in the magiſtrates way, begged
the count to puſh the matter no farther. At which he
ceaſed to oppoſe Leonora's will; ſhe diſengaged herſelf
from his hands, and immediately retired.

She made directly to her governante, Come, Madam, ſaid ſhe, break off this impertinent converſation:
we are impoſed on; let us leave this dangerous houſe.---
What is the matter, child, anſwered Marcella, with
aſtoniſhment, what makes you want to be gone in ſuch a
hurry?---You ſhall know, replied Leonora: but firſt let
us fly; for every moment I ſtay here gives me freſh pain.
As eager as the duenna was to know the occaſion of this
haſty parting, ſhe could not be informed upon the ſpot.
She was obliged to yield to Leonora's inſtances; and
accordingly they flew out of doors, in an inſtant, leaving
la Chichona, the count and his valet, in the greateſt con-
fuſion.

When Leonora ſaw herſelf in the ſtreet, ſhe began to
give her governante an account of what had paſſed in la
Chichona's cloſet. Madam Marcella heard her very at-
tentively; and when they came home, I muſt confeſs,
child.

child, said she, what you have told me mortifies me extremely. How, in the name of wonder, could I be so
over-reached by that doating old woman? I made a difficulty to follow her at first. I wish I had persisted in
it. I ought to have distrusted the fair face she set upon
the matter. I have committed a folly not to be forgiven
one of my experience. Why did you not let me know
the cheat while we were in the house? I would have
belaboured the faces of them; I would have given Count
Belflor his own in both ears, and pulled off the beard of
the counterfeit old man in a trice. But I will step back
this moment, and return the money I received there as
the restitution of a real debt, and if I find them together,
they shall lose nothing by waiting. At this away she
rushed full speed to la Chichona's lodgings.

The Count was still there: he was distracted at the
ill success of his stratagem; and another, in his place,
would have abandoned the design; but he was not at
all disheartened. With a thousand good qualities he
had this ill one, that he resigned himself too much to
the strong disposition he had to love; and when he liked
a woman, pursued her favours too impetuously; and
though he was naturally an honest man, he was capable
at such a time of violating the most sacred rights, to accomplish his desires. Reflecting therefore, that it was
impossible for him to carry the point he proposed without madam Marcella's assistance, he resolved to spare
no cost to bring her into his interest. This duenna, as
severe as she seemed to be, would not be proof, he
thought, to a considerable present; and he was not mistaken in his opinion; and if there are governantes who
are faithful, it is because the gallants want either generosity or riches.

As soon as madam Marcella entered the door, and perceived the three persons there she wished for, she burst
into scolding like a fury; she called the count a million
of scandalous names, and sent the restitution-ducats in
a volley at the valet-de-chambre's head. The count
                                                    sustained

sustained the tempest with unparalleled patience, and
falling on his knees before the duenna, to make the
scene more affecting, pressed her to take the purse
again, and offered her a thousand pistoles, besides, con-
juring her to pity him. As her compassion had never
been sollicited so powerfully before, she was not inex-
orable. She presently hushed all her invectives, and
comparing in her thoughts the sum now tendered her
with the slender recompence she expected from Don
Lewis, Leonora's father, she saw she should get more
by mis-leading Leonora from her duty than by retaining
her in it. Accordingly, after some slight contention,
she took the purse again, accepted the offer of the pistoles, and promised to serve the count in his amour;
and accordingly set about the execution of her promise
without delay.

As Leonora, she knew, was of virtous principles, she
was very cautious not to give her any suspicion of her
intelligence with the count, lest she should acquaint her
father; and projecting to ruin her in an artful manner,
she thus began with her on her return: I have satisfied
my indignation, Leonora; I caught the three deceivers
on the spot, who were all amazed at your couragious
retreat. I have threatened la Chichona with your father's resentment, and the rigour of the law, and heaped upon Count Belflor all the ill names my passion
could suggest. I hope his lordship will make no such
attempt again, and that his galantries will cease here-
after to exercise my vigilance. I thank Heaven that by
your resolution you have escaped the snare which was
laid for you! I weep for joy, and am in a transport
that he has reaped no advantage by his artifice; for
these great lords make a diversion of seducing young
women. The generality, even of those who value
themselves upon their honesty, make no scruple of it:
as if there was no evil in blemishing a family. I do
not say absolutely that the count is one of this character, nor that he means to delude you; we must not al-

ways

ways judge ill of our neighbour: perhaps his defigns towards you are lawful; for though by his rank he may pretend to the firft alliances in the court, your beauty may have
made him refolve to marry you. I remember alfo that
in the anfwers he made to my reproaches, he intimated
fomething of it to me.---What do ye fay, good governante? interrupted Leonora; if he had fuch a defign,
he would have afked me of my father before now, who
would not have refufed me to a perfon of his rank.

What you fay, replied the governefs, is very juft, and
I am of the fame opinion; this irregular ftep of the
count looks fufpicioufly, and perhaps his intentions
may not be good. I could like to run back once more,
and gave him another lecture.---No, Madam, faid Leonora, it is better to forget what is paft, and revenge
ourfelves by flighting it.---Very true, anfwered madam
Marcella, I believe that is the beft way; you have
more difcretion than I. But, on the other hand, don't
we mif-judge the count's fentiments? How do we
know he did not contrive this in order to declare his
paffion in a more delicate manner? Perhaps he is willing, before he obtains your father's confent, to pay
you long fervices, in order to deferve your favour,
aud affure himfelf of your heart, that your union may
be the more fixed and charming. If it were fo, daughter, would it be a mighty crime to hearken to him?
Open your mind to me; you know my tendernefs for
you; tell me, plainly, do you perceive an inclination
in yourfelf to the count, or have you an averfion to marry
him?

At this artful queftion, the too fincere Leonora caft
down her eyes, and blufhing owned, fhe had no diflike
to him; but as her modefty would not fuffer her to declare herfelf more fully, the duenna preffed her again
to conceal nothing; and the governante's affectionate
declarations vanquifhing her; Since you will have me
fpeak freely, Madam, faid fhe, know I efteem count
Belflor deferving to be loved. He looks fo handfome,
and

and I have heard him spoken of so advantageously, that
I could not help being moved by his gallantries. The
indefatigable application you have used to disappoint
them, has often made me very uneasy, and I confess I
have lamented it sometimes, and by my sighs recom-
penced the trouble your vigilance has made him suffer.
I will acknowledge also, that instead of hating him for
this rash action, my heart, in spite of me, excuses him,
and charges the fault upon your severity.----Child, said
the governante, since you give me ground to believe his
addresses will be agreeable to you, I would have **you**
manage this lover.----The service you offer to do me,
replied Leonora, wins my heart. Though the count
were not of the first rank in the court, though he were
only a private gentleman, I should prefer him to all other
men; but let us not flatter ourselves; Belflor is a great
lord, and is undoubtedly destined for one of the richest
heiresses of the kingdom. Never let us fancy he will
stoop to the daughter of Don Lewis, who has only a
moderate fortune to offer him. No, no, added she,
he has no such favourable sentiments for me. He does
not look on me as one who deserves to bear his name;
he only designs to delude me.

What! cried the Duenna, do you think he does not
love you enough to marry you? Love works the greatest
miracles every day. It seems, according to your opinion, there is an infinite distance between the count and
you. Do yourself justice, my good child! it will be
no abasement to him to marry you: you are of an
ancient family of quality, and he need not be ashamed
of you ralliance. Since you have an inclination towards
him, continued she, I must talk with him: I will know
the bottom of his designs; and if they are such as they
ought to be, I will flatter him with some degree of
hope.----By no means, cried Leonora; I am against your
going to him; for if he should suspect my having any
part in such a step, he would value me no longer.----O,
I have more discretion than you imagine, replied the

lady

lady Marcella ; I shall begin with reproaching him for
having a design to deceive you ; upon which he will not
fail to be eager to justify himself; I will mind what he
says, and shall discover what he means. In short, child,
leave it to me, I will be as careful of your honour, as
of my own.

The duenna then put on her cloak, and went out at
the beginning of the evening. She found Belfor lingering about Don Lewis's house, and gave him an account of the conversation she had had with her mistress,
and did not forget to boast how artfully she had discovered that she loved him. Nothing could be more
grateful to the count than this discovery ; he thanked
the good lady Marcella for it in the strongest terms ;
that is, he promised to pay her the thousand pistoles the
next day, and presumed upon the good success of his
enterprise, because he knew a young woman, whose
affections are engaged, is half conquered. They parted
then, wonderfully satisfied on each side, and the reve-
rend duenna returned to her lodging.

Leonora, who waited for her with much uneasiness,
asked her what news she brought ?---The best in the
world, answered the governante. I have seen the count.
I tell you, child, his intention is not criminal ; he has
no other aim than to marry you. He has sworn so to me
by every thing that is most sacred among men. I was
not wheedled away by this, as you may think I was. If
this is your purpose, said I to him, why do you not make
the usual advances to Don Lewis ? Ah ! my dear Marcella, answered he, without seeming embarrassed at the
question, would you have approved it, that before I
knew what Leonora thought of me, and following the
transports of a blind passion, I should have tyrannically
obtained her of her father ? No ; her repose is dearer
to me than my own, and I am too much a man of
honour to think of rendering her unhappy, by an im-
plicit obedience.

While

While he was talking after this manner, continued
the duenna, I obferved him with the ftricteft attention,
and exerted all my experience to difcover by his eyes,
whether he was really fo heartily in love as he reprefented.
He feemed to me to be feized with a fincere paffion ;
which made me fo glad, that I had much to do to hide
it from him. However, when I was convinced of his
fincerity, in order to fecure you fo important a lover, I
judged it proper to let him underftand your fentiments.
My lord, faid I, Leonora has no averfion to you. I
know fhe efteems you, and as far as I can judge, her
heart will not fly from your purfuit.----What do I hear?
cried he, in a tranfport of joy ! Is it poffible the charming Leonora fhould be difpofed in my favour ? How infinitely am I obliged to you, good Marcella, for having
refcued me from fuch a tedious uncertainty ; I am the
more tranfported with the news, as it comes from you ;
you, who were always fo prejudiced againft me, and
have made me fuffer fo much : But compleat my happinefs, my dear Marcella ; introduce me to fpeak with
the divine Leonora : I will plight my faith to her,
and fwear before you to marry no other, To all this,
purfued the governante, he added other things even
more moving. In fhort, my daughter, he begged me in
fo preffing a manner to promife him a private interview
with you, that I could not refufe him.----Ah ! why did
you make him fuch a promife ? cried Leonora, with
emotion. A difcreet young woman, you have told me
a thoufand times, ought abfolutely to avoid thofe con-
verfations, which are always dangerous.----I agree, faid
the duenna, that I have told you fo, and it is a very
good maxim : but you may difpenfe with it upon this
occafion, fince you may look upon the count as your
hufband.----He is not fo yet, replied Leonora, and I
ought not to fee him till my father has allowed of his
application.

The lady Marcella at this repented fhe had brought
up the girl fo well, fince there was fo much difficulty to

overcome her modesty. However, resolving to carry her point, whatever it cost her, My dear Leonora, said she, I am rejoiced to see you so reserved. Happy effect of my honest care! you have profited by the lessons I have given you. I am charmed with my labour! but you go beyond what I taught you, and carry my instruction too far. Your virtue, I find, is too rigid. As much as I am for encouraging severity, I cannot approve of that rigid discretion which is prejudiced against overtures without distinction. A young woman does not cease to be virtuous by giving a lover a hearing, when she knows the chasteness of his desires; and it is not more criminal to answer his passion, than to be sensible of it. Rely upon me, Leonora; I have too much experience, and am too much in your interest, to put you upon any thing which may injure you.

Alas! where would you have me see the count? said Leonora.—In your own apartment, answered the duenna; that is the safest place. I will introduce him thither to-morrow in the evening.—You cannot have such a thought, replied Leonora; shall I suffer a man---Yes, you shall suffer him, interrupted the governante; it is no such extraordinary thing as you imagine. It is done every day, and would to Heaven all the ladies who receive such sort of visits had such good intentions as yours. Besides, what should you fear? Shall not I be with you?--- If my father should surprise us? replied Leonora.---Make yourself easy as to that, answered the lady Marcella; your father is very well satisfied with your conduct: he knows my fidelity; and has an entire confidence in me. Leonora being so strongly urged by the duenna, and secretly incited by her love, could resist no longer, but consented to what was proposed.

The count was soon informed of it; and was so overjoyed, that he gave his agent five hundred pistoles upon the spot, with a ring of the same value. The lady Marcella seeing he kept his promise so well, scorned to be less punctual in keeping hers. Accordingly, the

next

next night, when she thought the house was all settled, she fastened a ladder of silk, which the count had given her, to the balcony, and thereby introduced him into her mistress's apartment.

The young lady in the mean time was full of alarming reflections. As much inclined as she was to the count, and in spite of all her governante could say to her, she reproached herself for having had the weakness to admit a visit which would blemish her duty ; to receive into her chamber by night a man who had not her father's approbation, and of whose real sentiments she herself was ignorant, seemed an action not only criminal, but what even her lover must condemn. This last thought gave her most pain, and she was taken up with it, when the count came in.

He immediately threw himself at her feet, to thank her for the favour she had done him. He seemed to be wholly possessed with love and gratitude, and assured her it was his design to marry her ; yet as he did not enlarge upon that so much as she could have wished ; Count, said she, I am very willing to believe you have no other intention than what you mention ; but whatever assurances you are able to give me of it, I shall always suspect them, till they are authorized by my father's consent.---Madam, answered Belflor, I should have asked it long ago, if I had not been afraid of obtaining it at the expence of your repose.----I do not blame you for not having done it as yet, replied Leonora ; nay, I approve your nicety ; but nothing restrains you now, and you must either speak to Don Lewis, or resolve to see me no more.

And why should I not see you, beautiful Leonora ! said he ; I wish you were more sensible of the sweets of love. If you understood how to love as well as I, you would find a pleasure in receiving my addresses in private, and in concealing them, at least for a time, from your father's knowledge. How charming is such a secret intelligence to two hearts closely united !---It may be such to

you,

you, said Leonora, but it would only give me trouble.
This extravagance of affection does not suit with a
young woman who is virtuous. Extol no more to me
the pleasure of such a blameable commerce. If you
have any esteem for me, you will not propose it ; and
if your intentions are such as you would persuade me
they are, you ought in your heart to censure me for not
being offended at it. But, alas! added she, letting fall
some tears, I must impute this affront only to my own
weakness; I have deserved it, by condescending thus
far.

Adorable Leonora! cried the count, you do me the
highest injury. Your virtue is too scrupulous, and takes
a false alarm. What, because I have been happy
enough to prevail on you to be favourable to my love,
are you afraid I should cease to honour you ? How unjust is this! No, madam, I know the inestimable value
of your kindness. It can never lessen my esteem for
you; I am ready to do what you require of me. I will
speak to Don Lewis to-morrow. I will use all my
power to get him to consent to my happiness; but I will
not conceal from you, that I see little appearance of it.
---What do you say? replied Leonora; can my father refuse the application of a man of your rank at court ?---It
is my rank, returned Belflor, which makes me fear his
refusal. You are surprised at my words; but you will
soon forbear to wonder. Some days ago the king declared he would dispose of me in marriage ; he has not
named the lady he designs for me ; he has only given
me to understand she is one of the first quality; and that
he **has** this match very much at heart. As I was ignorant what your sentiments might be towards me, for
your severity, you know, has not suffered me to discover
them, I did not express any repugnance to his will.
After this, judge, madam, whether Don Lewis will be
willing to run the risk of drawing the king's resentment against him, by accepting me for his son-in-law.

No,

No, undoubtedly, faid Leonora; I know my father, how advantageous foever your alliance may be
to him, will fooner renounce it, than expofe himfelf to
the king's difpleafure.   But though my father fhould
not oppofe our union, we fhould not be the better for it;
for how can you give a hand, which the king intends to
difpofe of elfewhere?---Madam, anfwered Belflor, I will
freely own to you, that this circumftance embarraffes
me extremely.   However, I hope, by obferving a very
nice conduct with the king, I fhall manage fo well the
friendfhip he has for me, that I fhall find a way to avoid
the misfortune which threatens me.   You will be able to
affift me in it, beautiful Leonora, if you think me
worthy of your alliance.---In what manner, faid fhe,
can I contribute to break off the marriage the king has
propofed to you?---Ah! madam, replied he with a paffionate air, if you will receive my vows, I can eafily
referve myfelf for you, without offending my prince.
Permit me, lovely Leonora, added he, cafting himfelf
at her feet, permit me to marry you in the prefence of
the lady Marcella, who will be a refponfible witnefs for
the facrednefs of our engagement.   I fhall thereby deliver myfelf without trouble from the cruel bands which
are preparing for me: for, after this, when the king
preffes me to take the lady he defigns, I will throw myfelf at his feet, and tell him I loved you long fince, and
have efpoufed you privately.   As defirous as he may be
to marry me to the other, he is too gracious to tear me
from her I love, and too juft to put fuch an affront upon
your family.   What do you think, prudent Marcella,
continued he, turning toward the governante, what do
you think of this invention with which love infpires me?
---I am charmed with it, faid the lady Marcella; it muft
be owned love is very ingenious.---And you, fair Leonora?
faid the count, what do you fay to it? Will your mind,
prejudiced with diftruft, refufe to approve it?---No, anfwered Leonora, provided you will bring my father
hither;

hither; I do not doubt but he will subscribe to what you mention.

We must by no means acquaint him with it, interrupted the duenna; you do not know Don Lewis; he is too delicate in points of honour to agree to it. The proposal of a secret marrriage will offend him. Beside, his prudence will not fail to make him fear the consequences of an union which will seem to clash with the king's designs. By this indiscreet proceeding you will give him a suspicion; his eyes will be always watching our actions, and he will deprive you of the means of seeing one another.----Ah! I should die with grief at that, cried the count. But, madam Marcella, pursued he, affecting a troubled air, do you really think Don Lewis would reject the proposal of a concealed marriage?---Never doubt it, answered the governante; though I should be glad if he would like it: But regular and scrupulous as he is, he will never agree that the ceremonies of the church should be omitted; and if they are performed at your marriage, it will soon be divulged.

Ah! my dear Leonora, said the count then, tenderly pressing her hand, must we, to humour an idle notion of delicacy, expose ourselves to the dreadful danger of being separated for ever? You need no one besides yourself to give yourself to me. Your father's consent, perhaps, may make you less uneasy; but since the lady Marcella has shewn us the impossibility of obtaining it, yield to my innocent desires; receive my heart and my hand; and when it shall be a fit time to inform Don Lewis of our contract, we will acquaint him with the reasons we had to hide it from him.----Well, count, said Leonora, I consent to your not speaking of it to my father so soon; but sound the king's mind, and before I receive your hand in private, talk with him, and tell him, if there should be occasion, that you have espoused me secretly. Try by this false declaration------O, no, madam, replied Belflor, I am too great an enemy to

lying,

lying, to dare to undertake such a fiction; I cannot de-
base myself so far. Beside, I know the king, if he
should happen to find out that I had deceived him, would
not forgive me while he lived.

It would be endless to repeat all that Belflor said to
seduce this innocent lady. But though he swore he
would as soon as possible publicly confirm the faith he
gave her in private, and called Heaven to witness to his
oaths, he could not triumph over Leonora's prudence;
and the day beginning to appear, obliged him, re-
luctantly, to withdraw.

The next day, the governante believing it concerned
her honour, or rather her interest, not to abandon her
enterprise; Leonora, cried she, I am at a loss what to say
to you. I see you are set against the count's passion, as if
it were intended only for galantry. Have you observed
any thing in his person that offends you?---No, madam,
answered Leonora; on the contrary, he never seemed
more amiable; and his conversation has made me discover new charms in him.---If it is so, replied the governante, I do not comprehend you. You are prejudiced in his favour; yet refuse to agree to a thing,
the necessity of which has been shewn you.---Mother,
returned the daughter of Don Lewis, you have more
prudence and more experience than I: but have you
well considered the consequences of a marriage contracted without my father's leave?---Yes, yes, said
the duenna, I have made all the reflections necessary
upon it; and am sorry to see you so obstinately
oppose the shining advancement Fortune offers you.
Take care your stubbornness does not weary out your lover.
Be afraid lest he should turn his eyes upon the promotion
of his fortune, which the violence of his passion now
makes him neglect. Since he is willing to give you his
faith, accept it without hesitating. His word binds
him; nothing is more sacred to a man of honour. Besides, I am witness that he owns you for his wife. Do
not you know that such an evidence as mine is sufficient

to

to cast a lover at law, who should presume to perjure himself?

It was by such discourses as these that the perfidious Marcella staggered Leonora, who in a few days after resigned herself very innocently to the evil intentions of the count; whom the duenna introduced every night into her mistress's chamber by the balcony, and let him out before day.

One night, when she had summoned him away something later than ordinary, and the morning already began to peep, he started up in haste to get down into the street, but had the misfortune to take his measures so wrong, that he fell to the ground. Don Lewis de Cespedes, who lay in the chamber over his daughter's, and was up early that morning about some very urgent affairs, heard the noise of the fall; he opened his window to see what it was, and perceived a man endeavouring to rise with much difficulty, and the lady Marcella in his daughter's balcony, who was pulling up the silk-ladder, which the count had not made such good use of in descending as in mounting. He rubbed his eyes, and took this spectacle at first for an illusion; but having thoroughly considered it, he concluded it was real, and that the day-light, as weak as it was, discovered his dishonour too clearly. Being alarmed at this fatal sight, and transported by a just fury, he went to Leonora's room, with his sword in his hand, in order to sacrifice her and the governante to his resentment. He knocked at the chamber door, and ordered them to open it: They knew his voice, and obeyed him trembling. He entered with a furious air, and shewing his naked sword to their astonished eyes; I come, said he, to wash out with the blood of an infamous child, the affront she has done to her father, and to punish, at the same time, the faithless governante who has betrayed my trust.

They both threw themselves on their knees before him; and the duenna beginning, Sir, said she, before we re-

ceive the chastisement you prepare for us, vouchsafe t^o
hear me a moment.----Well, base wretch, replied the old
man, I consent to suspend my vengeance for an instant.
Speak, let me know all the circumstances of my misfortune ; but why do I say all the circumstances ? I am
ignorant but of one, and that is, the name of the audacious villain who dishonours my family.----Sir, answered
the lady Marcella, the count de Belsior is the gentleman concerned.----The count de Belsior! cried Don
Lewis ; where has he seen my daughter ? By what means
has he seduced her ? hide nothing from me.----Sir, returned the governante, I will relate you the story with
all the sincerity I can.

She repeated to him then very artfully all the discourses she had made Leonora believe the count had
held with her ; and painted him in the brightest colours
of a lover, tender, nice and sincere. As she could not
escape discovering the truth, she was obliged to speak
it : but enlarged on the reasons which they had to make
that private marriage without his knowledge, and gave
them so happy a turn, that she appeased the passion of
Don Lewis. She discerned it ; and in order to bring
him perfectly into temper, This sir, said she, is what
you desired to know. Punish us now, plunge your
sword in Leonora's bosom. But what do I say ? Leonora is innocent, and has only followed the counsels of
her to whom you committed her conduct. It is myself
alone upon whom the stroke ought to fall. It is I who
have introduced the count into your daughter's apartment. It is I who have made the knot which binds
them. I shut my eyes to all the irregularities of a
contract, which was not authorised by you, in order to
secure to you a son-in-law, through whose hands all the
favours of the court at present are dispensed. I had no
other view than Leonora's happiness, and the advantage your family might derive from such an alliance,
and the excess of my zeal has made me betray my duty.

While

While the crafty Marcella was pleading in this manner, her mistress wept without ceasing, and shewed so deep a sorrow, that the good old man could not resist it. He was softened, and his anger changed to compassion. He dropped his sword, and putting off the air of an incensed father, Ah! my daughter, cried he, with tears in his eyes, how fatal a passion is love! Alas, you know not all the reasons you have to afflict yourself! The shame alone which arises from the presence of a father who has surprised you, now excites your tears. You do not yet foresee all the occasions of grief, which your lover perhaps is preparing for you. And upon what a rock, imprudent Marcella, has your indiscreet zeal for my family thrown us? The alliance of such a man as the count, was enough, I confess, to dazzle you; and it is that alone which saves you in my opinion; but wretch as you are, should you not have distrusted a lover of his character? The more interest and favour he has, the more ought you to have been on your guard against him. If he should make no scruple to violate his faith to Leonora, what must I do? Shall I ask the relief of the laws? A person of his rank will easily protect himself from their rigour. I wish he may be true to his oaths, and keep his promise to my daughter; but if the king, as he told you, designs to marry him to another, it is to be feared he will oblige him to it by his authority.

As for obliging him to it, sir, interrupted Leonora, we have no cause to be alarmed at that. The count has very well assured us, the king will not offer so great a violence to his inclination.----I am persuaded of it, said Marcella; the king loves his favourite too much, to use him so tyrannically; and is too generous to bring such a mortal affliction on the brave Don Lewis de Cespedes, who has spent his best days in serving the state.----Heaven grant, replied the old man, sighing, that my fears may be vain! I will go to the count, and demand him to explain himself on this subject. A

father's

father's eyes are quick-sighted. I shall see to the bottom of his soul. If I find him in the disposition I wish, I shall forgive what is passed; but, added he in a severer tone, if in his discourse I discern a perfidious heart, you shall both away to a retirement, there to lament your imprudence the rest of your days. At these words he took up his sword, and leaving them to recover from the fright in which he had put them, he returned to his chamber.

Early in the morning Don Lewis went to the count, who not imagining that he was discovered, was surprised at his visit. He came out to meet the old gentleman, and having embraced him; Don Lewis, said he, I am overjoy'd to see you here. Is there any opportunity for me to serve you?---My lord, answered Don Lewis, give orders, if you please, that we may be alone. Belflor obeyed; and being both seated, Don Lewis thus began: My lord, said he, my honour and my repose require an explanation from you which I came to ask. I saw you this morning go out of Leonora's apartment. She has confessed the whole to me, and has told me--- She has told you that I love her, (interrupted the count, in order to turn off a discourse he was unwilling to understand,) but she has very faintly expressed to you all my sentiments towards her. I am charmed with her, she is beyond description. Wit, beauty, virtue, and all other accomplishments, are hers to perfection. I have heard you have a son also, who follows his studies at Alcala; pray, is he like his sister? If he has her beauty, and resembles you in other respects, he must be a compleat gentleman. I die with desire to see him, and offer you what interest I have to serve him.

I am greatly indebted to you for this offer, returned Don Lewis gravely; but let us come to that which--- He must be put into the service immediately, interrupted the count. I undertake his fortune, and can assure you, he shall not grow old among the croud of inferior officers.----Answer me, count, replied the old gentleman roughly,

roughly, and ceafe to divert the difcourfe. Do you
defign, or not, to keep your promife ?—Yes, undoubtedly, interrupted Belflor, a third time ; I will keep the
promife I make you to fupport your fon with all my
interest. Depend upon me ; I am a man of integrity.—
This is too much, count, cried Cefpedes rifing ; after
having feduced my daughter, you have the infolence
alfo to infult me. But I am a gentleman, and the affront
you offer me fhall not go unpunifhed. Having faid
thefe words, he went away, with a heart full of refentment, and revolving a thoufand projects of revenge
in his mind.

When he came home, fays he to Leonora and the
lady Marcella, with the highest agitation, It was not
without reafon that I fufpected the count ; he is a tray-
tor, and I will be revenged on him. As for you, to-
morrow you fhall both go into a convent. You have
nothing to do, but to prepare for it, and thank Heaven
that my anger is contented with this chaftifement. Thus
faying, he fhut himfelf up in his clofet, to confider fe-
rioufly what meafures to take in fo difficult a conjuncture.

What was Leonora's grief, when fhe heard that Belflor was falfe ! fhe ftood fome time without motion. A
deadly palenefs overfpread her countenance ; her fpirits
forfook her, and fhe fell down in the arms of her governante, who thought fhe was going to expire. The
duenna tried every way to bring her out of her fwoon ;
fhe fucceeded, and Leonora came at length to her
fenfes ; fhe opened her eyes, and feeing the governante
bufied in helping her, How barbarous are you ! faid fhe,
fetching a profound figh ; why have you brought me
back from the happy condition in which I was ? I was
not then fenfible of the horror of my deftiny. Why did
you not let me die ? You, who know the forrows which
muft difturb the quiet of my life, why have you recalled
me to a fenfe of them ?

Marcella

Marcella endeavoured to comfort her, which only made her grieve the more. All your words, cried the daughter of Don Lewis, are superfluous. I will hear nothing. Do not lose time in opposing my despair, you ought rather to promote it ; you who have plunged me in this abyss. It was you who answered for the count's sincerity ; and without you I should not have yielded to the inclination I had for him. I should have vanquished it by degrees ; at least he would have received no advantage from it. But I will not, pursued she, impute my misfortune to you ; I charge it on myself. I should not have followed your counsels, in accepting the vow of a man without my father's knowledge. As flattering as the courtship of the count de Belflor might be to me, I should have despised it, rather than encouraged it at the expence of my reputation. In short, I ought to have distrusted him, and you, and myself, after having been so weak as to resign myself to his perfidious oaths ; after the affliction I have caused to the unhappy Don Lewis, and the dishonour I have done my family, I abhor myself ; and, far from fearing the retreat with which I am threatened, I could willingly hide my head in the most hideous obscurity. As she spoke thus, she was not contented to weep plentifully, but rent her garments, and tore her beautiful hair for the injustice of her lover.

The duenna, in order to conform herself to her mistress's sorrow, did not spare her grimaces. She dropped some tears which she had at command, and made a thousand imprecations against men in general, and against Belflor in particular. Is it possible, cried she, that the count, who appeared to me so full of truth and probity, should be wicked enough to deceive us both ? I cannot recover from my surprise, or rather I cannot persuade myself of it.

Indeed, said Leonora, when I represent him to myself at my feet, who would not have trusted his tender air, and his oaths to which he so boldly called Heaven

to witnefs, and the tranfports he conftantly expreffed ?
His eyes alfo fhewed even more love than his tongue
uttered : in fhort, he feemed to be enchanted with the
fight of me. No, he did not deceive me : I cannot
think fo. My father, perhaps, has not talked to him
with fufficient difcretion : they were both angry, and
the count has anfwered him more like a haughty noble,
than a fond lover. Yet perhaps I flatter myfelf : I muft
get out of this uncertainty. I will write to Belflor, and
acquaint him, that I expect him to-night ; I muft have
him come to fatisfy my heart, or confirm his treachery
himfelf. The lady Marcella applauded the defign, and
had even fome hope that the count, as ambitious as
he was, would be touched with the tears which Leonora
would fhed at the interview, and refolve to marry her.

In the mean time Belflor having rid himfelf of honeft
Don Lewis, began to reflect on the confequences which
might arife from the reception he gave him. He rightly
judged that the family of the Cefpedes, being provoked
at the injury, would meditate revenge. But this troubled him very little. The intereft of his love affected
him much more : Leonora he thought would be fent to
a monaftery, or at leaft that fhe would be kept up ; and
that in all appearance he fhould fee her no more. This
apprehenfion afflicted him : and he was ftudying fome
means to prevent this misfortune, when his fervant
brought him a letter, which the lady Marcella had juft
put into his hands. It was from Leonora, and thefe
were the contents :

" TO-MORROW I muft leave the world, and bury
" myfelf in a retreat. To fee myfelf difhonoured, and
" become a difgrace to my family and myfelf, is the
" deplorable condition to which I am reduced by hav-
" ing liftened to you. I expect you to-night. In my
" defpair I feek for new torments. Come, and own to
" me that your heart had no part in the oaths your
" tongue pronounced ; or juftify them by a behaviour
" which

" which alone can foften the rigour of my deftiny. As
" there may be fome danger in this meeting, after
" what has paffed between you and my father, bring
" fome friend with you. Though you make all the
" unhappinefs of my life, I feel myfelf yet concerned
" for yours."

The count read the letter two or three times, and
reprefenting to himfelf Leonora in the fituation fhe
defcribed, he was moved. He turned his thoughts in-
ward; reafon, probity and honour, all the laws which
his paffion had made him violate, began to refume their
empire over him. He became enfible of his bafenefs
at once; and as a man coming out of a violent fit of a
fever blufhes at the extravagant words and actions
which efcaped him, he was afhamed of all the mean
artifices he had employed to accomplifh his defires.
Wretch, faid he, what have I done? What dæmon has
poffeffed me? I have promifed Leonora marriage; and
have taken Heaven to witnefs. I have feigned that the
king had propofed a match to me. Lying, perfidiouf-
nefs, and facrilege, all I have made ufe of to corrupt
the innocent. What a madnefs was it! Would it not
have been better to have exerted my endeavours to fubdue my love, than to have fatisfied it by fuch criminal
ways? In the mean while here is a virgin of rank feduc'd;
I abandon her to the rage of her relations, whom I dif-
honour with her; and I make her miferable for having
rendered me happy. What ingratitude is this! Ought
I not rather to repair her honour, and the outrage I
have done her? Yes, I ought; and I will, by marrying her, fulfil the promife I have given. Who can oppofe fo juft a defign? Should her favours prejudice me
againft her virtue? No; I am fenfible how much it coft
me to overcome her refiftance. She furrendered not fo
much to my tranfports, as to the faith I fwore: But,
on the other hand, if I acquiefce in this choice, I do
myfelf a confiderable injury. I, who may afpire to the
most

moſt noble and the richeſt heireſs of the kingdom, ſhall I content myſelf with the daughter of a private gentleman, who has only a moderate eſtate? What will they think of me at court? They will ſay I have degraded myſelf.

Belflor, divided thus between love and ambition, knew not what to reſolve; but though he was uncertain whether he ſhould marry Leonora, or not, he yet determined to go to her the next night.

Don Lewis, on his part, ſpent the day in conſidering how to reſtore his honour. He thought it was a very delicate conjuncture. To have recourſe to the laws, would render his diſgrace more public; beſides, he feared juſtice would be on one ſide, and the judges on the other; and he dared as little to go and fling himſelf at the king's feet. As he believed the king had a deſign to marry Belflor according to his own intereſts, he was afraid his application would be in vain. There remained no remedy, therefore, but that of arms, and this was what he fixed on. In the heat of his reſentment, he was tempted to ſend the count a challenge; but reflecting that he was too old and too feeble to venture to truſt his arm, he choſe rather to commit it to his ſon's. Accordingly he ſent a ſervant to Alcala, with a letter for his ſon, in which he charged him to come to Madrid, immediately, to revenge an affront offered to the family of the Ceſpedes.

His ſon, whoſe name was Don Pedro, was a young man of twenty years old, perfectly well made; and ſo brave, that in the town of Alcala he paſſed for the completeſt chevalier among the ſcholars in the univerſity. He was not then at Alcala, as his father imagined; for a deſire of ſeeing a lady whom he loved, had drawn him to Madrid: the laſt time he had been there to viſit his family, he had made this conqueſt at the * Prado. He

* A large foreſt with a pleaſure-houſe, near Madrid, belonging to the kings of Spain.

did

did not know her name; and was injoined not to enquire after it; and he submitted, though with a great
deal of difficulty, to this cruel neceffity. It was a young
lady of quality, who had conceived a kindnefs for him,
and thinking fhe ought to diftruft the difcretion and
conftancy of a fcholar, fhe judged it proper to prove
him well before fhe difcovered herfelf to him. Don
Pedro's head ran more upon his unknown miftrefs, than
upon Ariftotle's philofophy; and the fhortnefs of the
way from Madrid to Alcala invited him frequently to
play the truant to fee her. To conceal thefe amorous
journies from his father, he ufed to lodge in a publick
houfe at the end of the town, where he took care to
conceal himfelf under a borrowed name. He never
went out but in the morning, at a certain hour, when
he repaired to a houfe where this lady, who fpoiled his
ftudies, was fo kind as to meet him, accompanied with
her duenna. After which he kept clofe in his quarters,
the reft of the day; but to make amends, when night
came he rambled over the whole town.

It happened, one night, as he was walking through
a by-ftreet, he heard fome voices and inftruments which
feemed to deferve his attention. He ftopped to liften:
it was a ferenade. The cavalier who gave it was fud-
dled, and naturally brutal. He no fooner difcerned
our fcholar, than he went up to him haftily, and without other compliments, Friend, faid he, in a furly
tone, go your way, I love no impertinent hearkeners.----
I might have withdrawn, anfwered Don Pedro, fhocked
at thefe words, if you had defired me with a better
grace, but now I mean to ftay, to teach you how to
fpeak to a gentleman.----Let us fee then, replied the
mafter of the concert, drawing his fword, which of us
fhall give place to the other. Don Pedro laid his hand
alfo on his fword; and they began to fight. Though
the ferenade-gentleman acquitted himfelf with fkill
enough, he could not parry a mortal pufh, which laid
him flat on the ground. All the partners in the mufic,

who

who had thrown by their inſtruments, and drawn their ſwords to run in to his aſſiſtance, came up to revenge him. They attacked Don Pedro in a body, who on this occaſion ſhewed what he was able to do. Beſide his parrying all their paſſes with a ſurpriſing agility, he made home-thruſts, and held them all in play at a time. However, they were ſo many in number, that as good a ſwords-man as he was, he could not have ſaved himſelf, if the count de Belflor, who was then paſſing by, had not taken his part.

The count had courage, and reſolution. He could not ſee ſo many upon a ſingle man, without interpoſing on his ſide. He drew, and planting himſelf by Don Pedro, preſſed the ſeranaders ſo warmly, that they all took to their heels, ſome being wounded, and others fearing to be ſo. After their retreat, the ſcholar would have thanked the count for the ſuccour he had given him ; but Belflor interrupted him ; by ſaying, Are you not wounded ?---No ; anſwered Don Pedro. Let us make off then, replied the count ; I ſee you have killed a man ; it is dangerous for you to ſtay longer in this place ; the officers of juſtice may ſurpriſe you. They poſted away, and turned into another ſtreet, and being got to ſome diſtance from that where the combat happened, they ſtopped.

Don Pedro, urged by gratitude, begged the count not to conceal from him the name of a cavalier, to whom he was ſo highly obliged.---Belflor told it him very readily, and also aſked him his. The ſcholar, not caring to diſcover himſelf, anſwered, He was called Don Juan de Matos, and aſſured him he ſhould always remember the ſervice he had done him.---I will give you an opportunity, ſaid the count, this night, of getting out of my debt. I have a meeting upon my hands, which may prove dangerous ; and was going to look for a friend to bear me company. I know your bravery ; may I aſk you, Don Juan, to go with me ?---To doubt it, returned the ſcholar, is to affront me ; I cannot make a better uſe

of

of the life you have faved, than to rifk it for you.
Come on ; I am ready to follow you. Belflor then carried Don Pedro to Don Lewis's houfe, and both of
them mounted the balcony, to Leonora's apartment.
As Don Lewis had removed fome days before to another
quarter of the town, his fon did not know it was his
father's houfe into which the count introduced him,
neither did he perceive it was the good lady Marcella
who uſhered them in, becauſe ſhe received them without
a light, in an anti-chamber, where Belflor defired his
companion to ſtay while he went into the lady's room.
The ſcholar obeyed, and fat down in a chair, with his
fword in his hand for fear of a furprife. He began to
think upon Belflor's fuccefs in his amour, and wiſhed to
be as happy as his new friend : for though he was not
uſed ill by his unknown miſtreſs, yet ſhe was not quite
fo gracious to him as Leonora was to the count. As
he was purfuing thefe reflections, he heard fomebody try-
ing gently to open a door which was not that of the
lover's chamber, and he faw a light through the key-
hole. He ſtarted up, and advanced towards the pafs,
and haftily prefented his fword at his father, who was
coming to Leonora's apartment, to fee whether the
count was not there. The good man did not believe
that, after what had paffed, his daughter and Marcella
would dare to admit him again, and therefore he had
not caufed them to lie in another apartment. However, it came into his mind, that before they went into
the monaſtery the next day, perhaps they might be willing to fee him for the laſt time. Whoever thou art,
faid the ſcholar, come not in here ; if thou doſt, it will
coſt thee thy life. At thefe words Don Lewis looked
on Don Pedro, who alfo looked earneſtly on him. They
knew each other ; Ah! my fon, cried the old man,
how impatiently have I expected you ! Why did not you
let me know you were come ? Were you afraid of dif-
turbing my reſt ? Alas ! I can take none, in the cruel
fituation I am in !---O my father, faid Don Pedro very
much

much troubled, is it you I see? Are not my eyes deceived by some false resemblance?---Whence proceeds this astonishment? replied Don Lewis; are you not in your father's house? Did not I send you word that I removed hither eight days ago?---Just Heaven! answered the scholar, what is this I hear? I am then in my sister's apartment.

Just as he ended these words, the count, who heard a noise, and thought somebody was attacking his friend, came with his sword in his hand out of Leonora's chamber. When the old man perceived him, he flew into a passion, and shewing him to his son, There, cried he, is the audacious wretch who has robbed me of my repose, and fixed a mortal stain upon our honour. Let us be revenged, and make haste to punish the traitor. Thus saying, he drew his sword, which he had brought under his night-gown, and would have assaulted the count, but Don Pedro held him. Hold, my father, said he; moderate, I pray you, the transports of your anger.---What do you design, son, answered the old man, by holding my arm? You imagine, without doubt, that it has not strength enough to revenge me. Well, do you then take satisfaction for the insult which is done us; it was for this I sent for you home to Madrid. If you fall, I will take your place; the count must either perish by our swords, or take both our lives, after he has taken our honour.

Sir, replied Don Pedro, I cannot grant what your impatience expects of me. I am so far from attempting the life of the count, that I came hither only to defend it. My word is engaged, and my honour requires it. Let us be gone, count, pursued he, addressing himself to Belflor.----Ah! cowardly wretch, interrupted Don Lewis, looking on his son with resentment, dost thou thyself oppose a revenge which ought to awaken all thy soul? My son, my own son is in the interest of the villain who has corrupted my daughter! But do not imagine to elude my resentment. I will call in all my domestics,

tics, and will make them revenge me on his treachery
and thy cowardly bafenefs.---Sir, replied Don Pedro,
be more juft to your fon : call him not coward ; he does
not deferve fo bafe a name. The count has faved my
life to-night. He asked me, without knowing me, to
bear him company where he was going : and I offered to
fhare the dangers he might run, without knowing that
my gratitude would imprudently engage my arm againft
the honour of my family. My word obliges me, therefore, to defend his life here. By this I acquit the debt
I owe him ; but I fhall not lefs ftrongly refent the injury he has done us, and to-morrow you fhall fee me
ready to fhed his blood with the fame zeal as you fee
me now defend it.

The count, who had not fpoken yet, fo amazed was
he at this adventure, now began ; Perhaps, faid he to
the fcholar, you will not eafily be able to revenge this
injury by arms. I will offer you a more certain way to
reftore your honour. I confefs, that till this day I had
no defign to marry Leonora ; but this morning I received a letter from her, which has conquered me, and
her tears have compleated the victory. The happinefs
of being her husband is now my fole ambition.---If the
king has defigned another lady for you, faid Don Lewis, how will you excufe yourfelf ?---The king has propofed no one to me, interrupted Belflor, blufhing. Forgive that fiction to a man whofe principles were warped
by paffion. It is a crime which the violence of my defires made me commit, and I atone for it by confefling
it.---My lord, anfwered the old man, after this confeffion, which becomes a noble mind, I do not doubt your
fincerity. I fee you really mean to repair the affront we
have received : my anger yields to the affurances you
give me ; fuffer me to forget my refentment in your
arms. Thus faying, he went up to the count, who
ftepped forward to prevent him. They mutually embraced ; when Belflor turning to Don Pedro, And you,
counterfeit Don Juan, faid he, who have already gained

my

my esteem by your valour, and the generosity of your
sentiments, come hither, and let me vow to you the
friendship of a brother. At this he embraced Don
Pedro, who received his salute with a respectful air;
and answered, My lord, in promising me so valuable a
friendship, you command mine. You may depend
upon a man, who will be devoted to you to the last moment of his life.

In the mean while, Leonora, who was listening at her
own chamber-door, did not lose one word of all that
was said. She was tempted at first to have shewn herself, and have run in between their swords, without
knowing why, but Marcella prevented her; but when
the skilful duenna saw matters were accommodated
peaceably, she thought her mistress's presence and
her own would not hurt the new agreement. They
both appeared therefore, at this crisis, and weeping
ran to prostrate themselves before Don Lewis. They
were justly afraid that having been surprised the last
night, the old gentleman's rage might flame out again;
but he made Leonora rise, and said, My daughter,
dry your tears: I will not reproach you again: since
your lover will keep the faith he swore to you, I consent to forget what is past.

Yes, Don Lewis, said the count, I will marry Leonora; and the better to repair the injury I have done you,
and to give you a more compleat satisfaction, and your
son a pledge of the friendship I have vowed him, I offer
him my sister Eugenia.—Ah! my lord, cried Don
Lewis with transport, how am I overwhelmed with the
honour you do my son! What father was ever more
pleased! You now give me as much joy, as you have
given me grief.

If the old man seemed charmed with the count's
offer, it was otherwise with Don Pedro. As he was
strongly smitten with his unknown lady, he stood so
confused, that he could not speak a word. But Belflor,
without observing his perplexity, went away, saying, He

was going to order the preparations for this double
union, and that he thought it long till he was joined
with them by such intimate bands.

After his departure, Don Lewis left Leonora in her
apartment, and returned to his own with Don Pedro;
who said to him with all the franknefs of a fcholar, Sir,
pray excufe me from marrying the count's fifter.   It is
enough that he marries Leonora; that marriage is fufficient to fecure the honour of our family.----What! faid
the old man, do you decline marrying the count's fifter?
---Yes, fir, replied Don Pedro; this union, I own, would
be a cruel punifhment to me, and I will not conceal from
you the caufe.   Six months ago I fell in love with an
amiable lady.   She alone can make my life happy.---
How wretched is the condition of a father, faid Don
Lewis, never to have his children difpofed to do what
he defires! But who is this lady who has made fuch a
mighty impreffion on you?---I know her not, anfwered
Don Pedro; fhe promifed to inform me when fhe fhould
be convinced of my prudence and conftancy; but I am
perfuaded her family is one of the moft confiderable in
the court.----And do you think, faid his father, changing
his tone, I fhall have the complaifance to approve this
romantic love of yours, and that I fuffer you to renounce
the moft glorious advancement Fortune can offer you,
in order to preferve your fidelity to one of whom you
know not fo much as the name? Expect it not from my
indulgence; fupprefs rather the fentiments you have
for one who perhaps does not deferve them, and think
only of meriting the honour the count is willing to con-
fer on you.----All this difcourfe, fir, replied the fcholar,
is to no purpofe; I feel I can never forget my unknown
miftrefs: nothing can difengage me from her.   Though
an Infanta were propofed to me—Hold! cried Don
Lewis roughly, it is too much infolently to boaft of a
conftancy which provokes my anger.   Be gone, and
never appear in my prefence more, till you are ready to
obey me.

Don

Don Pedro durſt not reply to theſe words, for fear of drawing upon himſelf others more ſevere. He retired into a chamber, where he paſſed the reſt of the night in a train of reflections, both afflicting and agreeable. He conſidered with ſorrow that he was going to embroil himſelf with his whole family, by refuſing to marry the count's ſiſter. But he was perfectly comforted, when he reflected, that his dear unknown would recompenſe him for ſo great a ſacrifice. He flattered himſelf, that upon ſo ſhining a proof of his fidelity, ſhe would not fail to diſcover to him her condition, which he imagined was little inferior to that of Eugenia. In this hope, he went out by break of day, and walked at the Prado till the hour came for him to be at the lodging of Donna Juana, which was the name of the lady, at whoſe houſe he uſed to meet his miſtreſs every morning.

He found there his unknown fair, who reſorted thither ſooner than ordinary ; but he found her diſſolved in tears with Don Juana, and full of ſorrow. What a ſight was this for a lover ! He approached her with great concern ; and falling at her feet, Madam, ſaid he, what am I to think of the condition in which I ſee you ? What misfortune is foreboded to me by theſe tears ?---You do not expect, anſwered ſhe, the fatal blow. Our cruel fortune is going to ſeparate us for ever. We ſhall ſee one another no more.

She accompanied theſe words with ſo many ſighs, that it was doubtful, whether Don Pedro was more affected with what ſhe ſaid, than with the trouble ſhe ſeemed to feel as ſhe ſpoke it. Juſt heaven ! cried he in a tranſport of paſſion which he could not command, can you ſuffer an union which you know is innocent and pure to be deſtroyed ? But, madam, added he, perhaps you have taken a falſe alarm. Is it certain you are to be torn from the moſt faithful lover that ever lived ? Am I indeed the moſt unfortunate of men ?---Our misfortune, anſwered the lady unknown, is too ſure. My brother, who has the diſpoſal of me, marries me to-day : he has

told

told me fo himfelf.----Ah ! who is this happy man? replied Don Pedro with precipitation ; name him to me, madam : in my defpair I-----I do not know his name, interrupted the lady ; my brother did not care to tell me. He faid, he wifhed I would fee the gentleman firft.----But, madam, faid Don Pedro, will you fubmit without refiftance to a brother's will, and be dragged to the altar without complaining of being made fo cruel a facrifice ? Did you do nothing in my favour ? Alas! I was not afraid to expofe myfelf to my father's refentment, to referve myfelf for you. His menaces could not fhake my fidelity, and let him ufe me as rigoroufly as he can, I will not marry the lady propofed to me, though fhe be of a very confiderable rank.----And who is this lady ? faid his unknown miftrefs.----She is the fifter of the count de Belflor, anfwered the fcholar.---- Ah ! Don Pedro, replied the lady, joyfully furprifed, you certainly miftake ; you are not fure of what you fay. Is it in truth Eugenia the fifter of Belflor that is propofed to you ?---Yes, madam, replied Don Pedro, the count himfelf has offered me her hand.----What, faid fhe, is it poffible you fhould be the perfon for whom my brother has defigned me ?---What is it I hear ? cried the fcholar in his turn : Is Eugenia de Belflor my unknown miftrefs ?---Yes, Don Pedro, replied fhe ; but I can fcarcely think myfelf fo at prefent, I have fo much difficulty to believe the good fortune of which you affure me.

At thefe words Don Pedro embraced her knees ; **and** afterwards took one of her hands, which he kiffed with all the tranfport which a lover can feel, who paffes fuddenly from an extreme forrow to an excefs of joy. While he was abandoning himfelf to the emotion of his love ; What a world of trouble, faid Eugenia, would my brother have faved me, if he had named the hufband he defigned me ? What an averfion had I conceived for my fpoufe ? Ah, my dear Don Pedro ! how have I hated you ?--Fair Eugenia, anfwered he, how charming is this hatred to me! I will deserve it, by adoring you all my life.

After the two lovers had given each other the most moving tokens of mutual affection, Eugenia desired to know how the scholar had been able to gain her brother's friendship. Don Pedro did not hide from her the amour of the count and his sister, and related all that had passed the preceding night. It was an additional pleasure to her to understand that her brother was to marry her lover's sister. Donna Juana was too much interested in the fortune of her friend, not to be touched with this happy event. She rejoiced at it, as well as Don Pedro, who at last parted from Eugenia, after they had both agreed not to appear to know one another when they came before the count.

Don Pedro returned home; and his father finding him disposed to obey him, was pleased with it the more, because he imputed his compliance to the resolute manner in which he had spoken to him the night before. They expected to hear from the count, who sent them a letter, and acquainted them, that he had obtained the king's consent to his marriage and that of his sister, with a considerable post for Don Pedro; that both the marriages might be performed the next day, because the orders he had given about them were expedited so well, that the preparations were already very far advanced. In the afternoon he came himself to confirm what he had written, and to present Eugenia to them.

Don Lewis received her with great respect, and Leonora embraced her several times. As for Don Pedro, agitated as he was with the impulses of love and joy, he over-ruled himself so far, as not to give the count any suspicion of his former acquaintance with Eugenia. As Belflor was particularly careful to observe his sister's behaviour, he thought he perceived, in spite of the constraint she imposed on herself, that she was not displeased with Don Pedro. In order to be better assured of this, he took her aside for a moment, and made her confess

5

confefs that fhe liked her intended fpoufe very well. He told her then his name and his family, which he had refufed to inform her of before, left the difparity of their rank fhould prejudice her againft him ; and fhe pretended to hear it, as if fhe had been ignorant of it till then.

At laft, after a variety of compliments on both fides, it was concluded that the nuptials fhould be held at the houfe of the count de Belflor ; where they were cele-brated with univerfal joy ; only the lady Marcella had no fhare in the mirth ; fhe wept while the others were rejoicing ; for after his marriage the count confeffed the whole intrigue to Don Lewis, who difpatched the bafe duenna to the monaftery * de Arrepentidas, where the thoufand piftoles fhe had infamoufly received for feducing Leonora, ferved to fubfift her in a courfe of penance for the remainder of her days.

* Monafteries in the Popifh countries, in which women of lewd lives are confined, and kept to penance.

END of the THIRD VOLUME.